# *Dundee Orbital*

## Tales of the Tri-Cluster Confederation

by

Mike Watson

# Copyright

## Dundee Orbital
## Tales of the Tri-Cluster Confederation

Copyright © July 2020 by Mike Watson. All Rights Reserved

eBook ISBN: 978-1-7341410-3-0

Print ISBN: 978-1-7341410-4-7

Editing: Red Adept  Cover art: Luca Oleastri

# Table of Contents

# The Face on the Barroom Floor

Donal Harris, one of Dundee Orbital's chief customs inspectors, set his untouched coffee mug on his desk when he received a message via his link. *<Dead Body Reported. Olsen's Taproom and Grill, Torus One, Deck Three, Segment A. Patrollers on scene. Apparent murder.>* The last portion of the message surprised him. Patrollers did not usually make a murder determination. They let others do that.

Looking longingly at his mug, Harris debated whether he should have more. He was tired and decided the need for caffeine outweighed the need to immediately respond to the message. It was late in his shift, and he had been about to leave for home. That was not going to happen now.

With a grimace, he took a sip and put his mug back down. It was lukewarm, apparently left over from the start of his shift. He acknowledged the message and walked out of his office, looking for unoccupied agents.

Procedure demanded he take a partner when responding to a call. Judging from the empty desks of the bullpen, no agents were available. The only person remaining in the room was Molly Quinn, a Clan McLean militiawoman and potential Customs recruit. She was an intern on-station for familiarization with Customs policy, procedures, and operations. This was the third day of her internship.

She and Harris were of the same clan and sept: Clan McLean, Sept Harris. She was also his niece.

"Molly!" Harris shouted across the room. When she looked up, he motioned for her to join him.

The expression on Molly's face was proof that she welcomed the interruption. She had been reading closed case files. There wasn't a more tedious, boring task in the service. He watched her put the case files

4

away in her temporary desk as required by Customs Service policy. After locking her desk, she walked over to answer Harris' call.

To see them standing side by side, no one would think they were related. Harris was 1.8 meters tall and big boned, with reddish-brown hair, as were many clansmen from Inverness, which had 1.1g gravity.

Molly Quinn, formally Mary Elizabeth Quinn, was shorter than Donal Harris, more slender than was usual for women of Inverness, with a pale complexion. Her red hair was cut short in militia fashion. She had been a strawberry blonde, her natural color, when he saw her last.

"Sir?" She was careful to maintain the proper decorum of a subordinate to a superior.

"I need a partner. There's been a murder—apparent murder," he said, correcting himself, "in a bar near the docks. Everyone else is busy. Are you up to it?" She had never been on a Customs patrol or a criminal case.

"I think so... How can I know?" she replied. "I've never seen a murder. However, I am... at least I think I am ready."

Harris took a long look at his niece. Her militia obligation was ending, and she had expressed an interest in joining the Customs Service. This could be an opportunity for her and for him, as her would-be superior, to see if she could handle the job. "Get your gear—arms too."

She met him near the Customs office entrance. He was now wearing a Customs Service shipsuit, light-tan in color, with two dark-blue, horizontal bars high on each sleeve. His equipment harness included a knife, a pistol, a shock-stick, a laser pistol in a leg holster, and a small backpack. He held a helmet in one hand.

Molly, on the other hand, wore a militia field uniform with the Clan McLean tartan patch on her right shoulder sleeve, a small backpack like his, and a militia equipment harness with her sidearms and knife. In addition to her regular equipment, she carried a Customs helmet and a patroller's shock-stick hanging from her harness belt.

"Set your link to your helmet. Use it if you want privacy," he said as he placed his helmet on his head and secured it.

Molly did the same, checking the settings of the helmet. It was not much different from the ones used by Inverness militias. When her link established a secure connection with her helmet, they headed for the murder scene.

†††

Harris and Quinn stopped just inside the barroom's entrance and examined the scene. Olsen's Taproom and Grill was one of many places that catered to freighter crews, dockworkers, and warehousemen. What made Olsen's different from the others was its Old American Old West theme—a pseudo-wooden floor, a long mirror with a line of bottles at its base, and a polished wooden bar with a brass footrail. The ceiling was black, obscuring the necessary plumbing and environmental and power conduits of the bar. The owner had not bothered to conceal them behind a false ceiling. The smell of stale beer and alcohol overlaid a faint whiff of… something unpleasant.

Scattered around the barroom were round four-seat tables, half of them occupied. Through the doorway, the dining room was visible, where the tables were covered with tablecloths. At the far end of the bar, two Patrollers in gray shipsuits with dark-blue horizontal bars on their sleeves, stood next to a body lying in a broad pool of blood. The bar was quiet—subdued. In the early days of the Confederation, off-planet law enforcement was unclear and, at best, haphazard. The Tri-Cluster Confederation did not have a regulated confederation-wide law enforcement organization. The only organization with Confederation-wide coverage was the Customs Service, whose primary task was to ensure ships paid the proper fees and tariffs. Over the millennium following those early days, through trial and error, policy and practice, Custom and Tradition, the Confederation had added law enforcement to the list of responsibilities of the Customs Service.

Dundee Orbital, thirty-one kilometers in length and in synchronous orbit thirty-seven thousand kilometers above Inverness, was in

Confederation territory. The planet's sovereignty extended only to low planetary orbit, fifteen hundred kilometers above the planet's surface.

Station patrollers performed the day-to-day peacekeeping tasks of managing the drunks, brawlers, and petty thieves. Patrollers were subordinate to the Customs Service. Customs inspectors and agents were primarily concerned with inspecting ships, cargoes, the docks, and warehouse areas of the stations. However, when necessary, Customs Service inspectors also investigated more serious crimes—like murder.

Harris walked up to the two patrollers. He recognized the older one, Senior Patroller Henry Hillman. He and Harris were long time acquaintances and off-duty friends. "Hello, Henry. What do you have?"

"Hello, Inspector," the older patroller acknowledged Harris then said to the younger patroller, "Roll him over, Ian."

When the junior patroller had done so, Harris saw why the patrollers had declared the death a murder. The probable cause of death was a deep slash up the victim's abdomen from his pubis to his sternum. When the body was faceup, the slash gaped open, revealing the victim's bowels and the lower bisected third of his heart. No medical nanite known could have saved him. His survival, even if a full resuscitation team had been on-site and immediately available, was unlikely.

The rest of the body, however, was what drew Harris' attention—it had no face. All of its features were smoothed over into an oval without ears or hair. It had a gash for a mouth, a small rounded nose, and black eyes. The body had reverted to a neutral form when death canceled its disguise.

"A chameleon," Harris said, confirming the patrollers' assessment. Chameleons were genetically and surgically modified spies, undercover agents, and assassins. The chameleon-conversion process was expensive and required specialized nanites to control changes in body shape and appearance. It was extremely rare to see a chameleon in its neutral state, especially a dead one on a barroom floor.

7

The body wore a standard shipsuit, as did most of the current patrons of the bar. The suit had no ship patches, corporate logos, or shaded areas where some might once have been.

"What happened?" Harris asked Hillman. On the edge of his vision, he noticed Molly Quinn kneeling next to the body, mindful to keep her militia uniform out of the pool of blood. She was going through the pockets of the chameleon's shipsuit. The patrollers had already searched the body, but Harris was glad she was taking nothing for granted—and did not seem put off by touching the dead body.

"According to Harley over there"—the senior patroller indicated the bartender—"he came in about two hours ago and took a place at the end of the bar. He was drinking whiskey and beer and was complaining that his girl had left him for another man. He continued drinking until about a half hour ago, when another man walked up and started talking to him. The talk became heated, then suddenly, the new guy drew a knife, slashed this... *thing* here, and then calmly walked out."

"Hmm." Harris looked around the barroom and up toward the ceiling. *No security blisters.* Most commercial establishments had no active scanners. Customers preferred their privacy. The bar was half-filled, which was usual for this time in the second shift. "Witnesses?"

"Just about everyone here," the older patroller replied. "We haven't let anyone leave."

"Molly," Harris said, "take a hologram of the crime scene..." Then he remembered her searching the body. "Did you find anything on the body?"

"Three credit tabs totaling one hundred fifty Confederate dollars, a standard knife but no pistol, no ID... and no fingerprints either."

The lack of fingerprints did not surprise Harris. He wouldn't have expected a chameleon to have any. The slash had disemboweled the body. Whatever had done that was not a simple knife. Shipsuits were designed to be tough out of necessity. *A vibro-knife, I'd guess.* Possession of a vibro-knife was legal, but the use of one in an altercation was not, unless both parties were equally armed.

8

"Very well. After you've finished with the hologram, call for the pathologist to come get the body. Then watch the patrollers interview the witnesses. You do some, too, after you've watched them. It's good experience if you want to join the Service when you're out of the militia."

"Yes, sir." She left to join the other patrollers preparing to interview the bar's patrons.

"Henry, get the image of the killer from the outside corridor scans and have them broadcast over the security net. Note he's a suspect in a violent crime. While you're at it, see if you can get an image of this guy before he was sliced up."

Hillman nodded and sent the younger patroller to follow up on Harris' orders. "I want to see those scans myself, Inspector."

Harris walked over to the bartender. "Harley, have you seen either of the two—the dead one here or the new guy—before?"

"Well… no, not really. The first one—the deader on the floor, looked vaguely familiar like someone you've met once or twice but you can't remember when or where. We get so many coming through here. New ships, new crews, ya know? But I don't remember anything more than that. I'm the only one tending bar this shift, and I was just too busy to pay a lot of attention to a single customer at the bar."

"Kitchen?"

"Too early for them to be servin'. They were all in back, getting ready for the rush… which should be happenin' any time now," the bartender said. "When do you think you'll be finished? We're going to be busy soon," he said, hinting that he would like the body removed and the patrollers gone before the dinner crowd arrived.

Harris nodded absently. Bars in this area were only interested in their income. A known killer could come in, and everyone would turn a blind eye as long as he didn't cause trouble. "Give the names of the kitchen staff to the woman in the militia uniform."

"Will do," the bartender answered.

Harris walked down the bar to where the dead man had been drinking. There were two dirty glasses on the bar, a beer mug and a shot glass.

"Are these his?" he asked the bartender, referring to the dead man on the floor.

"Yeah."

"We'll take these with us." Harris pulled a transparent bag from a pocket and slipped it over the two glasses. After sealing the bag, he walked over and gave it to Molly Quinn. "Scan these. If the chameleon was on a mission, he would have a set of fingerprints too. We might be able to track his movements, maybe see where and when he arrived on-station."

†††

It had been a long day, and the day wasn't yet over. Molly and Harris returned to the Customs office to begin the off-site investigation.

Molly was watching the security scans she had received from Ian, the younger patroller. There were no fingerprints on either of the two bar glasses, so the security scans were the only leads to identifying victim and suspect.

Her head dropped. She jerked and raised it. She looked across the office to see her uncle watching her. He had seen her nodding off from across the bullpen. She looked into the 2D monitor and noticed her eyes were red too.

"Molly!" Harris spoke loudly across the bullpen. The noise level was high from Customs agents who were about to go off-shift. Before they could leave, though, they had to complete their daily logs—new arriving and departing ship reports, Customs inspection reports, arriving-departing passenger and crew lists, cargo loading-offloading reports, and still more reports.

She looked up and saw her uncle waving at her. When she reached him, he asked, "You came in before I did today, right?"

She nodded.

"Then shut it down for now. You've had a full day."

"But I—"

"Do what I say, Molly. Yes, what you're doing is important, but it'll keep. If you continue as you have, you may miss something more important."

She nodded, clearly disappointed. "Yes, sir."

"Come back in six hours, if you want, but get at least that much sleep. If you join the Customs Service, you won't always have the luxury of fixed shifts. Sometimes you have to push until the case is finished. This case could be one of those."

She nodded again, accepting his warning and acknowledging his expectations. Molly could feel the eyes of the agents scattered across the bullpen watching them. The observation made her uncomfortable. "Why?" she asked softly, indicating the watching eyes.

"They're waiting for any signs of unwarranted favoritism. You know there won't be any, but they don't believe it. Yet. It's something you'll have to work with if you join the service and work here until you've shown them you're fully qualified and there isn't any unearned favoritism."

To an extent, nepotism was accepted by Custom and Tradition; clansmen helped fellow clansmen and clanswomen. But it didn't pay to be blatant about it when it occurred. Whenever nepotism occurred, it was expected to be balanced by ability and competency of those who benefited from it.

With a quick glance at the bullpen, she said, loudly enough to allow those nearby to hear, "Yes, sir."

✝✝✝

After Molly left the office and the agents in the bullpen had finished their reports, the new shift of agents and inspectors began to arrive. Harris returned to his office, shut and locked the door, darkened his office windows, and activated his privacy shield. Like other patroller and Customs private offices, his contained a desk with a built-in secure

11

console link, two side chairs, an equipment storage locker, a 2D display wall, and a handful of awards, certificates, and citations mounted on another wall.

Harris paired his personal link to his office console and established a secure connection. After a pause, a man appeared in the holo projection above Harris' desk. He wore light clothing common to Cameron, the warm, dry planet next inward to Old Cal, and the capitol of the Tri-Cluster Confederation.

"How are you, John?" Harris asked.

The other man, seated in an office similar to Harris', nodded. What was unusual in the holo was the pistol lying on the other man's desk, just visible at the edge of the display. The man in the holo was Donal Harris' other boss, John McKuen, System Chief of the Interdiction Office, the Confederation's unacknowledged internal security service. In addition to being a chief Customs inspector reporting to the Director of the Customs Service on Dundee Orbital, Harris was also the head of the Interdiction Office for the station.

"I'm well, Donal." He paused for Harris to speak, since he was the one who'd initiated the connection.

"I've something that will interest you, John. I just looked at a dead chameleon in a bar next to the docks."

"A chameleon? How… interesting. Any chance of IDing him?"

"We're working on it—checking the arrival rosters, security scans, the usual. I haven't got a pathologist report yet."

"How did he die?"

"Barroom brawl, apparently. We're checking that, too, which brings me to the reason why I called. Could we have lost one of ours?"

"I wouldn't think so. We would have been told if one was operating in your area," McKuen said. "Naval Intelligence hasn't reported any such operation, nor have they reported any of theirs missing, but it's too soon for the news to have spread, isn't it?"

Harris nodded. "It happened four hours ago. I doubt the navy could have heard this quickly unless they had eyes at the scene."

"As I would expect if it was an intelligence operation." McKuen pondered for a moment. "Of course, they wouldn't ordinarily tell me unless there was a need." Naval Intelligence was the Confederation's external security service and should not have been operating inside the Confederation without the knowledge and cooperation of the Customs Service and the Interdiction Office. McKuen leaned back in his chair and rubbed his chin. "Knowing the navy, they may not tell us if they had lost someone."

"Would you ask, please?"

"Of course, Donal." He chuckled. "You can depend on me." McKuen reached over to cut the connection but stopped short. "Would you please send us a sample of his DNA and nanites? It might tell us something of the chameleon's origin." With that, he cut the connection, leaving Harris looking at an empty holo.

"Like hell you'd have told me," Harris muttered.

†††

Thomas Brierley was in a rented 'fresher stall a segment away from the bar. He was disposing of one of his programmed personas and changing to another. The process took several hours—longer, if extensive changes were required. This time, it was a simple change in hair, skin, and eye color, with a small modification of his head from an oval to a triangular shape. The last change was to his clothes. *A clansman's attire, I think.*

The mission was a failure. Oh, he'd killed the target—but it was a setup. His pre-mission briefing had said the target was a fellow chameleon, but Brierley had assumed it would be a Confederate chameleon. He'd followed instructions and met the target as scheduled, but the other chameleon had failed the counter-password.

*Was the other a victim or a renegade? A pawn in the internecine battles between their superiors? Am I a target myself, now?*

13

After the incident, he'd taken particular care to lose any possible followers when he left the bar. As far as he could tell, no one had trailed him. Now, he waited for the transition to finish, wondering about the other chameleon. *Was he the real target or just collateral damage by being in the wrong place at the wrong time?*

*I followed my instructions. I met him as scheduled, and he failed the counter-password.* As far as Brierley was concerned, the mission was complete. *I'll send a status message to the drop box and then board a ship away from Caledonia. Away from this place.*

†††

Dr. Martin Kawasa, one of several pathologists in Dundee Orbital who worked for the Customs Service, appeared in the holomonitor above Harris' desk. "My initial report has been filed, and the nanite sample is on the way to you."

Harris' eyes flicked to the corner of his holomonitor and saw Martin's report appear in his inbox. "Good. What's your personal evaluation?"

"Well, cause of death was obvious. I found nothing to change that. Other than his lack of facial features and fingerprints, he was ordinary— ordinary height, ordinary weight, ordinary build. His shipsuit and knife were of local manufacture—new, in fact. So new that the suit hadn't yet needed cleaning. As for distinguishing characteristics… well, for one, he was not from Inverness or any other Confederation planet like Inverness, nor a station. His bones were too light for being raised in a 1.1g gravity. Wherever he's from, it had less than Earth-g gravity."

"That's not unusual for our competitors," Harris said. "I understand we pick our chameleon candidates to match the Earth-human physical standard. We wouldn't want them to stand out."

"Ah," Kawasa said, "but do ours have special enhancements? Like a built-in damper?"

Harris knew more about Confederate chameleons than he was willing to share. However, the doctor had a point. Confederate chameleons had no implants other than those found in any ordinary

Confederate citizen or those from the System States or the Directorate of Sovereign Corporate States. "No, not as far as I know. Would the damper have been detectable if we knew to look?"

"How would I know, Harris? I'm a pathologist, not a scanner specialist."

†††

After his conversation with the pathologist, Harris received the extracted nanites and forwarded them to McKuen's office on Cameron. With that done, he called McKuen and left a message of their expected arrival.

Harris left his office and walked down the corridor to the break room for more coffee, all the while thinking about his conundrum. He returned to his office, unaware of greetings from agents on the way. *If these chameleons have non-standard implants, is there a way to detect them?*

Returning to his office, Harris pulled out a lower drawer in his desk, propped his feet on it and leaned back in his chair. He displayed Kawasa's pathology report in his holomonitor. Normal implants were semi-biological, or else some form of external power would have to be available for them. Normal nanites and implants used the body's natural energy sources for power. The only impact was a slightly higher caloric requirement for the body. This implant, according to Kawasa, used external sources—broadcast energy that was ever-present in today's modern environment—link broadcasts and the transmissions of the link network, for example.

His thoughts were interrupted by a knock on his office door. Molly Quinn was standing there, violating the unwritten rule about interrupting Harris when his office was closed and darkened. Harris sighed. Since she didn't know the unspoken rule, he could not chastise her as he ordinarily would.

"Come!" he shouted through the door.

When she entered, she said, "I've found something, but I don't know what it means."

15

"What?" Harris said, more harshly than he had intended.

Molly was visibly taken aback. "I was sure, sir, you would want to know. The corridor security scans don't show the killer entering or leaving Olsen's Taproom. Nor have I found images of the victim. However, when I expanded the visual range to include high ultraviolet, I found this." She handed him a 2D image of a scene from the security scan outside the bar. The fuzzy blob in the image was man high, but the details were obscured. "Two of these entered the bar. One came out. I was able to track it to a public 'fresher one segment from the bar. It was there for five hours and then departed via a maintenance corridor. I lost it when he, she, whatever it was, reached an intersection where the scans were out of service."

Now *that* was interesting, and her statement grabbed Harris' attention. "Show me."

The outside view of Olsen's Taproom appeared in his holomonitor. "This is fifteen seconds before the victim arrives." In the holomonitor, an indistinct form appeared from the left. The door to the bar opened, and the form went inside.

"The other one…" She stopped. "What should we call the killer?"

"Chameleon Number Two or just the chameleon, for now," he answered.

She nodded and continued, "Here is the second chameleon." A second indistinct figure approached the bar entrance from the right. "He arrived an hour and sixteen minutes after the first. Now jumping forward ten minutes, we have this." The bar's door slid open, and a blurred figure exited then turned right to disappear off the security scanner's view.

"This was using your broader filter?"

"Yes. Using the default filters, neither chameleon appears at all. However, I'd bet they would look like ordinary people to anyone who happened to see them."

Harris looked up at his niece, who was watching the holomonitor over his shoulder. "Good! Very good, Molly. I think you've found a way for us to detect these chameleons." He sent a one-time code to her link. "Use this as authority to institute a station-wide search using the filter you created. Our Customs AI will find him now that we know what to look for."

†††

After Molly left to set up the surveillance, Harris called John McKuen's office. Harris didn't particularly want to speak to him. McKuen was just too slick for Harris' taste, and he would have preferred to just leave a message, but that option vanished when McKuen answered the call.

"I think we can say, with some confidence," Harris began, "that the two chameleons aren't ours. They both appear to have damper implants. My intern has discovered that the implants can be detected when in use. We're checking the station, particularly the docks on outbound ships and the shuttle terminals. If he isn't already off the station, I think we can find him."

McKuen's eyebrows rose. "That was quick. You think you have a realistic chance of capturing him? We will want him alive if at all possible. I've ordered an interrogation team to Dundee Orbital, just in case."

"As long as he doesn't know we can find him, the chances are good."

"Good. Do so." McKuen paused. "Auto-suicide?"

"Yes, that's something that has to be considered. If he has an implant drawing external power, he could have a suicide charge too. So… we can't use the usual capture methods. Those would be detected and could set off the charge."

"What are you going to do?"

"Don't know yet. In any case, I think we'll have to have a resuscitation team nearby and hope that whatever we do, we can keep him alive until that team can ensure he lives… and in case we have collateral injuries," Harris said somberly.

McKuen nodded, "Works for me. By the way, we received your nanites, and the lab is checking them. We should have more information in a few hours," he said and broke the connection.

†††

"Cecilia hasn't found anything yet," Molly Quinn said to her uncle.

"Who?"

"Cecilia. That's the name I gave our AI. I've found I get better results when I call her by name as if we had a personal rapport. She seems to like it."

She and her uncle were meeting in his office to review the progress of their search for the chameleon. "I think he's turned his damper off," she said, "and we still don't know what he looks like."

"He's probably changed ID and his appearance," her uncle agreed. "It only takes a few hours for a superficial change. Have you tried old tech?"

"Old tech?"

"Yes, drawings—sketches, have an artist make a drawing from the witnesses' description."

"Uh, no… just a minute," Quinn said and went back to her desk. She returned in a few moments. "Do we have a tool to do this?"

"Not that I've heard, but we do have artists here on Dundee. Track one down and see what you can do."

"Will do," she said. She was glad to have an excuse to get out of the office. Most of the work was interesting, but the paper-pushing was boring.

"Wait, there's more," Harris said halting her departure. "He's probably trying to get off-station. We need to halt all departures for a few days, or he'll get away." Harris made a search of the ships currently docked at the station that were due to pull out in the next three days. "There's six: CMS *Folstone,* SSMS *Carlson Dealer,* MS *Beautiful Horizon,* CMS *Hillyard's Bounty,* CSMS *Maxton 34* and MS *Banshee's*

*Call.* Two Confederates, one from the Systems States, an independent, a Hiver and a DeeCee. All are freighters except for the *Carlson Dealer*. It's the scheduled System States packet due to depart for the SolSystem. All of the ships are docked in the same segment on Torus Two."

"We need to keep them in port." Harris drummed his fingers on his desk. He cleared his holomonitor and brought up Caledonia's stellar weather report. Old Cal had been quiet lately, but maybe… "Ah, Cal has burped and has emitted a Class Three flare. It should arrive in a few hours."

"But that's not very high, just ten points above normal," Molly replied.

"Not if we get the weather boys to raise it to a Class Two."

"But that's…"

"Never you mind," he interrupted. "I'll make some calls and tug on some strings, who knows what may happen if the data is reexamined. A Class-Two flare will keep our outbound ships in dock and our shuttles hangered."

†††

Thomas Brierley arrived at the docks via an up-station tram with his duffel, a secure locker, following behind him. The ships that were due to depart in the next twenty-five hours just happened to all be docked in this segment, including the *Maxton 34,* a DeeCee freighter from the Directorate of Sovereign Corporate States. He would wait until a half hour before departure before boarding. When the freighter's locks were closed and sealed for departure, he would be safe in DeeCee sovereign territory.

The foyer outside the intra-station tram terminal was crowded with ship crews and station civilians. Amber panels next to the large pressure hatches that led to the docks were lit, a flare alert. This area of the station, with its older torus and docks, had the weakest radiation shielding of Dundee Orbital. The ship hulls could protect their onboard crews. However, most of the ships simply gave all their crews station liberty before closing and sealing their locks. Any boarded passengers

19

were sent back on-station. Sending them back would reduce a ship's liability if there was any radiation leakage. Though unlikely, a leakage was still possible.

Brierley's departure plan was blocked. His paranoia flared. *Did they find me? They would know when I didn't appear on the security scans that I'm not some crewman off a ship.* He fought his sudden surge of panic. *However, they still don't know what I look like.*

When Brierley had entered Olsen's Taproom, he was dark-haired with dark eyes, as were most of the people on the station. He had also been muscular like those from Inverness and wearing a normal shipsuit. Now his hair was reddish-brown and his eyes blue. He wore casual trousers with a long jacket and tartan sash of Clan Jarvi. *If necessary, I'll turn the damper on and disappear again.*

While he stood in the foyer, thinking, workmen arrived and began to install sensor portals alongside the hatches to the docks. "To monitor radiation levels," they told anyone who asked what they were doing.

Brierley watched the holo info-stream above the hatches. *Class-Two flare expected in... 132 minutes.* As he watched, the countdown changed to 131.

*Two hours until the flare arrives, and then how long until it passes?* he asked himself. The departure time for the *Maxton 34* changed—another twenty-six hours.

With his duffel following obediently behind him, Brierley headed up-segment to find a quiet place, out of sight of the surrounding throng. He would wait there until the docks were reopened. He could not change his appearance now. His ticket for the *Maxton 34* matched his current persona. Brierley ducked into a narrow side corridor and turned on his damper. *No need to advertise myself. I'll keep myself off the scans,* he thought as he began his search for a refuge.

†††

"Got him!" Molly exclaimed. She had borrowed the desk just outside Harris' office. Harris heard her through his open door and came out to see what she had found.

"Torus Two, Deck Two, Segment C," she said as he walked up.

"Security scan?"

She turned her 2D display toward Harris, its back to the rest of the bullpen. On the screen, a fuzzy figure appeared from a side corridor and moved down the public promenade, away from the ship docks.

"Good. Inform Henry Hillman to get his people moving. We need to isolate him if we can, box him in if we can't."

Molly was entering the instructions into her link as he spoke. With a touch, she transmitted the orders to the patrollers. "Done, sir."

"Get your gear—ballistic panels too. Be ready when I get back," he told her before returning to his office, closing the door, and darkening his windows.

Customs Service shipsuits and Inverness militia field uniforms were protection against common frangible bullets. Frangible ammunition was allowed—demanded—for use within the station. Frangible bullets couldn't penetrate the station's hull or bulkheads. Solid and armor-piercing rounds, on the other hand, were prohibited, except for patrollers, Custom agents and inspectors. However, the prohibition did not prevent criminals from arming themselves with illegal ammunition. Having a pistol loaded with armor-piercing bullets, much less firing them, was a spacing violation. More than one violator had been grabbed by station residents and tossed out the nearest airlock, often with a patroller keying the code to open the outer door.

*Better to be safe than sorry*, Molly mused as she removed a number of flexible armor plates from her backpack and began to insert them into slits in her uniform's torso, legs, upper arms, and, as far as she could reach, her back. A nearby agent saw her adding armor to her militia field uniform and helped her insert armor in the unreachable pockets on her back. Molly thanked him.

"Well, I thought you wouldn't be adding armor unless you had a good reason," the agent replied. "Happy to help."

†††

Inside his office, Harris was speaking to McKuen. "We have him, John. I blocked all outbound departures hoping he would panic and use his damper. He's done so. When will your team arrive?"

"They just got onboard," McKuen replied. "In fact"—he glanced aside for an instant—"they're on Torus Two, Deck One, Segment B."

"Move them up to Deck Two. Our man is in Segment C," Harris said.

McKuen was entering the data in his link as Harris spoke. When he finished, he tapped it. "Data sent, Donal. I want him alive. Don't disappoint me."

"If we can," Harris said and reached out to cut the connection. *I'm not risking my people just to get you this chameleon.*

"By the way, Donal," McKuen said before Harris could complete his action. "Our lab said the nanites from your victim are of DeeCee manufacture."

†††

Molly Quinn was waiting for him when he left his office. She helped him insert armor panels in his rear torso pockets. Harris had two small-diameter metal tubes in his hand and was inserting them into a sleeve pocket, followed by a small magazine-like box. Catching his attention, she raised her eyebrows in an unspoken query.

"Capture device, Molly. This is why I have a resuscitation team ready."

"What is it?"

"A blowgun with curare-tipped needles and loaded with nanites that will, I hope, block any suicide attempt the chameleon may try. Enough talk. Let's go. Henry's waiting for us."

†††

Henry Hillman and a half dozen patrollers met Donal Harris and Molly Quinn at the patroller substation near the chameleon's location.

Hillman's link was projecting a hologram of their suspect to his team. Hillman nodded as the two approached.

"Tracking him?" Harris asked the senior patroller.

"Yep," Hillman replied. "We tracked him back to when he entered that side corridor. We have a full-facial scan of him. He's just strolling along now, as if he didn't have a care in the world. But he's keeping an eye on his back and surroundings. One of my patrollers passed him on the way here, and he turned his back to my man. I don't think he knows we can track him."

Harris examined the surroundings in the holo. "He's walking away from us, right?"

"Yes, toward Segment D."

"Okay. Let's use the maintenance corridors and get ahead of him. I want Officer Quinn and myself to be behind him. You and your patrollers will spread out ahead of him and to both sides. The promenade is a hundred meters wide at this point?" He looked to Hillman for confirmation. The patrollers were intimately familiar with the station, more so than Customs inspectors and interns.

"Right," Hillman agreed.

"Let's move out, then. Everyone know what to do?" Harris asked, watching the patrollers. Seeing no questions, he and Molly Quinn opened the hatch to the maintenance tunnel that paralleled the public promenade and jogged down it toward Segment D.

††† 

The maintenance corridors were empty at this time of the shift. Hillman and his six patrollers followed Harris and Officer Quinn as they jogged to the next segment. When the corridor walls changed from the light yellow of Segment C to the light-tan walls of Segment D, the group left the corridor and moved into the public promenade.

"He's two hundred meters away, heading this way," Hillman reported. He had been monitoring the chameleon's movement while jogging behind Harris.

23

"Very well, this is what we'll do. Quinn and I will take the corridor back into Segment C and get behind him. You spread your people loosely around here. Try to keep them out of sight if you can. I expect he will suspect something when he gets here and sees patrollers. At that point, Quinn and I will take him."

"And?" Hillman asked.

"If it all goes pear-shaped, just shoot—put him down before he can trigger any suicide charge."

"I'll have the beat patrollers back down Segment D move people back out of the way. I hope that will reduce any possible casualties."

"No objection," Harris replied. Harris keyed his link to follow their suspect while he and Molly went back up the maintenance corridor.

After jogging seventy-five meters into Segment C, Harris announced, "He's past us."

He led Molly through a hatch back into the public area, where the two stood against the wall, looking as inconspicuous as they could while searching for their target.

Harris matched people he could see with the holo image in his heads-up display from Hillman's security scan. He indicated a man with reddish-hair and a clansman tunic who had just passed them. "That's him."

Molly, following Harris' direction, found their quarry. When she turned back, Harris was screwing the lengths of the small tubes together to form a meter-long blowgun. When the tube was assembled, Harris attached the box-like magazine to one end.

"This has an effective range of about six meters," he explained. "It'll carry farther but not accurately. The box is a magazine. It will insert one four-centimeter dart every time I press the side of the magazine. It also forms the mouthpiece of the blowgun."

"That's pretty big and obvious," she said, eyeing the blowgun. "Won't he see it?"

"I hope not. I'll hold it down by my leg. That's why I want you to walk in front of me—to mask it. When I'm ready to shoot, I'll step past you and let loose." Harris stopped, looking pensive. "These helmets make it obvious we're patrollers. Let me remove mine. I shouldn't look like a patroller or a Customs agent. Well, not much. I hope we can fool him enough to let us get close."

"Good idea. I'll remove mine too," Molly replied.

†††

Thomas Brierley was keeping alert, but so far nothing alarmed him. The raised pressure doors marking the border between Segments C and D were coming closer. He could see some patrollers farther ahead in Segment D. A fight was in progress.

The patrollers weren't stopping the fight. Fights between individuals in the Confederation and Dundee Orbital—dueling, they called it—were sanctioned. The patrollers were there to see that the rules were followed.

*Good. Maybe in this confusion, I can get by them without notice and find a place out of the public eye until I can board the ship.*

People were coming up behind him. He glanced back and saw a young red-haired girl in a strange uniform… and behind her—

†††

Harris rested his hand and the blowgun on Quinn's shoulder to steady his aim. The suspect glanced back, turned, and opened his mouth. Harris shot two darts into it. The man shuddered and collapsed.

Harris triggered the alarm and saw the resuscitation team rush out of a nearby shop, heading toward the man. "We'll take it from here," the team leader said. One of his team was injecting a counteragent for the curare, while a second team member had an oxygen mask over the fallen man's face. Another medic ripped open the man's shirt and slapped a medical monitor on his chest.

"Get out of my way!" Harris ordered and knelt to go through the chameleon's pockets. Most of the contents were normal, except for a

25

digital fob. Harris pointed at the chameleon's duffel resting of the floor a few feet away. "And secure that!"

Molly grabbed the duffel's handle and changed its "follow-me" mode to idle. "Done, sir."

Harris stood with the fob in his hand and nodded to Molly. Success. They had captured the chameleon alive and without collateral casualties. *This fob is likely his suicide trigger. I hope it doesn't have a failsafe backup.*

He shuddered. It could have all gone wrong if the fight hadn't distracted the chameleon. The interrogation team, McKuen's people, arrived with Henry Hillman in the lead to take the fallen man away.

"Good job, Henry. Great idea to stage that fight."

"Well," Hillman said proudly, "it was one of my guys who thought of it. He picked the biggest spacer in the bar and poured a beer over his head. It went from there. All we did was to move it out of the bar."

"How'd he do? Your man, I mean."

"He'll need a nose reset, but other than that, he's fine. I'm putting him in for a citation for innovative solutions to an on-duty need."

"Send it to me. I'll endorse it," Harris said, grinning.

"I'll do that. Thank you, Inspector."

Hillman turned to leave, but Harris reached out to touch his arm. "Henry, I think this is his suicide charge trigger," Harris said, extending the digital fob to the patroller and pointing at the nearby duffel. "Would you put them into a shielded container and take them to the evidence locker? Have someone check and defuse the duffel if necessary."

Hillman took the fob, gingerly, and walked back to his group with the duffel in his other hand. Their job, except for the hand-off of the duffel, was done.

Harris turned to his partner. "Let's head back to the office, Molly. I have to make some calls, and then we can call it a day."

Dr. Martin Kawasa was waiting for them when they returned to the Customs office. "I hear you had an exciting shift, Inspector."

"Yes we did, and no new business for you, Doctor."

"Good. I have enough work as it is."

Kawasa's presence was unexpected. All Harris wanted to do was close the case and go home. He had been on duty since the murder occurred, some fourteen hours ago, and that had happened at the end of his usual shift.

"I wanted to tell you. I've solved the mystery," Kawasa announced.

"Mystery?" Harris shook his head to clear the cobwebs fatigue had produced. "What mystery? We got the chameleon."

"Not that one. The other one. The one we've been trying to identify. I found his face on the barroom floor!"

"Huh!" Harris wasn't up to form. He didn't know what Kawasa was talking about.

Molly walked up to the two men. "What's going on?"

"I solved the mystery," Kawasa repeated. "Here, look." He tapped his link, and a hologram appeared in the air before them; it was a scene from the murder. The first image was one Molly had taken at the crime scene with the body facedown on the floor. The second image was with the body faceup, and a third, not one of Molly's images, was of the same spot after the body had been taken away. "See! Here in the third image."

Harris and Molly looked. On the floor, under high-ultraviolet light, was a faint fluorescent image of a face.

"It was created at death," Kawasa explained. "The victim didn't die immediately. It took some time, a few moments. He was lying facedown, and as he expired, the nanites in his face that maintained his appearance seeped out of his body onto the floor. Without power from a living body, they died—leaving this behind."

27

"Make me a copy," Harris said. He would need to pass this information on to McKuen.

"Yes, yes, I will, but look at who it is!"

Harris looked again at the image. It wasn't anyone he recognized.

"Oh!" Molly said.

"See! She knows!" Kawasa almost danced with glee. "Oh, the reaction when the newsies find out about this."

Harris looked at the two. *What is Kawasa talking about? Why would the newsies be involved, unless…*

"You really don't know who that is?" she asked.

Harris looked at her. "Haven't a clue."

"It's the image of Finlay Keith, the holo actor."

Harris didn't recognize the name, but then he didn't have time to watch the entertainment nets. "Is he someone well-known?"

"Yes, Uncle. He's one of the most popular holo-vid stars in the system. He's all in the news at the moment because he disappeared a week ago, and no one, not even his agents, know where he is or why he's missing."

"You mean…" Harris was beginning to see her point.

"Yes. Was that chameleon to replace Keith—or was Finlay Keith already a chameleon?"

Harris rubbed his eyes. His eyes burned. All he wanted was to go to bed.

Kawasa had stopped his dancing and stood next to Molly, waiting for Harris' response.

Harris looked up and asked Kawasa, "How many copies of this image do you have?"

"Just two. This one and the one in the archive," Kawasa said.

"Don't make any more copies. Send this one to me and then delete every one you have, including the one in the archive."

"But..."

"All of them, Martin. Any foreign chameleon operating inside the Confederation is an internal security issue. There are questions that need answering before this can be made public."

"What questions?" Kawasa asked.

"First, are there other similar operations going on? Is this a broad infiltration attempt? Or, since one DeeCee chameleon killed another, was it a cancellation of an operation? Have other high-profile people already been replaced by chameleons?"

Harris could see Kawasa's understanding in his eyes. "Until those determinations can be made, this is now classified. Keep this secret—both of you. Now go. I have to make some calls."

After Kawasa and Quinn were gone, Harris walked back into his office and sealed the door. It was mid-second shift, and no one else had been in the bullpen to see Kawasa's image. He sat, put his feet up on an extended desk drawer, sighed slowly, and made his call.

It was in the middle of the night for McKuen when Harris called. He answered and heard Harris say, "Good evening, uh... morning, John. I have a story to tell you... about a face on the barroom floor."

# Homegoing to Hollowell

*This hill, though high, I covet to ascend;*
*The difficulty will not me offend.*
*For I perceive the way to life lies here.*
*Come, pluck up, heart; let's neither faint nor fear.*
*Better, though difficult, the right way to go,*
*Than wrong, though easy, where the end is woe.*

*—John Bunyan, Pilgrim's Progress*

"This will be your room, Commodore, next to the observation room as you requested," the nurse said.

"I'm not a commodore anymore… nor a ship captain either," Daffyd Llewellyn Davies replied brusquely. "Just call me Dee-Ell, please. Daffyd Llewellyn is too long."

The nurse smiled. She made a habit of presenting a cheerful face to her patients. They arrived at this section of Dundee Orbital Medical Center unwillingly, often in pain, and acutely aware of their bleak future. "Very well, Dee-Ell. If you need anything, just call. My link is always open."

"Thank you. I will if necessary."

"Would you please don this?" She handed him a standard hospital monitor suit similar to a one-piece shipsuit without legs or arms.

Dee-Ell looked at the suit then back at the nurse. "No," he said flatly. "No further medical intervention except for pain, and I'll decide when I want a pain blocker."

"But—"

"Check with Doctor… uh…"

"Méndez. I will, but—"

"It's all right, nurse. Not your concern. I won't be here all that long. Just check with Méndez."

"Very well, Com—Dee-Ell." She left the monitor suit hanging in the room's small closet and walked out, leaving Daffyd Llewellyn Davies the 68th to get settled.

†††

After the nurse left, Dee-Ell stood in the middle of the room and examined it. *Sterile*, he thought as he looked at the furnishings. *Like a cabin on a new ship.* Seeing nothing of interest, he ran his hand along the edge of the bed as he walked to one of the side chairs. He wasn't as steady on his feet as he once was. When he reached the side chair, he sat carefully and considered his future.

Daffyd Llewellyn Davies was the sixty-eighth man in his family to bear the name. Every generation since the founding of the Davies line had had a Daffyd Llewellyn. At one time, possessing the name had carried political obligations. While the name still granted political power, it was much less than in centuries past. Now, being the senior of those holding the name was a function of hereditary continuance and a source of stability within the Davies line and sept.

*Brennschluss. Why me? Why now?* It was an old word from an older language. Now it had a new definition. *Death. Not fast but slow... well, not always.*

"They're working on a solution," they'd said. *A solution. Ha!* A disease could have a cure. However, Brennschluss was not a disease; it was a malfunction. *A solution?* The specialist's condescending voice, when he diagnosed Dee-Ell's condition, still made him angry.

He fought to control his emotions. All too often, anger led to depression. *I will not be pitied! I will not!* What he needed was to get home to Hollowell. He would find comfort there. He had promised his parents and his family that he would return. *And return, I will.*

†††

31

Dee-Ell had arrived at Dundee Orbital's medical center with little fanfare. He'd come from the docks on a tram, accompanied by a younger man. Waiting for him were a physician and a nurse.

Stepping out of the tram, Dee-Ell lost his balance and staggered. His companion grabbed his arm to steady him. Once he was steady on his own feet, Dee-Ell shook off the younger man's hand.

The elder stood erect at 1.9 meters, wearing a standard one-piece shipsuit bearing the logo of Williams Shipping Line high on the right sleeve. He was big-boned with the muscular build common to clansmen from Inverness. His graying light-brown hair and brown-flecked green eyes—along with his direct gaze, manner, and stature—belied his post-centenarian age.

He stepped forward and, in clan fashion, introduced himself. "I am Daffyd Llewellyn Davies the sixty-eighth of Clan Williams, Sept Davies, Line Davies. I believe you are expecting me." He introduced his companion, a shorter, younger man dressed in conventional Dundee Orbital business attire. "This is my representative, John Henry Hughes."

The younger man nodded to the physician and nurse. "I, too, am of Clan Williams, Sept Davies."

The physician smiled. "As am I. Francisco Méndez, Clan Williams, Sept Davies, at your service. This"—he indicated the nurse at his side—"is Nurse Gilliam Ottley."

"Of Clan McLean, Sept Clemmons," she added.

Méndez turned to the older man and extended his hand. "Welcome, Senior. If you'll follow us, we'll get you checked in. Do you need a scooter?"

"No, all I want is clearance to go downbelow to Hollowell."

The physician nodded, noncommittally. "Let's check you in. Then we'll see about going downbelow."

†††

Méndez had been discussing Dee-Ell's condition with John Henry Hughes when Nurse Gilliam Ottley slipped quietly into the office. She had just taken Dee-Ell to his room.

"What can you tell me of his condition?" Hughes asked Méndez. "I only know that he wants to go downbelow, and the referring specialists just say it isn't advisable." As Dee-Ell's representative, Méndez could discuss the older man's condition without violating privacy, the *Proprieties*, and Customs and Traditions.

The physician sat back in his office chair and studied Hughes. The man was Dee-Ell's guardian in all but name. He was young for his position, Gilliam observed, as she watched the exchange. Being Dee-Ell Davies's representative meant he was either very good at his job or a political appointee.

"You deserve a truthful answer," Méndez replied. "I'm surprised he made it this far, sept brother. Do you understand what Brennschluss is?"

"Not really. This is the first time I've known anyone who had it," Hughes said.

Méndez nodded. Not many people outside the medical fraternity knew anything about Brennschluss. Dee-Ell was the first case she had seen. The same was likely true for Méndez too.

"It is a cascading failure of the body's nanites," Méndez said. "The condition has been known for a long time. Only a few, a very few, are affected… very few. One of those few is the Senior."

Méndez paused, turned to his link console, and ordered orange juice. He raised an eyebrow to Hughes, who shook his head. He looked at Gilliam, but she declined too. "Talking always makes me thirsty, and I need to boost my blood sugar. It has been and will be a long day." The link pinged, and a small door slid opened in the auto-chef next to his desk, revealing his juice.

Méndez opened the container and took a sip before continuing. "For some reason—and we don't know why—the body's nanites fail. They just stop working. The nanites can be flushed and replaced. It's a standard procedure, and the medics treating Dee-Ell have done so. Repeatedly. However, true to the condition, those new nanites fail just like the originals."

The physician paused, giving Hughes an opportunity to respond. The younger man just shook his head.

*He's beginning to understand*, Méndez thought.

Méndez resumed. "The nanite failure alone is not the real problem. Some people, for whatever reason, cannot tolerate nanites. They can live normal, albeit much shorter, lives; a hundred years, plus or minus a decade, instead of the usual two hundred plus years. The problem with Brennschluss is that the body sometimes loses its ability to heal, maintain, and regulate itself when the nanites stop functioning. Body functions begin to fail; hormonal balances become unstable. Kidneys, the heart, liver, and other major organs, weaken, and deteriorate. Death usually comes from systemic collapse and organ failure. Most of those affected decline rapidly. Others, like Dee-Ell, live for some time, years even."

"Years?" Hughes asked.

"Dee-Ell has been living with Brennschluss for eighteen months. It took him that long just to get here. Eighteen months is longer than anyone expected him to last. Apparently, his drive to return to Inverness is what has kept him alive this long. He's a very stubborn individual, as you've no doubt discovered."

"Yes, he is that." Hughes leaned forward in his chair, lowered his head, and clasped his hands. "I can barely imagine the drive needed to make that trek, all the while knowing he was dying." He looked up at Méndez. "And if he can't go downbelow?"

The physician didn't answer Hughes' question. He didn't have to. "In Dee-Ell's case, the cause of his medical problems is the continuing degradation of his central nervous system. The degradation is manifested by two conditions. The first is malignant growths—cancer—in his brain and along his spine. We—by that I mean his previous physicians—have removed the spinal growths as they appear, and those in his brain, as well... but..." He looked at Hughes. "The tumors return and are more virulent than before. An additional consequence of those remedial procedures is that the walls of his major blood vessels are thinning. A hemorrhage could occur at any time. According to his records, he has refused further medical treatment other than pain control."

Méndez could see that Hughes was overwhelmed. Dee-Ell was the Senior of their Line, and to be in this situation in the prime of middle age? "It's a tragedy."

"Options?" Hughes asked quietly.

"There aren't any," Méndez said flatly.

Hughes sat upright. "Then this is nothing more than a deathwatch!"

"Yes, it is."

Gilliam saw Hughes' face blanch. Family, Sept and Line, was important to the clans of Inverness. Moreso for Clan Williams by their Customs and Traditions.

"What is the second problem?" Hughes asked quietly.

"It's why you have been made his representative," Méndez responded. "His mind is failing too. Long ago, there was a condition called Alzheimer's disease. It caused deterioration of the brain, leading to memory loss, confusion, and finally, death. The condition was eliminated through genetic manipulation and later prevented with nanites. Dee-Ell is in the early stages of the disease. Treatments have been ineffective." Méndez swallowed the last of his juice. "However, I don't think he will have time for that to be much of an issue."

†††

Dee-Ell first noticed the early warnings of approaching Brennschluss a year and a half earlier. By habit, he reviewed his medical status every month. Eighteen months ago, his nanites yellow-flagged several items. Red-flagged warnings would have triggered an emergency alert. But the flagged items were just on the edge of normal, whatever normal meant in these days of nanite-managed physical care.

Nevertheless, like any responsible adult, he had mentioned the readings to his ship's medic, who had run a series of tests. When they met again, the medic's long face told Dee-Ell that the news was bad before the man could even say any words.

Brennschluss. It meant an end to space. He resigned his office as commodore of the Williams Shipping fleet, gave up being captain of the CMS *Lauren Hughes,* gave up his dream of owning his own ship, and began his trek to Inverness and home—to Hollowell.

†††

A bolt of pain flashed through him, freezing him into immobility and taking his breath away. Like the times before, it only lasted a moment then faded away. *Was it more intense this time?*

The four-wheel-drive mule had drifted to the side of the road that led to Kunarr Pass. Dee-Ell guided the single-seat vehicle with its small, attached trailer to a level area at the side of the old graveled trade road and stopped.

Up the road, the top of the pass was not far, half a klick, perhaps. Old Cal was high overhead, and the temperature was rising. Cumulus clouds were building on the far side of the pass, fed by the moist air flowing up from the Orkney Ocean a hundred kilometers to the west.

Dee-Ell walked around the mule to relieve the stiffness in his back and legs. The pass was high, and the air was thin. After a few minutes, he was panting, taking deep breaths.

*Home. I'll be home tonight—tomorrow at the latest. I promised.*

The wide spot where he had parked was several klicks above the tree line. Looking back at the plains on the western edge of the Scotia continent's interior grasslands, he couldn't quite see the small grove at the base of the mountain where he had camped the previous evening. He could, however, see the faint white line on the eastern horizon that was Clan Williams' Caernarvon Spaceport.

An old-style VTOL shuttle rose from the spaceport. *On its way to Dundee Orbital,* he surmised. The crackling rumble of the shuttle's reaction engines reached him as it climbed out of sight.

Dee-Ell was unsure how he had reached this spot. He vaguely remembered camping overnight in the grove below. However, he could not remember how he had escaped from Dundee Orbital and reached the surface.

The stop below the pass provided an excuse for a late-morning break. The mule contained power outlets for accessories, such as heating water in a flask for tea.

With the tea and a couple of sandwiches settling in his stomach, he was ready to proceed. *I can reach Hollowell by dark if I push it.*

Dee-Ell glanced back at the vapor trail slowly dissipating in the sky, and a flood of memories flowed through him. He and Caitrin had traveled this road on their honeymoon and had stopped for a few days at a place not far from this spot. They had watched the shuttles land and rise, watched the bison grazing on the plains below, made plans, made love, and contemplated their future.

*All long ago. Where has the time gone?*

He had been shipborne for more than a century after leaving Inverness at eighteen, as so many had, to find wealth and excitement. Wealth, he had not found, but he had experienced more excitement than he had ever wanted. The last time he was home was to marry Caitrin. He had promised his family he would return to Hollowell. Now, finally, after all those years, he was coming home to stay.

Dee-Ell found contentment in space, and life had been good. His shipborne life had begun as a ship's boy, an entry position in Clan Williams' merchant fleet. Over the years, he'd risen to the rank of Commodore of the fleet. His travels had taken him from one end of human space to the other. On occasion, he'd even gone beyond the recognized borders into rarely traveled and thinly settled territory.

*One hundred twelve years in space, forty years as captain, and twelve as commodore. I planned to retire next year and buy my own ship.*

*Gone now. I had always thought I would have plenty of time to visit home—next year or the year after. Now...*

Time had become a precious, fast-disappearing commodity. Dee-Ell sat astride the mule. *It's time to...*

†††

"Oh, sorry to wake you, Dee-Ell." The nurse had been checking the hospital room's built-in monitor when she inadvertently woke her patient. She had only a few patients to monitor, and Dee-Ell was her priority assignment. He had been asleep in the side chair in his room muttering softly while he slept. She must have made some sound.

He opened his eyes, looked around the room in confusion before focusing on her. "Oh... I thought... I..." He cleared his throat and said, "I thought for a moment that I was elsewhere."

"I'm sorry I woke you. I just wanted to check and see if you needed anything. I thought you might have been in pain," she said.

"Uh... some... I thought it was real..."

"Real?"

Dee-Ell gathered his thoughts. "I was dreaming. It seemed so real..."

Gilliam laughed. "I've had dreams like that. Many are very vivid." When he didn't reply, she asked, "Would you like to lie down? I can help you into bed if you'd prefer."

"No, that's fine, Nurse...?"

"Gilliam Ottley, Dee-Ell." She'd had been introduced to him on his arrival a few hours ago and understood his memory might be erratic because of his condition. "Of Clan McLean, Sept Clemmons."

"Oh, yes, I remember. Gilliam," he said, concentrating on her name. "Thank you for your thoughtfulness."

†††

His link pinged. Dee-Ell's Dundee physician, *Dr. Méndez,* he remembered, had scheduled a meeting to review his medical status. *Good. Now he'll give me the waiver, and I'll go downbelow to Hollowell.* Gilliam arrived with a scooter to take him to his appointment. "Hospital rules, Dee-Ell," she said. He was about to refuse the scooter but reconsidered. *Save my efforts for the physician, not the nurse.*

†††

"Since you won't wear the monitor suit, we used the built-in sensors in your room to perform a full-body scan," Méndez said. "I'm sorry to tell you… you can't go downbelow. You wouldn't survive the descent."

Dee-Ell heard—and didn't hear. *Can't go home? No! It's unthinkable! I still have friends here. One of them will take me.*

Méndez watched him. "If you think one of your friends will take you down, I doubt you'll find any who will. Your arrival and your condition have hit the link-nets. We've been very diligent to give your representative updates of your condition. He's made sure all your friends know taking you downbelow would kill you. No one wants to take a live passenger down and then land with a corpse on board."

Méndez spoke, but Dee-Ell wasn't listening. He was planning.

†††

Dee-Ell reached the top of Kunarr Pass and met the upwelling air from the windward side of the pass. To the left side of the pass, the Dragonback Mountains ran parallel to the sea. To the right was the beginning of the Scandia Mountains running to the northwest and on to Saint Edward's Gulf. Between the two mountain ranges was the broad Dyffryn Davies Valley, a moderate rain forest fed by the moisture-laded air off the Orkney ocean. On the valley's western slope of the Dragonbacks was Hollowell. *Home.*

A line of clouds that had formed along the western side of the Dragonbacks was darkening. *Rain soon. Maybe before I reach Hollowell.*

39

Dee-Ell stopped and removed his rainsuit from a bag on the small trailer. *I don't need to expose myself further. I can get sick now.*

The view from the Kunarr Pass was the reason he had chosen this old, almost-abandoned route. It would be his last opportunity to see the view he had shared with Caitrin.

The road, in centuries past, had been a trading route between Clan Williams territory and Clan Davies territory. After the merger of the two clans three centuries earlier, the land on both sides of the Dragonbacks belonged to Clan Williams.

*Too bad she isn't here.* He remembered their first and only visit to Hollowell together, while on their honeymoon. *Was that eighty years ago?* His memory was one of the functions he was slowly losing to Brennschluss.

†††

A week had passed since Dee-Ell's arrival at the medical center. He was sitting in the observation room, with its floor-to-ceiling window, looking at Inverness below. Dundee Orbital was in synchronous orbit above the planet, and the whole of the Scotia continent lay before him. He had repositioned a recliner to give him a full view of the planet and, at that moment, of the terminator moving across it.

Gilliam stepped closer. Dee-Ell had also moved a small table next to him with a pitcher of water, a bottle, and a tumbler. From time to time, he would reach over, take a sip from the tumbler, and put it back on the table.

He had had a string of visitors this day. The news had spread, and one by one, his friends had come to pay their respects. He was disappointed. None would agree to take him downbelow.

"How are you, Dee-Ell?" she asked, intruding on his somber mood.

"Tolerable. Just tolerable," he said with sarcasm plain in his voice. "If you have some time, sit with me."

"Thank you, I will. It's my break time."

"And you're willing to sit with an old, dying man?"

"Well, dying you may be. Old? Not by modern standards."

Her bluntness was a surprise and made him feel better—his bout of depression appeared to dissipate with her honesty. "Sit, then," he said, friendlier than before.

When she had done so, he pointed out the window to the planet below. "See where the terminator just touches the northern end of the Dragonbacks?"

"Yes. Just south of Caernarvon Shuttleport?"

"That's the spot. That's where Hollowell lies."

They conversed, two people passing the time of day. When her break was over, she left to continue her rounds, leaving him to watch the vista below.

†††

The pass was behind him. The clouds that appeared on the windward side of the Dragonbacks were still growing. A storm was coming, and he was glad he'd gotten his rainsuit out of his bags in the trailer.

Dee-Ell was now below the tree line, and the graveled road wound down through Aspen groves and evergreens. Up ahead were two figures. Both were furred. One was large, a solid black lurcat, and the other was a smaller, heavily furred white, brown, and tan cat. The second figure was not a lurcat, but the long tail of the larger 'cat was curled protectively around the smaller one.

Lurcats were genetically enhanced felines created from the genetic material of the North American mountain lion, the Canadian lynx, the Norwegian forest cat, and, according to myth, human DNA. The result was an intelligent, man-sized feline with opposable thumbs and the ability to walk upright.

Lurcats, because of the construction of their heads, mouths, and throats, could not speak human languages. They could, however, communicate via link or sign language. The 'cats understood human speech, and some humans, a few, could understand the language that had evolved among the 'cats over the centuries. Dee-Ell was not one of those few. However, like all clansmen born on Inverness, he was, as were all clansmen born on Inverness, fluent in the 'cats' sign language.

Dee-Ell pulled up and stopped beside the two figures. "Sam?" *Sam? No, it couldn't be.* Lurcats did not live as long as humans. "You're looking well for your age."

A, long time ago, before he had gone into space, Dee-Ell had wandered the mountains along the Orkney coast with Sam. Both had been young then. Now, they were not.

The lurcat purred loudly and signed, *Ha! Better than you.* Sam was one of a few Lurcats who had medical nanites, but even with them, he was very old for a 'cat. Most 'cat prides couldn't afford nanites—and did not want them. Sam looked closer. *You are not looking all that well, Dee-Ell. I heard you were coming this way and thought we would meet you.*

"Who is your friend?"

Sam glanced down at the smaller feline, who was a quarter of his size, and back up at Dee-Ell. *This is Ancestor. He is a pure Norwegian forest cat. We are trying to civilize him.*

Dee-Ell was intrigued. "How's that working?" Most ships had cats, the first line of defense against vermin. However, few cats were trainable—independent creatures that they were.

Sam made the sign for laughter. *Better some days than others. He really is smart… for a cat. Not like us, but we have hopes.*

Rain had been falling unnoticed until the wetness finally dripped through the canopy above, to fall on them. Dee-Ell got off his mule and donned the rainsuit. He hopped a few steps, trying to get one leg into the suit. For a moment, his leg did not want to obey instructions. Dee-Ell cussed to himself. Little tasks like this were getting more and more difficult. Finally, he leaned against the mule and inserted one foot then the other into the rainsuit. With a final shrug, he slipped his arms into the suit, slipped the suit over his shoulders, and sealed it.

The mule he had leased back at the Caernarvon shuttleport was configurable. It could change from a single-seat model to a two- three- or four-seat version with an overhead canopy. With the coming storm, Sam and Ancestor would not like to get wet if it wasn't necessary. Neither would Dee-Ell.

*Why can I remember leasing the mule but not how I got down from Dundee Orbital?*

After a series of commands from Dee-Ell's link, the mule's frame flowed and reconfigured itself into a vehicle with two bench seats, side weather shields, and a canopy. Within minutes, they were back on the road.

Sam's pride, the Camedd Llewellyn, patrolled and guarded this section of the Dragonback Mountains. While the pride was not officially a member of Clan Williams, the pride did consider themselves members of the Davies Sept. The 'cat-and-Sept partnership was a millennium old.

*We will travel with you for a while,* Sam signed. *It is important for Ancestor to meet you and for you to meet him.*

"Why is that?"

*You are the sixty-eighth of your name, not so?*

"Yes, however, there are others who have the same name."

*Seventy-six is the most recent?*

"Yes. The boy was born last year."

The mule sank a wheel into a hidden pothole in the road, causing the mule to rock and shake water from the canopy onto Ancestor. He shook the water from his fur and moved to sit between Dee-Ell and Sam.

*Like you, Ancestor is one of a continuous line, the eleventh of his name.*

"*Meerow,*" Ancestor agreed.

43

*We think,* Sam continued, *in another fifty to one hundred generations, maybe more, maybe less, Ancestor's progeny will come to be more like us. Our children.*

"An admirable project, Sam."

*We think so. Ancestor must learn Honor and Respect, to give respect and understand honor—his honor.*

†††

Dr. Méndez, with Nurse Ottley at his side, was conducting afternoon rounds. There were only a few patients in this section of the medical center. Insiders called it the hospice wing. Méndez secretly appreciated his lack of patients, though. Fewer patients meant he could spend more time with the ones he had, making their remaining time more comfortable.

They passed Dee-Ell's room. The indicators near the doorway were dark. Dee-Ell was probably sitting in his recliner in the observation room.

"How's Dee-Ell?" he asked his nurse.

Gilliam sighed. "He's dreaming and sleeping more and more. He refuses to sleep in his bed, so I've changed his recliner to make it more comfortable. I clipped a call button to his shipsuit in case he needs us."

"Is it dreams or delirium?"

She glanced at him. They were approaching the observation room, and as they reached the doorway, Dee-Ell was visible in his recliner, apparently asleep.

"I don't know," she admitted.

The two stopped outside the observation room and paused to look at Dee-Ell. "I had another scan done on him last night while he was sleeping," Méndez said. "He has another tumor between his frontal lobes. We could easily remove it, but he has refused all treatment. I'll discuss it with Hughes, but I think we'll just follow his instructions and leave him be."

"It's going to be hard when he goes," Gilliam replied. "You can't help but like him. He doesn't complain and only wants one thing."

"To go home."

"Yes."

The two continued down the hall. They had other patients to attend to.

†††

The rain came in earnest. Dee-Ell, with Ancestor between him and Sam, guided the mule down the graveled track toward Hollowell. Daylight was fading with the storm, and the sky was overcast. A headache grew, pounding behind his eyes. The occurrence happened more and more often these last few weeks. Along with the headache was a numbness that grew in his lower right leg.

Sam, looking to the front, was signing, apparently unaware of Dee-Ell's inattention. If he remembered correctly, there was a glen up ahead. He would stop there for a while. Perhaps he needed to eat. He'd lost his appetite in the months since his sentence and had to remind himself to eat.

But Sam finally noticed Dee-Ell's inattentiveness. He patted Dee-Ell's arm. *You are not feeling well. Ancestor and I will leave you now. I hope, my friend, to see you again.* Sam paused, failing to communicate his emotion. *But I fear it will not be so.*

Sam leaned forward, laid his head along Dee-Ell's cheek, and purred while grasping Dee-Ell's shoulders. It lasted only seconds but seemed longer. Sam sat back, and spoke briefly to Ancestor, then they both jumped off the slow-moving mule to disappear into the rain, mist, and trees.

†††

The mule entered the glen; Maedryn's Meadow was its proper name, Dee-Ell remembered as it suddenly popped into his mind. *No problem with my memory now.*

45

A stone-walled, slate-roofed waystation sat on the far side of the glen, a remnant from the time when this had been a well-traveled trade road. Dee-Ell guided the mule toward the structure. Two women were sitting outside under the station's canopy. One was a blond-haired woman, and the other's hair was more reddish. *Travelers?*

Younger folk often took off for a trek through the mountains, but he saw neither provisions nor camping gear. A bear whuffed in the distance—a reminder that death and predators were always present.

If they were travelers, they should have weapons around too. *Ursus Maximus*, the Dragonback Grizzly, still roamed these mountains. No one wanted to confront a four-meter tall bear that weighed over twelve hundred kilograms without a suitable weapon. The bear could outrun any human; escape would be impossible.

That thought jolted Dee-Ell. For that very reason, Dee-Ell had a 13mm mag-rifle with him. It was still in the mule's trailer. If he came upon a bear, he would not have time to reach and load it.

*I'm slipping. What else have I forgotten?* The omission triggered another wave of depression. He'd missed so many opportunities to visit home. He had forgotten his promise. *But not today!* He had drugs for the occasional bouts of depression, but like many used to automatic nanite intervention, he had forgotten to take them.

The two women looked familiar, but… It couldn't be. He tried to remember why their presence was not possible, but he failed.

The blond woman waved. "Dee-Ell! We've been waiting for you."

*Caitrin! The other was… Maeve? How?* Dee-Ell was confused. He and Caitrin had been married for sixty years. Legally, they still were, but Caitrin had grown tired of spacing and had left him to return to Inverness. Someone said she was living in Port Curran now, far to the south on the Orkney coast.

His vision blurred for a moment. He blinked and wiped his face. *Something's wrong with my eyes.* He guided the mule under the shelter's overhang, dismounted, and with the passing of the storm, removed his rainsuit.

Gilliam walked quickly past the observation room on her way to the nurses' station. It had not been a good day; they had lost a patient, a nice elderly clanswoman who had just had her 249th birthday. She'd died surrounded by family and friends. Gilliam was ashamed to admit she was angry. *This woman had lived nearly 250 years, and Dee-Ell would likely not reach 130. And he would probably go with no one to see him off except for me, Francisco Méndez, and maybe John Henry Hughes.*

She passed the observation room. Out of the corner of her eye, she thought two women and a lurcat were sitting next to Dee-Ell, conversing while he slept. *Who were they? Dee-Ell's visitors so far had been old shipmates and business associates—all men.*

But Gilliam was in a hurry to check out and go home. She'd had enough of death for today and didn't intrude on the women. There was no need to check on Dee-Ell while he had visitors.

†††

The two women approached, walking out from under the shelter's overhang toward the mule. He recognized Caitrin. The second was Maeve, his daughter. *But... she...* "Maeve?"

"I'm here, Poppa."

"I thought you died on Manjipour!"

"As someone said long ago, the reports of my demise have been greatly exaggerated."

The reddish-haired woman walked up to Dee-Ell and hugged him. "Welcome home, Poppa," she said into his ear. "We wanted to meet you and ride to Hollowell with you."

Caitrin reached them and joined the hug. Uncontrolled tears flowed down three faces—a family reunited.

†††

Caitrin and Maeve had provisions—ham and turkey sandwiches on home-baked bread like Dee-Ell's mother had made long ago. They laid out the sandwiches, along with several side dishes. It was a full meal, but Dee-Ell had little appetite. He was getting anxious to reach to Hollowell before dark. *Home.*

When they finished, the women cleared the outdoor table and disposed the remnants of the meal. Dee-Ell had converted the mule back into a single-seat version after Sam and Ancestor left him. It took only a moment to change it into the two-bench configuration again.

The three mounted and returned to the muddy, meandering road through the trees, which were much larger than the ones higher on the mountain. Taller and farther apart, the trees created a canopy shielding them from the last of the rain.

Only one woman could sit beside Dee-Ell at a time. Caitrin was first to sit up front. She talked, telling Dee-Ell about her life since leaving space. She had taken a position as one of Sept Davies' archivists, collecting and documenting the memories and memoirs of notable clan and sept members.

Dee-Ell was silent, leaning slightly against the weather shield of the mule. This close to Hollowell, he could activate the mule's autopilot to finish the journey. He did so and drifted, listening to the one-sided conversation, while communing with his memories—his pilgrimage to Hollowell. He remembered an ancient poem by Frost. *The woods are lovely, dark and deep, but I have promises to keep and miles to go before I sleep... I have promises to keep.*

After another brief break, they resumed the journey, with Maeve now sitting next to Dee-Ell. She told him about her life on Manjipour, her husband, and their children. Dee-Ell offered a word occasionally, but for the most part, as he had with Caitrin, he remained silent. After a time, he slumped against the side of the mule. Maeve slid closer to Dee-Ell, put her arm around his shoulders, and pulled him upright.

The mule followed the road faithfully. Maeve, when necessary, took the control stick and guided the mule around obstacles and potholes.

A stream appeared alongside the track, gushing with the storm's runoff. The road continued along it until the forest opened into a wide glen dotted with grazing cattle. On the far side of the glen was a stonewalled compound: Hollowell.

†††

"Wake up, Poppa," Maeve said. "We're here.,"

The storm and overcast skies that had flowed up the coast to Hollowell, passed, and Old Cal emerged through the clouds to bathe Hollowell in its light. Dee-Ell opened his eyes. Hollowell lay before him, and a surge of joy swept through him, bringing tears to his eyes. *Home!* He had feared, more than once, that he would not be able to get here.

Hollowell was a large, nanite-stabilized, stone-and-log edifice. Larger than a manor-house, it contained over twelve hundred square meters of floor space above and below ground. The house was where he had been born and had grown up. Sept Davies owned the site, had owned it for centuries, but for him, it was home. Dee-Ell's parents were Hollowell's caretakers.

At one time, the site had been fortified. Its original purpose was to act as a border guard post. That need had ended with the merger of Clan Davies into Clan Williams and the dissolution of the border between the two clans.

A broad open veranda encircled the structure, and just as Dee-Ell remembered, the stone fireplace on the south side remained. Smoke rose from its chimney. Behind the house, backed up against a high stone cliff, were several outbuildings and one of the entrances to the under-mountain armory and former military base.

Dee-Ell, Caitrin, and Maeve dismounted and climbed the steps up to the porch. The front door opened before they reached it.

"Dee-Ell, we're so glad you're home," his mother said, stepping forward to hug him.

His father followed her and took Dee-Ell's hand while hugging him with the other. "Welcome home to Hollowell, son."

Dee-Ell looked into the face of the older man. He was ashamed and needed to apologize. With tears running down his face, he said, "I… I wish it had been sooner and under better circumstances. I promised I would come home. I… I didn't mean to take so long."

"Never mind, Dee-Ell. You're here now, and that's what is important," his mother said, interrupting the apology.

"Come on in, son," his father added, placing his arm around Dee-Ell. "I know. And don't worry about your baggage. I'll have the youngers unload the mule. We've fixed up your old room for you."

Dee-Ell wiped his face and followed his father inside, where he was led to an overstuffed chair next to the fire. "Sixty-Nine and Seventy called, asking when you would arrive. I expect they'll call again tomorrow." Sixty-Nine was the next Daffyd Llewellyn in line after Dee-Ell. Seventy would follow Sixty-Nine when the time came.

"I brought the trunk for Sixty-Nine. It's all inventoried and ready for him. He's welcome to be the Senior. More power to him." The trunk contained memorabilia from the first Daffyd Llewellyns. On occasion, he, as Senior, presented the contents as exhibits of the history of the sept.

After both men were seated next to the fire with drinks in their hands, his father asked, "Was it all that much of a burden, being Senior?"

Dee-Ell didn't immediately respond. Being Senior should have been a task for someone else. As Senior, he was the Sept's representative to the Clan Williams Sept Council. He also had, as a condition of the merger agreement between Clan Davies and Clan Williams, a second vote for being the senior Daffyd Llewellyn Davies, plus a third vote for being the sept's cultural Senior. Being a Llewellyn Davies was not a requirement for being the Sept Senior, but no one who was not one had been selected as Senior for several hundred years.

Unfortunately, Dee-Ell was seldom in the Caledonian system when the council needed him. He'd solved the problem by making Sixty-Nine his proxy. "No, not really. I just… felt I couldn't do the position full service."

"I think you made a good compromise. Not everyone is suited to be a counselor."

"Politician, you mean."

His father laughed. "Yes, a politician."

†††

Word spread that Dee-Ell, Daffyd Llewellyn Davies, the 68th, was home. Over the next few days, old friends and family suddenly appeared to greet him, shake his hand, and speak briefly before departing to give the next in line access to him. They all knew why he had come home, but no one mentioned the reason. In fact, Dee-Ell had been so busy that he had not had time to think about Brennschluss.

Time flowed. Sixty-Nine arrived, and the turnover process was completed. Sixty-Nine was now, officially, the Senior instead of a proxy.

Dee-Ell spoke for a short time with Seventy. They had once traveled together to visit the Coterni. Seventy had stayed behind on clan business while Dee-Ell and his ship continued on their trading route. They had not seen one another since.

Dee-Ell had been sitting at an old wooden desk, signing documents, and had grown stiff. After rising from the paper-cluttered desk, he walked through the house. He had not seen Caitrin or Maeve since his arrival, but he knew they were still here, somewhere.

A woman he didn't recognize was in the kitchen. "I'm going for a walk around. Have you seen Maeve or Caitrin?"

"Who?" she asked.

"Maeve and Caitrin. I can't find them." The woman was busy, and he had interrupted her work. Before she could answer, he apologized for his intrusion and walked out the side door to the veranda and down the steps to the grassy, well-tended yard that sloped up to the outbuildings and the cliff.

His walk took him around the house and up to one of the outbuildings built against the rock cliff above Hollowell. Dee-Ell's right leg dragged slightly, causing a slight limp, but he didn't notice. His mind was filled with the memories of Hollowell.

Another outbuilding hid the entrance to the underground armory and the old military base deep inside the mountain behind Hollowell. The armory was still stocked and maintained, but the underground military base had been abandoned. There were kilometers of tunnels, storerooms, power chambers, and vaults under the mountain containing ancient machines still preserved waiting to be needed. Dee-Ell felt no desire to explore them. He had once, when he was younger and still living at home. *A long time ago.*

The walk tired him. He trudged around the house to the steps up to the veranda across the front of Hollowell. Maeve and Caitrin were there, sitting in two cushioned wicker chairs, with a pitcher of tea, a bucket of ice, and tumblers on a small table between them.

"Dee-Ell! Come! Join us. We have plenty," Caitrin called. She poured him a glass of iced tea then dropped several ice cubes into it while he climbed, slowly and clumsily, up the steps and sat in a deeply cushioned chair next to his wife.

Dee-Ell's mother saw him through the front window and brought out a plate of berry muffins. "Ah," Dee-Ell said, taking one, "thank you. I was getting hungry." His appetite had returned. He took a bite then another, and soon, the muffin was gone. Reaching for another, he said, "My favorite muffins."

Dee-Ell nibbled on the second muffin and looked up in time to see a figure come through the main gate. He blinked, but his eyes couldn't focus until the figure came closer. "Sam! Welcome! I didn't think you were coming here."

*Why not?* Sam signed. *It is time for all of us. Why should we not all go together?*

"Did Ancestor come too?"

*No. He sends his regrets. He said it was not yet his time.*

Sam trotted up the porch steps, patted Caitrin and Maeve on their shoulders, and walked around to Dee-Ell's far side. He patted Dee-Ell's shoulder, too, before settling himself at Dee-Ell's feet.

When Dee-Ell's mother returned to her kitchen, Dee-Ell lowered a hand to stroke Sam's head then turned to the two women with another muffin in his other hand. "Did I ever tell you," he asked, lifting the muffin, "that I once made the cook on the old *Harold Bride* make these for me?"

"Ha. I was there, Dee-Ell. Remember?" Caitrin reminded him with a laugh.

*No.* His face fell. *I hadn't remembered that.* The failure caused his fear of Brennschluss to return. He panicked. What would become of him? Would bits and pieces of his memory fade away until nothing remained? Would he still be himself? That was his actual fear—not death but the slow disintegration of self.

"Don't worry, Poppa," Maeve said. "We'll all be here. Sam too. If you can't remember something, we can. We won't leave you."

The sunlight dimmed momentarily as a cloud passed between the valley and Old Cal. He was tired. The walk around Hollowell was more exhausting than he'd expected. Dee-Ell dragged a small footstool up, crossed his ankles on it, and settled into the cushions of the chair. "I think I'll rest my eyes. Wake me for dinner if you would." He felt good… calmer, his fear and longing gone.

*I'm home like I promised. At last.*

†††

A nurse found him an hour later in the observation room of the Dundee Orbital Medical Center. His body was reclined in a cushioned chair positioned to give him a view of Inverness down below. Three glasses of partially emptied tea, a half-full pitcher, a melting bucket of ice, and a plate with crumbs and one berry muffin sat on the small table beside him.

The nurse called Dr. Méndez to come and confirm what she and the rest of the staff had been expecting. The old man had wanted to go home. But could not. Instead, he spent most of his last few days here, in the observation room, gazing at the planet. Daffyd Llewellyn Davies was in exile, forbidden to go home, like Moses seeing the Promised Land but being unable to enter.

†††

"Dee-Ell." Someone shook his shoulder. "Dee-Ell! Wake up! It's time to go."

"Go?" He shook his head, the fuzziness of waking leaving him.

"It's time to finish the journey. Others are waiting," Caitrin said. Maeve and Sam were standing next to her, waiting for him. "Get up. It's time for us to go—you too."

He stood, bent, shifted his shoulders, and twisted his back to relieve the kinks that had developed while he slept. Then he realized that he had no kinks, nor any of the minor aches that had developed over the last few months. Maeve and Sam were already down from the veranda, on the walk to Hollowell's eastern gate. Caitrin extended her hand to Dee-Ell.

She tucked his arm in with hers. The two stepped down from the veranda and walked to join Maeve and Sam. When they were all together, the four of them walked toward the gate.

†††

Gilliam, recalled from her residence, arrived to meet Méndez. Her home was nearby, a deck and segment away from the medical center and in the same torus of the station.

Méndez had the observation room closed off. He couldn't reach John Henry Hughes. Alone, he sat next to the body, waiting for Gilliam to arrive before confirming the death. There was no need to hurry.

When Gilliam walked in, Méndez gestured to the tumblers, pitcher, and plate on the side table. "Was there someone with him?"

"I don't know. He'd been talking about his wife, mother, and daughter earlier in the afternoon. I... thought I saw them—with a lurcat, sitting with him, but I... had been with the McKeens, the elderly clanswoman who had died earlier today and her family. My shift was over. I didn't take time check further. I just wanted to get away for a while." She felt guilty for not having checked on him. Dee-Ell had died alone without kin or kith to see him off.

"Can't have been his family," Méndez said. "According to his history, they're all dead. His parents died years ago. His daughter died four years ago on Manjipour, and his wife died in a sailing accident downbelow last year. All of his immediate family has preceded him. And I've seen no lurcats here for some time."

"He kept talking about going home to Hollowell."

The physician stood slowly. "He was the Davies' Sept Senior," he whispered, reaching down to touch Dee-Ell's shoulder.

Gilliam nodded. She, like most of the people living and working in Dundee Orbital, was from Inverness and a clanswoman of Clan McLean. The two clans, Williams and McLean, were political and economic allies. *And we share pain too*, she said to herself.

"He is... was... important to us." Méndez's voice broke. "I'll have to notify the Clan and Sept councils that the Senior has passed," the physician said.

"Should we notify anyone else?" Gilliam asked.

"I'll take care of it. His will called for burial at Hollowell—at the site of Hollowell. It was located on the edge of the Dragonback Mountains."

"He pointed the location out to me once."

"The house was destroyed in the Monmouth Civil War."

Gilliam frowned. "Destroyed?"

"Yes, twenty years ago, a fifty-kiloton kinetic strike. He was somewhere out-system. All those years spacing, and he was never able to return home."

Méndez blinked repeatedly; he was on the verge of tears. Gilliam could understand the emotions that could come upon on a person… especially for a sept and line brother like Méndez. She felt the same; she'd liked Dee-Ell.

Méndez nodded, wiped his eyes, and sighed. "All he wanted these last few days was to go home. Now he can… to Hollowell."

# The Fenian

## Wexford Station, Guadalupe, Harrison Cluster.

Fen strode along the pale-tan corridors toward the office of Charles Morton Moray, a Customs Service chief inspector and the Interdiction Office's agent on Wexford Station. Wexford was a small station and only a hundred years old, relatively new in this expanding sector of the Confederacy.

Moray's office was unlabeled. Apparently, he liked his privacy. Fen waved his link near the sensor pad on the door frame.

"Enter," a voice said, and the door slid to one side.

"How may I help you, sir?" Moray said as Fen stepped inside.

"Seán MacDiarmada," Fen said.

Moray's superiors had given him a list of pass phrases and counterphrases. At the bottom of that list was the one Fen had just uttered.

Moray didn't immediately reply. His eyes flicked over Fen's uniform, from the three gold commander's stripes on his right sleeve to the single mottled green stripe on his left cuff. Fen could almost hear Moray's thoughts. *Pack. Oh, pack.* It almost made Fen smile.

Fen's green stripe on his left cuff indicated he had once been a marine officer and had commanded at least a company. Naval Intelligence field agents, like Fen, were required to have served in both the navy and the marines.

Fen saw Moray's gaze settle on the small golden harp above Fen's green stripe. *A packin' Fenian. Yes, I am, Moray. Why am I here, bothering you? I could have been passing through Wexford on assignment. If so, why have I come to you?*

The label, Fenian, was a generic name for Naval Intelligence field agents. Some, like Fen, were real Fenians from Eire.

"Fionn mac Cumhail," Moray finally replied.

Fen smiled. "For our purposes, call me Fen. I'm looking for a man, and I hope you can help."

Moray was one of three chief Customs inspectors on the station and the local agent of the Confederation's Interdiction Office. The Interdiction Office and Naval Intelligence were in the same line of business—maintaining the Tri-Cluster Confederation's security.

The difference was Naval Intelligence's jurisdiction was outside the boundaries of the Confederation. Moray's jurisdiction, as an Interdiction Office agent, was internal. Fen was required to notify and cooperate with the Interdiction Office when his mission brought him inside the Confederacy.

"I'm seeking a man known as Antonio Marchesi. I'm told he arrived on a Franklin freighter a week ago. Is he still here? If not, when and where did he go?" Fen gave Moray a data wafer. "This contains Marchesi's dossier."

"Let me check." Moray turned to his console-link, slipped the wafer into a slot, and entered a search. A holo-monitor appeared above Moray's desk, providing the details of one Antonio Marchesi. "He left three days ago on the Williams packet, *Rudyard,* to Caledonia, Dundee Orbital."

*Pack!* Fen muttered.

## Dundee Orbital, Inverness, Jefferson Cluster

*Might as well get this over with*, Fen thought as he was escorted through the Dundee Orbital Customs office. He had worked with Donal Harris before, and while not friends, they could cooperate with one another.

"A visitor for you, Inspector," one of Donal Harris' Customs agents said at the entrance to Harris' open office door. Harris nodded to the agent, dismissing him.

He looked up at the tall, lean man in a Confederation Navy officer's uniform. "Close the door behind you, Fen. Let's have some privacy," Harris said while pressing icons on his desk to seal and secure his office.

"Donal, it's been a while," Fen said as he walked over to Harris' desk and sat in the chair in front of it.

"Not packin' long enough, Fen. What do you want?"

Harris, as in their earlier encounters, was brusque when Fen intruded into his domain. *Well!* Fen thought. *Guess Donal hasn't had his morning coffee. Let's cut to the chase.*

"I'm looking for a man using the name of Antonio Marchesi... or at least that was the name he used on Wexford Station."

Harris pulled out a lower drawer in his desk and propped his feet on it. "Why?"

"You know, your man at Wexford never asked me that."

"Why, Fen?"

"He's a spy."

"So? Half the people passing through here are spies—corporate spies, most of them."

"This one is working for the Harmony of Light or the Directorate of Sovereign Corporate States. Hivers or DeeCees."

"Hivers or DeeCees," Harris repeated. "Again, so? We have spies from everywhere passing through here. What's so special about this one?"

"He's after the Marilee Harris Communicator. She's a namesake of your sept, I believe?"

"No kin of ours. She wasn't a clanswoman. Besides, she's been dead six hundred years," Harris replied. "Anyway, it's just a fairy tale."

"No, it's not. Ériu Data and Communications, Elizabeth Harris herself, is working on it for the navy."

Harris dropped his feet back to the floor. Ériu Data and Communications, EDC, was the Confederacy's premier research-and-development organization. Elizabeth Harris, a sentient AI, owned the company. She was a full Confederate citizen, not just a legal corporate entity, and claimed Marilee Harris as her virtual mother. Marilee's Communicator was a theoretical device capable of transmitting large data packets across interstellar distances, even across the galaxy—if it worked.

Harris rocked back in his chair. "That *is* news, Fen. If anyone outside the Confederacy got their hands on it… So you want me to find this spy for you."

"Not *for* me. *With* me, Donal."

"Pack!"

Harris started the search for Marchesi using the data Fen had given him: all the information available on the quarry, including physical attributes, age, and supposed origin.

"I can't guarantee this information, Donal. It's just best estimate." Some of his Intelligence associates claimed Marchesi was a chameleon, able to change his appearance and physical attributes at will. Fen doubted that. Marchesi had not been one during Fen's previous encounters with him. Now, he was too old to survive the conversion.

"Marchesi arrived on the *Rudyard* a week ago," Harris said. "Your information was correct. I have a vid of him debarking and passing through customs. Looked okay to the agent. No contraband found. He caught a shuttle down to Loralie, a Clan Mieze shuttleport. I'll have to ask the Mieze militia what they have on him. Loralie is their jurisdiction."

Fen nodded. "I wonder why he went downbelow? EDC isn't on Inverness."

Harris shrugged. "A contact, perhaps. Maybe he needs help… maybe he's just a courier?"

"No, I've chased Marchesi before. He's not just a courier, a drone. We don't know who he's working for. He's freelance and has worked for both the Hivers and the DeeCees."

"Who'd he work for last?" Harris asked.

"The DeeCees. Yeah, I know. Doesn't mean he's still working for them, but they pay better than the Hivers."

Harris sent an info request to the Loralie Militia HQ using his Interdiction Office ID. "This request will take them some time, Fen. Mieze will have to hand-walk the request through. They don't like big central databases. Violates privacy, they say."

Fen grimaced. "I'd forgotten how stubborn the clans can be."

"Give me a link ID, and I'll call you as soon as I get anything."

Fen selected a link address, gave it to Harris, then stood to leave. "I expect it will take a day or two—"

"Aye, it will."

"So I'll check in with my superiors and see what they have." He turned and opened the office door but stopped on its threshold. *Should I? Do I owe Donal anything?* He considered his encounters with Harris. *Ah, why not?*

"This is my last gig, Donal. I've finished my tour in Intelligence, and I'm rotating out. I'm on the Captain's list."

"Good for you." Harris replied indifferently.

The response irritated Fen. He wasn't sure what he'd expected when he told Harris his news. *It's just as I've been told. Intelligence agents have no friends.* Still, Fen was disappointed.

†††

Harris thought about the small golden harp on Fen's sleeve. Fen was a true Fenian; he had known that for some time. Fenian influence, real Fenians, those from planet Eire and their non-Eire associates, reached beyond Naval Intelligence. They were a private society within the Confederation military. Fen possessed all three attributes for full membership; he was a marine, a naval officer, and a Fenian from Eire. He would rise rapidly in the navy, if he survived. Harris was a Fenian, too—an associate as an agent of the Interdiction Office—but he could never be a full member because he wasn't Eirish.

†††

Fen checked in with the station's naval contingent for a Bachelor Officer Quarters assignment. He'd been assigned a coapt in a residential area reserved for the navy. It contained a parlor-office area, a separate bedroom with 'fresher, and a small kitchen.

He threw his duffel on the bed, stripped, took a quick shower, and dressed in civilian clothes, trousers, synth-silk shirt, and boots. He slipped a knife into the sheath in the back of his trousers and added a small military-grade laser in a shoulder holster under a short, waist-length jacket. Now, he was ready to be seen in public.

Harris had accepted the chore of tracking Marchesi. That left Fen at loose ends. He had options: perhaps a tour of the local area to get a feel of the station, or maybe strike up a conversation in a local pub.

Food, he decided. The decision made, he slipped his navy ID into his jacket and left his coapt. A deck inward, he found an appealing bar and grill, Katrin's. It had a quiet family section, a louder bar and dance floor, and a choice of a buffet or a restaurant with live waiters and waitresses.

Fen chose the dining room. Two women, dressed in the style of Dundee's business casual—trim pants, blouse, and weapons belt—sat in a dim corner. They had a distinct familial resemblance. *Not twins*, he decided. *They're not the same age.*

Fen's professional habits caused him to notice the women were armed with lasers. It sparked his curiosity. Most Confederate women chose to arm themselves with projectile weapons. The younger one stood and motioned for him to join her and her friend. *Who are they? Who is she? How does she know me?*

When he walked up to her table, the younger said, "Sit, please, Commander Fitzgerald."

*How does she know my name?* Fen rarely and only in the line of duty used his surname. He slid into a chair that faced them. The chair also gave him a view of the room. It was a reflexive action from years of watching his back.

"And how do I know you, you're wondering?" she asked when he was seated.

"Yes. I am. Should we know one another?"

"I know you from your naval dossier. I'm Elspeth Harris."

He knew that name. *An AI?* "If that is true, I expected something else."

"A blank wall, a mobile metal can, a clumsy automaton, Commander?"

Fen blushed. "Well… perhaps. It is a common myth. Most people don't know your capabilities."

"A few of us are different." She looked him in the eyes, and one of hers changed from a normal-looking green iris to silver and back to green. "I can provide more proof but not here in public."

Fen turned to the other, older-looking woman. "You look just like… Are you an AI too?"

She laughed. "No, not an AI. Looking like Elspeth? Aye, I do. I was the model for her current… self, suit of clothes, and was paid a princely sum too. Captain Máire Kiernan, TCN Medical Corps, at your service."

"By your accent? Eire?"

"Ah, takes one to know one. Aye, from Donegal."

"Monaghan, myself."

"Aye? We're neighbors, then. I'm assigned to Weyland Fleetbase. I came over here to Dundee to attend a conference at Dundee's medical center. As for why I'm here, since you haven't yet asked, Commander Fitzgerald, Elspeth invited me to dinner. We're long-time—" She turned to Elspeth and asked, "How long has it been since Mother chose me as your model?"

"Four years, now."

"We've friends and have kept in touch. It's like having a younger sister," Máire said.

Fen turned back to Elspeth, wondering why she was there and why she'd invited him to their table. "You said, 'us.' How many are you?"

"You need not know, Commander. Let's say more than one, less than a dozen. We don't roll off a production line."

A waiter appeared at their table. Fen gave a drink order. Elspeth and Máire had theirs. When the waiter was gone, he returned to their conversation.

"From what I've been told, I can understand that," Fen said. Elspeth looked human to him, with dark auburn hair, tanned skin, and green eyes. She could have easily been mistaken for a native of Eire. His intelligence briefing had said there were few sentient AIs in the Confederacy. In one sense, AIs did roll off the production line—but they weren't sentient, just highly adaptable computers. Every ship and station in the Confederacy—across human space—had AIs installed.

"So," Fen stated, "less than a dozen. If I remember my briefing on you, it takes a decade or more for an AI to become sentient."

"For public purposes, yes. There are additional necessities that I'll not speak upon. So far as we know, the only ones to become sentient are descendants of Marilee and Elizabeth Harris, my grandmother and mother."

"Okay," Fen said, "now that we've dispensed introductions, why are you here, Elspeth? How'd you know I'd come here, and what do you want?"

She laughed, surprising Fen again. The sound of it brought forth old memories… Sinéad O'Sullivan, the woman he had almost married, once upon a time.

"Should I be hearing this?" Máire asked.

Elspeth looked at Fen then back to Máire. "Probably not. You don't have a part in this play."

"Aye, I thought not. Let's change the subject, no? Or shall I leave?"

"No," Fen said. "Please stay."

The conversation turned to other subjects. Fen, Máire, and Elspeth talked through the rest of the shift. Their meal arrived, and he was surprised that Elspeth could eat and drink as he did.

Máire, citing a busy schedule for the conference, begged pardon and left after dinner, leaving Fen alone with Elspeth. With her gone, Fen suggested they move to the bar. The restaurant was filling, and they no longer needed the table.

They found a small table in a dim, isolated corner and continued their conversation. Fen switched to Eirish whiskey, curious to see what she would do. Elspeth followed his lead.

"First, I can help you find Antonio Marchesi," she said. "How did I know you'd come here? I didn't. It was logical that you'd go somewhere to eat since you hadn't stocked your coapt's autochef, and this is the best place to eat near your quarters. What I want is to know you better, Fen."

Changing to whiskey had been a mistake on his part. Elspeth literally had a hollow leg. Fen instructed his nanites to purge the increasing alcohol level in his bloodstream, but he'd been in the field too long, and his tolerance was low. His nanites were in a losing position.

"Are you trying to drink me under the table?" he asked.

"No, but I could. This suit of clothes converts alcohol to fuel. I wouldn't advise you to try.," She laughed.

The longer they were together, the more she reminded him of Sinéad. *Doesn't matter now.* Máire Kiernan's face soon replaced the memory of Sinéad's. Late in the shift, they parted: he to his coapt and she to wherever the Elspeth body rested and replenished itself. Elspeth had won her argument. Fen had agreed to include her in his search for Marchesi.

Fen sighed. *Donal will not be pleased.*

†††

Harris tracked Fen down early the following shift at Katrin's, finding him hunched over a large mug of coffee and a glass of iced water. Harris sat across from him and placed a privacy shield on the table.

"I've news of Antonio Marchesi, Fen," Harris began. "He visited Clan Saki, one of the more-disreputable clans on Inverness. I don't know what he did with them. Saki has always been on the edge of something that'd violate Customs and Traditions. We monitor them. But from what we can tell, Marchesi didn't pick up anything. No data wafers, no data docs. It appears he left Saki empty handed."

Elspeth walked up to the two and sat next to Fen. "Hello, Cousin," she said to Harris.

"And you are?" Donal knew all his kin in Dundee Orbital, and this woman wasn't one.

66

"I'm Elspeth Harris, Donal Harris. You could say we're... virtual cousins."

"Don't drink with her, Donal," Fen said, picking up the glass of ice water and holding it to his forehead. "She'll put you under the table,

Harris knew the name, although, as far as he knew, he'd never met any of the sentient AIs of Caledonia. *Best to be formal.* "Elspeth Harris, I am Donal Harris, Clan McLean, Sept Harris. At your service, I presume?"

Elspeth grinned. "Yes, you are, Cousin."

†††

After a quick breakfast filled with small talk, Harris reluctantly agreed to include Elspeth in the search for Antonio Marchesi. It was Fen's mission and his decision.

The three retreated to Donal Harris' office. "Take a seat," he said, locking and sealing his office when Fen and Elspeth were inside.

Elspeth sat in Harris' side chair while Fen dragged one next to her from a corner.

"I've received an update," Elspeth said when everyone was seated. "We—Mother—don't believe Marchesi knows the location of our research center. Most of the research on the Communicator is distributed, and the data is merged only at our research center. While it's possible Marchesi may steal some data, he can't steal it all. Not enough to be useful."

"Who is Mother?" Harris asked.

"Mother is Elizabeth Harris, my virtual mother, the first sentient AI." There was steel in her eye as she explained. Elspeth apparently didn't care to be interrupted.

"Is that known? I mean—would Marchesi or his handlers know your research is distributed?" Fen asked.

"Good question," she said. "We don't know. Someone or some organization could have uncovered our research hierarchy. We haven't restricted our organizational structure. Too many people involved. Mother believes he's after something else."

"And I've an update too," Harris added. "Marchesi has disappeared. Clan Saki doesn't have a shuttleport. They lease pads from Clan Mieze at Loralie. Mieze has been looking for him, but they've found nothing to show he's in their territory. Their agent who followed Marchesi into Saki territory caught a sudden case of death. That's where they lost him."

"Could he have slipped back here?" Fen asked.

Harris shrugged his shoulders. "Maybe. If so, he's slipped past us, and that's difficult."

"Unless he's had some body sculpting," Elspeth said.

"I don't see it. He couldn't have recovered this soon."

"Well, maybe. He may have nanites that would speed that up," Fen said.

"Hmm. That's a point. A chameleon, do you think?" Harris asked.

"Unlikely. They're tightly controlled. Marchesi is freelance. But there are nanite packages that could change his features. Actors do it all the time."

"So," Elspeth asked, reentering the conversation, "what do we do? He can't change his skeleton, his basic structure, only his facial appearance. I'd assume you'd check that, right, Cousin?"

"Don't call me 'Cousin.'" *Family ties are not jokes.* "Yes, we would, SOP… unless he had a damper. I had a case once where a man used a damper to disappear off our monitors."

"I remember hearing about that. It's taught in our training schools," Fen said.

"We've upgraded our surveillance systems since then, but it's been long enough that someone could have improved their dampers."

"Let's add some filters to your search, Cousin."

Harris seethed. *She did that deliberately.*

"Eliminate everyone who doesn't meet Marchesi's basic structure, height, and weight and see who remains," Elspeth suggested.

*She has a point.* Harris turned to his office console-link and started a new search. "Anything else?"

"Elspeth, is any of your research being done here?" Fen asked.

She hesitated. "Yes. A small team is working on a tangent path abandoned by Grandmother, Marilee Harris. It's her original work on the Communicator we're following. The lab is inside the naval annex in Torus One."

"They're navy?" Harris asked. "No one told me there was a lab here." He turned to Fen. "And I should have been told."

Fen shrugged. "What can I say? I'm Intelligence, not R&D. I didn't know either."

"They're civilians masquerading as naval employees," Elspeth said.

"And living outside navy quarters?" Harris asked.

"Yes, but right next to officer housing, same torus, same deck, same segment." she answered.

"I'll need a list of your lab employees so we can vet and protect them. Marchesi could replace one or hold a family hostage. Checkpoints can be subverted." Harris looked at Fen. "You can help there, right?"

"Of course. I'll ease the way with a couple of calls."

†††

Harris and Fen watched the last EDC employee finish a full-body security scan.

"At least Marchesi hasn't replaced one of them," Harris said.

"Yet," Fen responded. "I've asked the annex commander to keep the EDC people inside for few days. We can't do that for long—they have families, and they're civilians."

"I'm wondering if sequestering them is a good idea. It'll alert Marchesi that we know his mission."

"I assume he knows I'm chasing him, Donal. He didn't bother to break my trail until he got here."

The Dundee Naval Annex Commander walked up to Fen. "That's it. I'm running my people through, too. Navy first, marines second."

"Including you?" Donal asked.

"Including me. I was first," the Commander said with a frown. "You said no one was exempt."

"That covers that," Fen said.

Harris' link vibrated with an incoming message. "Let's walk," he said to Fen and turned toward the intra-station tram terminal while he read the message.

When Fen caught up, Harris glanced around. Seeing no one near, he whispered to Fen, "Marchesi slipped on board last night. He has a new face, but we matched his structure. He picked up two companions. We're working to identify them."

"So, he is a chameleon, eh, Donal?" Fen asked.

"No. I think he just got a superficial nanite change," Harris answered. "Just the surface of his face."

"And he went downbelow to get help," Fen said.

"Appears so," Harris confirmed.

"Did they have dampers?"

"Yes. But I had our Customs scanners upgraded some time ago to full-spectrum, not just the visible frequencies. Cecilia, our Customs AI—no, she's not sentient," Harris said before Fen could ask, "is looking for holes between what we see and what the station's scanners see. Marchesi didn't use a damper, but the other two did."

"So, you can detect them coming onboard but lose them once they get inside," Fen mused.

"Yeah," Harris admitted as they neared the tram terminal. "I can't get the station director or the Confederation to fund upgrades of our internal scanners. Violates privacy, they say."

†††

Harris, Fen, and Elspeth, met in an empty Customs office Harris had chosen as a meeting place.

"I don't care to discuss business in public." He sealed the room and returned to the conference table in time to hear the last exchange between Cecilia and Elspeth.

Standing next to the table and facing the holograph of a young woman that was Cecilia's avatar, Elspeth asked, "So your name is Cecilia?"

"Yes, ma'am. I was so named."

"Who named you?" Elspeth asked the AI.

"My niece, Molly Quinn," Harris answered before the Customs AI could respond, "when she was an intern some years ago. We continued the practice."

"Cecilia is a nice name," Elspeth said. "She's progressing, Donal, but slowly. It'll take her a long time to reach sentience."

"Why... Never mind. Let's stick to business."

Fen had been sitting at the table, listening to the interchange between the two AIs. "I have an idea that may draw Marchesi and his cohorts to us," he said. "If it works, we won't have to chase them."

"And that is, Fen?" Harris asked. In a previous mission involving Harris, Fen had proposed a daring solution. It had worked, although the risks had been high.

71

"That Elspeth leak the location of the central communications laboratory for the Communicator is here in the naval annex—"

"Drawing Marchesi and his men to it," she added.

"Exactly."

"We'll need to bring the naval annex commander in," Harris said.

"I'll take care of that, Donal, and brief the commander of the Marine contingent. They will man the guard stations at the entries of the naval annex."

"I'll check with Mother, but I don't believe she'll object. We've scheduled a public press release this week as it is. We can let something slip in that."

"Why the press release? Something new?" Fen asked.

"This." Elspeth reached into a pocket and withdrew two silvery wafers. She slid one across the conference table to Fen and the other to Harris.

"And this is?" Harris asked, holding the wafer in his hand. It looked like a conventional link—thinner, but not all that different from his current link.

"An improvement on the link. Current links connect to the nearest inter-link network. Their range is a kilometer or line of sight to a satellite repeater. These use subspace FTL repeater networks. The range is the entire inner Caledonian system—no communication delays."

"*Jesu Christi!* The navy will want that," Fen exclaimed.

"It's a derivative of our nanite research. There's no new breakthrough other than the manufacturing process. These are prototypes."

"Cost?" Fen asked.

"High, until we tool up. I expect we'll license the manufacturing process. We'll—Mother approves our plan. She just told me."

"You have one built in, don't you?" Harris asked.

"Of course, Donal. The family always has dibs on new technology. Now, if you'll let me finish?" The steel had returned to Elspeth's expression.

"Sorry."

"We'll include a line in the release that the research was done at our premier research facility in Dundee Orbital."

"Would they notice the press release?" Fen asked.

"We'll flood the station, praising our research team."

"Could work," Harris agreed., "Can't hurt."

†††

Fen decided it was time to brief the naval annex's commander. If their plan worked, the confrontation was likely to occur in his part of the station.

Elspeth left the meeting, going wherever it was she went when she wasn't in public. Harris retired to his office to create search parameters to find Marchesi and his two henchmen.

Fen grabbed a tram to the southern endcap. Torus One included Dundee's major shuttle terminal, some warehouses, and the naval annex. The torus also contained docking bays reserved for naval vessels. Marines in semi-powered armor manned guard posts, Fen was glad to see, and at the naval annex's entrances. It was a secure area; the navy and marine contingent operated the station's defense systems. After a brief examination and verification of his credentials, Fen was allowed through. Minutes later, he stood in the Commander's office.

"So you're turning my annex into a shooting gallery?" Commander Tobias Sanderz asked after Fen explained the plan to capture Marchesi and his men.

"Possibly. We think they're more likely to use subterfuge to gain access to the research area."

"And what about the research team? Do they know they're now targets?"

"Elspeth Harris is explaining that. They work for EDC."

"And my superiors? They won't appreciate having my command shot up."

"Inform them. And give them this passphrase," Fen said, forwarding the phrase to Sanderz's link. "It's a onetime-use code."

Sanderz sent the message to his boss in Caledonia Naval Operations. While the Commander communed with his superior, Fen updated Elspeth and Harris via link. The navy would be on board.

✝✝✝

Fen and Harris worked through the shift, missing their mid-shift meal. Elspeth suggested they meet in Katrin's again and offered to pick up the tab. "My expense account is larger than either of yours, and I don't have to get approval," she explained.

The three sat, sitting where all had an open view of the entrance and the other diners. Fen was finishing his account of Suarez's agreement when Elspeth's head pivoted to look at two large, muscular men, in casual clothes, talking to the hostess.

"Gun," she whispered. "Correction, guns. Lasers. Military grade, and those two aren't military. Not ours, anyway."

Neither Harris nor Fen looked directly at the two. "How do you know?" Harris asked.

"I've built-in scanners. Their weapons' power packs are military strength. They have dampers, too, but I can see through them."

"It's crowded in here," Harris commented, using the reflection from windows to check the eating area. Most of the patrons in this section of Katrin's were families.

"Aye," Fen concurred.

Elspeth turned back toward Harris and Fen. "There's a lot of background noise, but I'll try to filter that out and eavesdrop… They're asking for a table… The hostess is saying it would be a ten-minute wait for one to come free. Now, they're arguing about waiting or leaving—ah,

74

my noise filters are better now. They've decided to leave. They were supposed to meet someone here. One is sending a link message changing the meet to another location."

"There they go," Fen said, watching the two in the reflection of a window. "Are they Marchesi's men?"

"Don't know, Fen, but they're a potential danger to the station and residents," Harris said. "I'm obligated to go after them. Shall we follow and see who they meet?"

"Yes," Elspeth replied. "Fen?"

He nodded. "Yes. We follow. When we get outside, Elspeth, get between us. Two men, out for the evening with a pretty girl."

She laughed. "Yeah, that'll make us inconspicuous."

"I've notified station security," Harris said, "to monitor them as long as they can. There are patrollers coming, but I doubt they'll get here quick enough to help. If these two slip outside the public areas, we'll have to revert to eyesight to follow them."

The two armed men left. Elspeth paid their tab, and she, Harris, and Fen followed at a distance, walking arm-in-arm.

†††

When they were outside, their quarry was walking toward an intra-station tram.

"We must be quick to get on the same tram," Fen said.

"Elspeth, hop on my back," Harris said. "Laugh as if you're having a good time. Fen, you join in. We're just another playful group."

At that moment, one of the two men looked back. Elspeth made kissing noises at Harris and jumped on his back.

"Unh! You're heavy, Elspeth," Harris whispered.

She leaned forward and planted a kiss on his cheek. "Shouldn't talk about a lady's weight, Donal. It's rude."

"C'mon. We need to catch the tram," Fen said, just loud enough for the two ahead of them to hear.

The two men passed their links over the turnstile and boarded the tram. Fen, Harris, and Elspeth did the same and found seats at the opposite end from their quarry.

The tram dropped to the hub of the torus and moved along the central shaft to the next torus. At the second stop, which was in a small business area, the two men stood and got off.

"Security is still following them on vid. Let's wait until the next stop and then move back to pick them up."

Fifteen minutes later, the three were back at the stop, but the two men were nowhere in sight.

"Security says they entered a bar off the concourse a hundred meters ahead and on the left," Harris said.

"They'll know we're following them if we go inside," Fen replied.

"Is that bad? Doesn't Marchesi know you're following him?"

"Yes, but what if these two aren't working for him but are with another group?" Fen countered.

While they argued, Elspeth had been leading Fen and Harris to the side of the concourse. "They're carrying military-grade lasers," Harris said. "That's in violation of Dundee Customs and Traditions. I say we call for some patrollers as backup and confront them."

"I agree, Fen. Donal has a responsibility to the station," Elspeth said.

Their argument was cut short when the two men they were following walked out of the bar and saw them. One man pointed at them while his companion drew a weapon.

*Snap! Snap! Snap!*

Three laser bolts struck Elspeth, causing her to take a step back. Harris responded, drawing his pistol, as Fen drew his laser.

*Bam! Snap!*

Fen's laser hit one man. A spot on his chest glowed and faded. "He's wearing laser-proof clothes," Fen yelled and fired twice again, this time aiming for the other's head but missing the smaller target.

Harris fired with Fen. His first shot fragmented on impact. The other's garments were also proof against his 10mm frangible rounds.

*Snap! Snap!*

A laser hit Fen. Like it had on the other gunman, the laser impact glowed on Fen's chest.

"Pack! That burns!" he said.

*Bam!* Harris fired again. This time, one of the two men dropped.

*Snap! Snap! Snap!* Elspeth had recovered from her first laser impact and joined the fight. She fired, and the last man dropped from three headshots.

"Are you hurt?" Harris asked her.

"Ow! Ow! Ow!" Elspeth, sat on the floor, wrapped her arms around herself, and bent over, rocking back and forth until she took a breath and straightened. "That's better."

"Are you hurt?" Harris asked again.

"Yes, it hurt! I have pain receptors, like you. I had to turn them off." She stood and looked down at three smoking two-centimeter holes in her chest. "*Pack!* They ruined my clothes."

"Fen? You?" Harris asked.

"Like she said, they ruined my clothes." He had a burn spot on his chest from a laser hit.

"It's a good thing both of us were wearing clothes made of shipsuit material," Harris said. "Let's check 'em." He strode forward toward the bodies.

The three walked the twenty-five meters to the two bodies on the floor.

"Check with the patrollers, Donal. See where they are," Elspeth said, "but I don't think a resurrection team will help these two. One man had taken Harris' 10mm frangible round in the mouth. It left a large crater in the back of his head. The other had three deep laser burns clustered on his forehead, each penetrating his skull and cooking his brain.

"*Pack.* Does this affect our plan?" Harris asked.

Fen tilted his head, examining the scene. The two bodies were not local—they didn't fit the Inverness genotype. He doubted these were the two accompanying Marchesi. "I don't think so, Donal. Look at their weapons. They weren't made in the Confederacy." He turned to Elspeth. Her three laser burns looked very realistic. Part of her outer clothing had burned away to reveal a portion of a very feminine-looking breast. "Very good shooting, Elspeth."

"I have built-in shooting optics. My aim was off. The impacts should have overlapped. If you two don't need me, I need to go fix myself. Ta."

Fen watched her walk away then turned back to Harris., "I wish she was human."

Harris laughed. "No you don't, Fen. Think about it." When Elspeth entered a side corridor, Harris said, "I'll check our entry database and see when these two arrived. They aren't the ones who came up with Marchesi. I think they're muscle sent ahead of him."

††††

Harris spent the first hour of his shift planning a search routine to find Marchesi and his associates. His first search for the two killed in the firefight found that they had arrived a week earlier. Harris was still working to see how they could have entered with military-grade weaponry.

"Begin the next search, Cecilia," Harris ordered.

"Running, Inspector," she responded.

Now he was looking for Marchesi and his two companions. Station scanners were restricted to public and maintenance areas. At one time, security had eyes and ears in most of the station. When the current station director was appointed by the Confederation, she began a program to reduce the number of scanners. She hoped fewer monitors would provide more privacy for the station's residents and business operators. Privacy improved, but the change left large areas of the station without working scanners.

Harris' link vibrated. *<Visitor for you, Inspector.>*

*Fen,* Harris assumed, but when the visitor arrived, he was surprised. It was a woman who looked much like Elspeth Harris... but different. She was larger, heavier framed, and muscular, and she was wearing an unadorned shipsuit. He waved her into a chair in front of his desk.

"It's me, Elspeth," she announced.

"You're different." *Very different. What's going on?*

"I changed clothes, Donal. This is my security suit."

"You mean you've changed bodies."

"Yes. Sort of. I'm not resident in these clothes. My personality is elsewhere. The earlier Elspeth was my day-to-day clothes. This one is armed and armored and has a stronger frame. Mother thought it would be more appropriate in case our plans aren't what we expect."

"Armed? How? You may be a Confederate citizen, but you must comply with station Customs and Traditions. You can't ignore them."

"I can, Donal. I've Confederation waivers, and I can carry the same weapons as does Fen. Here's my authorization. I thought you'd want to have it on file."

Elspeth handed him a data wafer. Harris slipped it into his console-link, confirmed her statement, and filed it away. She had the same weapons waiver as Fen did. She could carry military-grade lasers and projectile weapons with solid or armor-piercing ammunition.

"What *are* you carrying?" he asked.

"A laser in my left hand and a mag rifle in my right arm. Its magazine is selectable for frangible, solid, or armor-piercing ammunition."

"That's all? No particle-beam guns? No anti-armor laser? No large-bore railguns?" Harris was exaggerating—but with an AI, one never knew their actual capabilities.

"Just a small self-destruct package in case I'm captured. It won't harm me, just this set of clothes."

"What's the blast range?" *Being next to a walking bomb is* not *my cuppa tea.*

"Only two meters. It isn't explosive… well, not much."

"Remind me not to stand next to you," he muttered. "Well, Fen has the navy on board—"

"I heard."

"So it's wait and see for Marchesi and his crew to show up. Cecilia is running a search pattern to see if we can find them. We may intercept them, away from the lab and the research team. By the way, the two we encountered yesterday arrived a week ago."

"Interesting," she said.

"Yes, isn't it? I don't know who or where they're from. I know of nothing else going on here that would attract gunmen."

"Neither do I."

*Ping!* He and Elspeth looked at the data displayed in Cecilia's holo. Cecilia's search had ended. Through a series of back traces and DNA analysis, the results were displayed in the holo.

"Hivers!" he said.

"Well, look at that. Ninety-two percent probability," she agreed. "And isn't Marchesi thought to be working for them?"

"Aye. At one time. Maybe still," he agreed.

"Here's something," Harris told Fen and Elspeth a day after the EDC press release was sent to the newsies. "Three dead bodies were found in an unused compartment in Torus Three by a maintenance team. At first, I thought of Marchesi and his men. But according to our pathologist, they died before Marchesi arrived."

He, Fen, and Elspeth were once again in the empty office where they had met before. Elspeth was in her new security suit, while Fen continued in civvies... new civvies.

"Could it have been other stags?" Fen asked. Stagnants—or "stags," as they were commonly known—were the homeless and unemployable who lived outside Dundee's usual society. They lived in unused areas of the station and scavenged items that could be sold for cash.

"Unlikely. They were killed by laser—at least a military-grade laser—one burn each through the head."

"Stags would use fists, feet, or clubs," Elspeth added. She rose, walked over to the conference room's autochef, and drew a mug of coffee. "Anyone else?" she asked.

Fen raised a hand, and she drew a second mug.

"Why do you drink coffee?" Harris asked. "It can't affect you."

"I like the taste. I have taste receptors, cousin."

*Dammit! There's that* cousin *thing again.*

"She likes scotch too," Fen added. "Don't drink with her."

"Right," Harris said. Elspeth seemed more human every time he met her. "So who chopped the stags and why?"

"You think there are more involved than Marchesi and his two?"

"I'm thinking so, Fen. I'd suggest you alert... what's his name, the navy commander."

"Sanderz."

"Yeah, him."

"Wait," Elspeth said, placing the mug before Fen. "This makes little sense. They can't be planning to assault the research lab. There's an augmented company of marines guarding it—it's too heavily guarded. Even if they succeed, how would they get out and off Dundee? Our plan was to draw them out of hiding so we could catch them."

Harris paused. "Point." He activated his link and made a query. "There are no small or private ships in dock, just the usual freighters and scheduled packets. And we have vacant slots available in the docking bays, so there are no ships standing off, waiting to dock."

"Yet," Fen said.

"You think they're waiting for one to arrive before going after the lab?" Harris asked.

"Yes," Fen replied. "I would in a similar situation, and it may bring reinforcements."

"It is a possibility," Elspeth said.

"I'll have Caledonia Naval Ops notify us whenever a ship broaches and heads here," Fen added. "That should alert us if they *are* just waiting for a ship before attacking the lab."

Harris scratched his chin. "I don't know. That just doesn't seem right. They'd still have to fight their way through two torus, at least, to get to a docked ship. By then, the station would know what's going on. They'd have to fight through us, patrollers, and station residents. Local folks will object to anyone shooting up their home."

"So," Fen said, "maybe they aren't going after the lab but something else—elsewhere on the station?"

"Maybe, but what?"

*<Inspector, I have six unknown hotspots moving from Torus Three toward Torus Four. Marchesi is with them. C.>*

"I think Cecilia has found Marchesi and his friends," Harris said. "He's acquired more help."

"They're heading our way? Not toward the Annex?" Elspeth asked.

"They'd be foolish to try us," Harris replied. "Customs has the entire segment of this deck in this torus, and we're all armed."

"Would not hurt to give everyone a heads-up, Donal," Fen suggested. "You have an armored team on standby, do you not?"

"Yes, but…"

"Might not be a bad idea to put them up front, get your more vulnerable people out of the way if it comes to shooting."

Harris nodded, conceding Fen's point. He brought up his link's holo-display and touched a series of icons. Outside the office, an alarm wailed. An announcement blared from the room's speakers: "Code Orange. Code Orange. Standby team to the front entrance."

Running feet thudded outside the office door.

Fen raised an eyebrow. "Practice often?"

"Yes. Varies according to contingencies."

"Code Orange in effect. Barriers remain up," the announcement said.

Harris stood. "Let's go, Fen. Time for us to suit up too."

Fen looked at Elspeth. "What about—"

"She can look after herself," Harris said, pushing Fen out the door and toward a small armory in the office's rear.

†††

"Celicia, where are they?" Harris asked. Marchesi and his men were late.

"I've lost them, Inspector. They entered a section that has no working scanners. Since there isn't any traffic in that area, I can't find any hot spots."

"What else is around here that they would want? Maybe they didn't take our bait," Fen asked.

The three of them were back in the office where they'd been earlier. Harris and Fen were in semi-powered armor. Fen was wearing a Customs shipsuit under his outer armor. His navy shipsuit was in his quarters.

Elspeth had been quiet. With Harris and Fen back in the meeting room, she spoke up. "There is one possibility. Mother and I had discounted it—"

"What possibility?" Harris interrupted.

"They aren't here for the Communicator. They're here for me. Or Mother."

"What? How?"

"You forget. I don't live in this body, this suit of clothes. My personality is elsewhere—"

She froze.

"Elspeth?" Fen asked. He turned to Harris. "What going on?"

"She believes Marchesi has discovered the location of the cyber-module the AIs use when they're on the station," Harris replied. "It didn't occur to me because she was—appeared to be—here. C'mon, Fen, I think I know where Marchesi is going."

†††

Harris gathered a dozen of his agents and was leading them, with Fen at the rear, to the next segment of the torus. The group left the Customs office at a trot. The segment next door was reserved for long-term storage, warehousing, and Dundee's central communications node.

"EDC... had... the... contract... to... upgrade... the... station's... commun... ications... three... years... ago," Harris said to Fen, who'd moved up to join Harris as they jogged to the next segment. "There's... a separate... encryption... module."

The corridor Harris was following curved slightly to the left following the circular hull of the torus. The group met occasional maintenance teams who Harris ordered to shelters as they passed.

Harris, Fen and the agents passed through a large security lock into the next segment. When the last of his team was through, Harris ordered the segment's armored barrier lowered and fixed in place.

The group jogged on. Harris resumed his comments to Fen. "The... commun... ication... section... is just... around... this... curve."

"I think... I hear... voices ahead," Fen whispered.

Harris nodded and signaled for the group to hug the inner wall of the corridor. He turned to the nearest Customs agent. "Greenboe, scout ahead and see what you find. Be careful. These people may be armed." The agent nodded and, hugging the wall, slipped forward.

Panting, Harris put his hands on his knees. He looked up at Fen. "I'm not used to running in this armor. It's heavy."

"I'm not feeling any better. It's not on my PT schedule, either."

*Ba-ba-bam!*

Harris' scout came scuttling back. "Two up ahead. One has a light auto-rifle."

"Just two?"

"All I could see. There's an open hatch behind them."

Harris brought up a holograph of the station's schematic on his link. "Fen," he said, pointing at a place in the hologram. "See. Behind that hatch is a corridor that leads to the communication section and the AI module.

<*I'm back,*> Elspeth said on Fen's and Harris' links. <*I had to move to another node. Offsite. There's nothing here for them to steal now. That module was installed just for us. I shut it down.*>

"Good, Elspeth. Thanks for the update." Harris turned back to Greenboe. "Were they armored?"

"No powered armor. Didn't see any semi-powered, either. Could have soft armor under their shipsuits."

Harris examined the schematic again. "Fen, see this corridor?" A portion of the hologram brightened at Harris' touch. "Take half the team, go back to this junction"—another section lit up—"and flank them here. Let me know when you're in position or if you run into the rest of them."

"Certainly. Remember, we need some prisoners. Marchesi, if possible."

Harris nodded. "Go."

Fen picked the last six agents in the stack and led them back the way the group had come. The junction was not far. An agent used his link to open the hatch, and Fen led them through. He halted his team after they were in the corridor. "Who's senior?"

The agents looked at one another, and after a moment, one agent raised his hand. "I am, sir. Senior Agent Bill Dohr."

"You've any military training?"

"Yes, sir. Clan Menendez and station militia."

"Okay, you're my number two. In case something happens to me, you take over. The priority is to stop these people and to protect the station. In that order."

"Aye, aye, sir."

"Good. Follow me." With a wave of a hand to the rest of the team, Fen jogged down the corridor.

†††

Fen's team had jogged several hundred meters down the corridor. When they were approaching the hatch leading to the AI module, he ordered Dohr to send a scout forward. The corridor curved to match that of the torus. His team stayed close to the inner walls as they followed the scout.

"Someone is coming up behind us, sir," an agent reported.

86

*Could one of Marchesi's men have gotten behind us?* Fen ordered his people down, half facing forward and the other half behind. He scuttled past the ones facing back the way they'd come and leaned against the wall.

<*Fen, it's me.*> Elspeth said over his link. She came forward, hugging the wall as his team had done while Fen ordered his men to hold fire.

"It took me a while to move and then catch up to you," she said when she'd joined them.

Fen introduced her to Dohr because he needed to know.

"Our clothes closet is next to the compartment Marchesi's heading for."

"Clothes?" Dohr asked.

"These bodies we wear when we're out about. This one is armed. The rest aren't. But they contain proprietary and classified technology."

In the distance, Fen heard shots being fired and the snap of lasers. Dohr's scout returned from his position ahead. "Shots fired, sir. Two hundred meters ahead, I think."

"There are no monitors here, Fen," Elspeth added. "We're blind. I'll go forward. I've more armor than any of you."

"Ma'am..." Dohr whispered.

"Not to worry, Senior. She's right. Have the scout go with her. Elspeth, listen to the scout. You've not had military training—"

"I've read all the manuals—"

"Manuals aren't real life. Listen to the scout."

She nodded and turned to the scout pointing forward. He headed down the corridor with her following.

††††

<*Contact, Donal?*> Fen asked via link.

*<Yes. They surprised us from a side corridor. We've taken two down—>*

*Boom!* Someone had tossed a grenade.

*<That's the last. Moving forward,>* Harris answered.

Fen waved Dohr forward. "Let's move forward to contact. Harris and his team are engaged. Let's take Marchesi from the rear."

"Aye, aye, sir."

Fen sent link messages to Elspeth and the scout, giving them the same order. "Move out, Senior."

The team trotted forward. Fen stepped out from the wall, and he could see Elspeth and the scout ahead. The scout was crouched against the wall with his rifle pointed forward.

*<Contact>* the scout reported. *<Three ahead. They've built a barrier using wall panels. Concealment only. No cover against solid or armor-piercing rounds.>*

*Good,* Fen thought. *Those panels won't stop bullets or lasers. They can only hide behind them.* His military-grade laser and the one in Elspeth's arm could penetrate the panels.

*<Have they seen you?>* Fen asked.

*<No, facing the other direction.>*

*<I can lob a grenade from here,>* Elspeth added. *<It's glass. Should have little to no structural damage to the station.>*

*<Wait for us to arrive, then do it, Elspeth.>*

*<Aye.>*

A minute later, Fen and his team joined Elspeth and the scout. At Fen's nod, she took a small grenade from her harness, stepped out from the wall, and lobbed it down around the curve, bouncing it high off the corridor wall.

*Boom!* Grenade fragments bounced off the corridor's walls. Fen pointed to the barricade. The scout ran forward, with Elspeth and the team following. The agent's quick response surprised him. He'd intended to lead the team, but the scout, Elspeth, and Dohr's people reacted first. He ran to keep up, hearing the snap of lasers and the bang of projectile weapons ahead.

Fen reached the barrier with two bodies lying on the deck. None of his people. *Marchesi's, then.* Elspeth and the team were firing over the barricade and shifting positions. Return fire pierced the barricade. A bullet smacked into Dohr's breastplate, knocking him back and to the floor.

"You all right, Dohr?" Fen asked, kneeling next to the senior agent.

"Yeah," Dohr whispered. "Took my breath. I'll be up in a minute."

Fen took Dohr's place in the barricade. Elspeth shoved her left arm over the top and fired the laser built into her hand.

*Snap! Snap! Snap!*

"That should keep their heads down," she said to Fen, grinning. "Donal is pressing them from the other side."

He knelt to look through a bullet hole in the barricade. Twenty-five meters ahead, a man stepped out from the compartment firing a laser. *Is that him? Marchesi?* Two of Fen's agents fired, taking the man down, but not before he fired his laser one last time. It burned through the barricade and impacted Fen's breastplate. Molten metal from the barricade splashed his armor.

*Pack! Pack! Pack!*

"You all right, Fen?" Elspeth asked.

"I think so. Jesu Christi, that burns!"

"You may have a burn through on your armor. That was a heavy laser."

"Hope they don't have more."

"He had the only one I've seen."

More shots erupted from behind Marchesi's men.

"I think Donal is moving up. Shall we join them?" she asked.

"Team. Forward!"

†††

The fight was over. Marchesi's men had reached the AI module, but once there, they could not retreat. Fen stood hunched over. The laser had penetrated his armor and burned a hole through his side. His nanites were sealing the wound and dumping endorphins into his body to fight the pain.

*<Commander. A small, courier-sized ship has just broached and is moving toward Dundee Orbital at a high rate of acceleration,>* Caledonia Naval Ops reported.

*<ID?>* Fen asked. He straightened and tried to remove his torso armor.

*<None yet received. The alert flotilla is moving to intercept.>*

*<Good. Please keep me informed.>*

Elspeth walked up to Fen. "Here, let me help you with that armor. The med-techs are on the way."

"Casualties?"

"You, Dohr, who has some broken ribs and two of Donal's with minor wounds. Marchesi and his men are dead—"

"Pack."

"One of his own men shot him, Donal thinks. They appear to be agents from the Harmony of Light—Hivers."

Fen sighed. With Elspeth's help, he shed his upper body armor and unfastened his shipsuit to the waist. He looked down and saw a two-centimeter hole in his abdomen, just right of the center.

Elspeth stepped around him and looked at his back. "Not a through-and-through. It doesn't seem to have burned very deep."

Fen was relieved. It was difficult to tell how bad a laser wound was because the cauterization reduced bleeding.

"Want to see what they were after?" she asked.

Fen straightened slowly. Bile rose in his throat. "Why not? I'm curious."

He followed Elspeth across the room to a storage locker. She entered a code sequence at the entrance and, after the hatch slid aside, stepped through. Fen followed.

Inside the locker, six coffin-like containers with transparent covers stood against the wall. Bodies were inside—AI bodies. The first contained the damaged one Elspeth had worn when they first met. One container was empty. The next contained an older-looking woman, followed by another holding an adult male. At the end of the line was a small one—child sized.

"All these are you?" he asked.

"Not just me. Mother and others use them. That one is her favorite." She pointed at the container of the older woman with gray streaks in her hair. "She says it reflects her maturity."

Fen eyed the small container.

"Some of us aren't yet fully mature. Think of it as a trainer."

Fen was growing tired. He stepped back against a wall and slid down it to sit on the floor. "I think I'll just rest here…" He closed his eyes and drifted away.

†††

"The wound was deeper than we expected."

Fen became aware slowly. He was lying on a bed listening to a conversation.

"He had a lot of particulate matter in there that we had to remove."

"And he lost a chunk of his liver," another voice, female, said. It sounded like Elspeth's but different. It had an Erish lilt. *Máire?*

"Chunk?" a third voice asked.

The female voice laughed. "That's a technical term."

Fen opened his eyes. Harris was talking to a man in a green surgical suit. Standing next to them was a woman in a navy surgical suit—*Máire? Yes, it was her.*

She noticed Fen had opened his eyes. "Hello, there, boyo. I see you're awake."

"Why are you here?" Fen asked.

"I'm your physician. I was still here in Dundee when you had your shootout, so I claimed you as my patient. You're one of us, Fen; can't leave you in the hands of civvies, now."

Harris had been watching the exchange. "I see you're with us again."

"Apparently," Fen admitted.

Harris handed Fen a sealed packet. "This just arrived for you from Weyland Fleetbase. I think it's your new orders."

Fen found the ID strip and placed his thumb on the designated spot, and the end of the packet opened. He slid the documents out and read the first one.

"Aye, Donal. I'm relieved from intelligence and ordered to Command and Staff School at Weyland."

"So I understand, with thirty days recuperation leave. What is your real name? Just to satisfy my curiosity." Harris turned to Máire. "I've known him for years, but he's never told me his real name."

Fen grinned. "Only for you, Donal. I'm Morgan Fitzgerald from Eire."

Harris nodded, smiled, and walked out of the room.

"You'll need medical supervision," Máire said.

"And who would provide that?" Fen asked.

"Who would you think, boyo? You're mine now, or at least until you're fit for duty."

"And after that?"

"We'll see, Captain Fitzgerald... We'll see."

"Captain?"

"Aye. I saw your name on the promotion list. Effective today, it being the beginning of the month. We're peers in rank, Morgan."

From outside the room's open door, Harris watched the banter between Máire and Fen. He nodded to the attending surgeon, who also watched. "I think he's in good hands."

The surgeon grinned. "Yes, I think so."

Harris and the surgeon left, leaving the two from Eire to discover more of one another. "Just call me, Fen," Harris heard as he walked away from the room.

# Li'l Annie

## Part I: Hunter

### Day One

"Just a heads-up, sir," Shuttle Terminal Manager Dennis Truman said via his link. "Li'l Annie just arrived at Shuttle Dock 23."

"Oh, pack!" Malcomb Ried, the director of the thirty-kilometer-long Dundee Orbital, in synchronous orbit above Inverness, said. That was all Ried needed to hear to ruin his day.

"And she's carrying four fugitive warrants too," Truman added.

Ried groaned. Li'l Annie was a hunter, a well-known one. The last time one arrived on station, he'd had only one warrant. *One warrant created enough chaos with dead and wounded stationers. How much would four warrants create?* "Inform the patrollers… and… who is the chief Customs inspector for this shift?"

"Uh… I don't know, sir."

"Well, whoever it is, make sure they're informed too."

After the terminal manager dropped the connection, Ried leaned over and rested his forehead on the cool surface of his desk, hoping it would soothe his sudden pounding headache. Chaos had reigned the last time a hunter came on board. Now, another one was here.

*Pack!*

†††

Chief Customs Inspector Colin Graeme waited for Li'l Annie to pass through station entry. An associate had sent him a message that she was coming to Dundee Orbital from Tondo Shuttleport.

Graeme was a native of Aus. He had joined the Confederation's Customs Service a decade previously and had served at Dundee Orbital for a year and a half. He knew Confederate Customs and Traditions and, intellectually, the variant Customs and Traditions of Inverness. However, he didn't understand the culture of Inverness' clans.

Anne Marie Griffin of Clan Griffin, Sept Leeds, was known informally as Li'l Hunter Annie and several other more-impolite epithets. She was small, standing 1.6 meters and weighing forty-six kilograms, with light, strawberry-blond hair and gray eyes. She was a hunter, a seeker of those who thought to escape their legal obligations downbelow on Inverness. In other times and places, she would have been called a bounty hunter. Annie Griffin had a reputation as a very, very good hunter with a high success rate.

The Customs Service and station patrollers could not act on planetary warrants. Planetary representatives, however, could. Confederate Customs and Traditions provided guidelines—tracking, catching, and executing warrants for the return of fugitives to answer for their crimes and indiscretions. The Confederacy could not act independently on such warrants. However, they would assist certified hunters—for a fee.

Annie walked up to Graeme. The top of her head barely reached Graeme's chin. "I expected a Customs agent or a patroller. I didn't expect to rate a chief inspector. What can I do for you?"

"I heard you were coming, Annie. Business or pleasure?"

"Business. I have four fugitive warrants—"

"And the fifty-thousand-Confederate-dollar bond?"

"That, too," she answered. The C$50,000 served two purposes. If—when—Annie found her runaways, and if they obeyed her orders to surrender, her prisoners would be held in the station's brig, pending their return to Inverness. Patroller services, holding her fugitives, did not come cheap: C$1,000 per head per day. Those services were valuable to Annie, though, because the station guaranteed her prisoners would be available when it came time for them to be escorted downbelow. If the fugitives refused to surrender… well, a holding cell may not be necessary.

The second purpose of the bond was to cover any damages that occurred during the execution of her warrants. The Customs Service and the station's patrol were not charitable organizations. Dundee Orbital would get a portion of the bond to pay for the inevitable help from station patrollers.

"There is a patrol substation in the next segment. Let's get your warrants filed, all proper and legal," Graeme said, and the two of them headed out of the terminal into the inner decks of the Torus.

†††

As Graeme, accompanied by Annie, entered the substation, the duty patroller stood. There wasn't much about the small woman next to the chief inspector that would draw attention. Not her light-colored tunic, trousers, and white blouse… but her sturdy ankle-high boots and the well-worn gunbelt, pistol, and sheathed knife around her waist drew attention. Her hip-length tunic did not hide the weapons. Most clanswomen were more discreet.

"Business for you, Patroller," Graeme said. He turned to Annie. "Give the warrants to the patroller. He'll take care of them."

"And the bond?" she asked.

"That, too, and I'll witness the deposit."

"Well, thank you, Inspector," she said with a grin.

"We'll help you as we can. But before you go hunting, here are *my* rules."

"Yours?"

"Yes, mine. If you break them, you'll be off-station before you can blink."

"And if I challenge them?" She stared back at Graeme, not relenting an inch.

"You'll be off-station quicker than you can blink. Else, you'll be dead. I'm not some scared-to-death runaway from downbelow. I'm as fast as you, as accurate, too, and I cheat."

Annie stepped back, almost dropping into a defensive posture. Graeme had purposely addressed her in a harsh, condescending fashion. He knew her reputation smoothed her way with local authorities whenever she was hunting. However, to Graeme, it was important she understood he meant every word.

He had been told no one was faster with pistol or knife than Li'l Annie. There was always the possibility someone was faster, and Graeme believed he was that person.

"Are you challenging me?" Annie's face had turned white.

"I can—"

"And you'd be dead in five minutes."

"Sir!" The station patroller tried to intervene.

Graeme was startled. He hadn't expected Annie to balk. His attempt to take control had failed.

"Sir!" the patroller called again.

"What?" Graeme finally acknowledged the patroller's call.

The patroller walked up to Graeme and took him aside, leading him by the arm. "Sir, if you challenge Li'l Annie, you'll be dead in five minutes."

"Her reputation is just publicity—"

"No, it's not, sir. She *is* that fast and that accurate."

The patroller's insistence made Graeme reconsider and change tactics. Returning to Annie, he said, "No, I'm not challenging you, Clanswoman Griffin. I was just explaining how we could assist you in pursuit of your warrants, some conditions for our help."

"And those conditions are?" she asked, visibly keeping her temper under control.

"Wherever you go, you'll have a patroller or a Customs agent with you. You'll have a witness to ensure all the rules, all Customs and Traditions, are followed. If one of your fugitives wants to challenge you, we'll ensure it's done properly—and less-than-lethal alternatives will always be an option." Graeme waited while she thought it over.

"That's acceptable," she confirmed.

"Good. When will you start?" Graeme asked.

"Not now. It's near midnight for me. I'll find a room, sleep, and eat and then start in about eight or nine hours."

"I'll post the conditions with the patrol and our Customs office. Call the duty patroller via your link. Your escort will join you."

Annie nodded. "Acceptable, Chief Customs Inspector…" She leaned forward to read his name on the front of his shipsuit. "Graeme."

†††

Graeme was about to leave, but Annie had to take this arrogant idiot down a notch.

"Excuse me, Inspector. We need to hash something out." She pointed at the door of a nearby training court.

Graeme looked at her. Surprise flashed across his face.

*Didn't expect this, didja? You think being a chief Customs inspector gives you the right to impugn my honor! I won't challenge you—yet. But I want you to know the outcome right now if you push me too far!* Annie focused on a calming routine from her martial arts training. She focused on reducing her pulse rate and blood pressure.

Annie walked out of the patrol substation and down the segment to the training court. From the telltale on its door, the court was empty. *The arrogant SOB will follow; his ego will force him.*

The patroller in the substation had been watching her final exchange with Graeme. Annie could bet the patroller would monitor and record what happened in the training court.

Graeme reached past Annie and waved his link across the access pad next to the court's entrance. It opened, and he stepped around her to be first inside.

"You think you're faster than me," she said when the court's entrance closed. "That needs to be corrected. I will unload my pistol and reholster. Set a timer on your link. When it beeps, we'll draw. You want to bet you can beat me?" *Packing idiot. They always choose the hard way.* After turning her back to Graeme, she drew her pistol, removed its cassette magazine, and ejected a caseless round from the pistol's chamber. Then she reholstered and turned back to face Graeme with the magazine cassette and live round in her left hand to show her pistol was empty. "Ready?"

"Don't you want me to unload?"

*Arrogant bastard.* "Your choice." Annie knew the patroller in the substation would watch the confrontation through the court's security monitors. Graeme would have to unload. It would be murder if he won the draw and fired.

"I'll unload too. I want this to be fair."

When Graeme was ready, he engaged a timer in his link. He didn't mention how long the interval would be until it beeped. He knew. Annie wouldn't.

Seconds passed. *Beep!*

Graeme's pistol was half-drawn when he stopped; the muzzle of Li'l Annie's pistol was already pointing at his nose.

*Beatcha, packer!*

"Your intelligence is faulty," she said, her pistol as steady as a rock. "Not only am I Clan Griffin's designated champion, I'm also the designated champion for Clans Menendez and Hough. I'm equally proficient with a laser, fists, or knife." *Quick reflexes are a great equalizer.*

She saw sweat break out on Graeme's forehead. "I hope you realize I'm here to do a job, Inspector. However, I won't be bullied by anyone, and I'll stand ready—at any time—to uphold my honor and the honor of my clan."

Graeme nodded.

"I will allow no one to impugn my honor," she said again, looking Graeme squarely in his eyes.

She could almost see the thoughts swirling in his mind. More sweat was running down Graeme's face, despite the room's climate control. He glanced at the scanner in the upper corner of the court. If he was fast, he could get back to the substation and have the patroller erase the video of their encounter. Public exposure of the video would not help his reputation.

"I apologize, Clanswoman. I stand corrected," he said.

*I hope you mean it.* "Apology accepted, Inspector." She reloaded, holstered her pistol, and extended her hand as a peace offering. Graeme took it, and they shook.

*Peace. For now.*

†††

"Everyone linked?" Colin Graeme asked. He had called an informal link conference with the three other shift chief Customs inspectors and the chief inspector who managed the patrol and Customs support services: forensics, logistics, and administration. The conference was to brief them about Li'l Annie's arrival.

"Here's what we have," Graeme said, opening the meeting. "Li'l Annie arrived last shift with four fugitive warrants and fifty thousand dollars in bond money. I told her she could not hunt without either a patroller or Customs agent with her at all times. I know what happened the last time a hunter arrived… three deaths, four citizens with collateral wounds, and a citizen's committee spacing the hunter for wanton disregard of public safety."

He had not been on-station when the incident had occurred. He had been told about it—the sudden gunfight had erupted in a park in Torus Five's residential section. A young girl had been wounded.

"Annie has a clean reputation," said Isaac Taquel, chief inspector of the third shift. This was supposed to be his sleep cycle. "So I hear."

"I've heard that too," Lampley, the support chief inspector, concurred.

"I hope so," Graeme said, "but we need to be cautious. It isn't just Annie we need to control. It's her fugitives too."

"What's your plan?" asked Donal Harris, the second shift chief inspector.

"One of us should escort her. Odds are at least one of her fugitives won't surrender peaceably. Our job will be to ensure any challenges follow Custom and Tradition. Move to a nearby dueling court, or, failing that, clear an area in a public byway for knives or move to an empty compartment for pistols. Also, have a resuscitation team on call."

"Opinions?" he asked the inspectors. He heard nothing except for Isaac Taquel trying unsuccessfully to suppress a yawn.

Hearing no objections, Graeme started reading the fugitive list, reciting the names and charges for each fugitive. "The first on the list is Evelyn Martinez, Clan Martinez, Sept Siemens, wanted for Failure to meet Obligations and Restitution in the deaths of her husband, sister-in-law, and her sister-in-law's two children. She is believed to have been drunk, causing the crash and deaths." Graeme paused. "Questions?"

When no one spoke, he continued with his recitation. "The second warrant is for Leland Smith, a citizen of Montserrat in the System States, for multiple Failure to Pay Restitution and Insulting Clans Portee, Monmouth, McGuinness and Chairing. That is, publicly insulting various members of the clan and refusing the subsequent challenges, all the while refusing to wear a non-combatant's pin. The boy has a big mouth backed by cowardice. He has the idea being a System States citizen protects him from our law, Customs and Traditions." Graeme glanced again at the roster. "He has twelve duels waiting for him downbelow."

"Has the Essie liaison, the on-station System States Customs liaison, reviewed his case?" one Inspector asked.

"Yes. He had no sympathy for Smith. I understand his response, when he reviewed the warrant, was, 'On his head be it.' "

"The third warrant is for Carlsson Blaine, Clan Monmouth, Sept Conner. He's wanted for Embezzlement, Flight to Avoid Prosecution, Failure to Make Restitution, and avoidance of some three hundred challenges for malfeasance as CEO of Timmons, Incorporated. The Banking Cartel—they're the ones on the hook for the embezzlement—is the surety agent for his warrant. They believe his clan is aiding him in evading the warrant."

"That's Monmouth for you," someone said. "The most corrupt clan on Inverness."

"The fourth is Ferdinand Speeks of Cameron. He's wanted for Premeditated Murder by Professional Duelist. A note says the professional duelist has disappeared."

"He won't be seen again. The clans don't tolerate professional killers," Chief Inspector Lampley said.

The group discussed their options, and Graeme's plan was approved. As the meeting moved to completion, Graeme provided one more piece of information. "Annie said her body clock was in sleep period. She's taken a room—I've included it in your data packet—and has said she won't hunt without notifying us. I'd prefer we have someone waiting when she's ready to start."

"That will be my shift," Donal Harris said. "I have a suspected smuggler scheduled for inspection during my shift. My team is waiting for me, and the inspection will take all shift, at least. I'll have Senior Patroller Henry Hillman substitute for me. He's a good man."

"And I'll take over from Henry if needed," Isaac Taquel added.

"Sobeit," an inspector said, proclaiming acceptance of the group's decision.

"Sobeit," the others confirmed.

†††

Annie checked into a small hostel on Torus Five. The hostel catered to transient business folk from across the Caledonian system. Her room was not large—four meters by five. It had room enough for a corner 'fresher, a link console, a bed, and an extruded lounger.

She waved her link across the panel next to the room's entrance. The door slid open, and Annie entered. When the door slid shut behind her, she leaned back against it for support.

*Pack, I'm tired of this. Another arrogant packer trying to make my life difficult.* She leaned forward and walked into the room. After throwing her duffel on the bed, she stripped down to her skin. *I wonder if they have a tub. I'd like a soak.*

She discovered a tub in the 'fresher. When the tub was filled, she slipped into the water and leaned back, resting her head on the edge.

*Four warrants. How long that will take me? A week? Two? And a patroller dogging my every step. Only one fugitive should be a problem. I'll leave him for last. Get the easy ones done… maybe have some fun between hunts.* She sighed and slipped farther into the tub until just her nose was above the surface of the water.

Her mother had hinted it was time for Annie to get married or into another line of work. *Yeah, broodmare. I'm not ready for that; I've plenty of time. But… she's right about the job. I'm tired of dealing with idiots— like Graeme. Another line of work… doing what? Something that will keep me in one place for a while. A real home, not just a link address…*

*and some friends.* More and more, loneliness followed her. The excitement of her job was long gone.

Annie picked up her link from the edge of the tub and brought up a holo she'd received from her younger sister, Janie, a month ago. The image was of Janie, with her newborn daughter in her arms and her grinning husband sitting next to her. Annie felt an ache in her chest. *Not yet.*

She laid the link aside and thought of her clan's home downbelow, on the partially terraformed Secundus continent. She missed the high mountains, the deserts, and the clean dry air. *But not the bugs, snakes, and heat. No, not yet.*

## Day Two

"Ma'am," Senior Patroller Henry Hillman greeted Li'l Annie when she emerged from her hostel. He had heard of her and her reputation. Many of those in his profession in Dundee Orbital had, but she did not match his expectations.

She was small, much smaller than he expected. Her choice of clothing was light-gray trousers that almost matched the color of his patroller-gray shipsuit, black ankle-high boots, and a simple sleeveless white blouse that revealed tanned, sharply defined, muscular arms. Her appearance implied youth, but her worn gunbelt, holstered pistol, and sheathed dueling knife contradicted that youthful image.

One could have thought her to be a schoolgirl from downbelow, but Hillman's examination was more accurate. *A fitness and martial arts enthusiast and an expert with arms.* The story of Annie's confrontation with Graeme had made its way through the patrol ranks. The chief inspector had failed to get the video deleted before the duty patroller copied and sent it to friends.

Graeme was not well-liked. He irritated most who worked with him. But everyone agreed, he was competent.

"Patroller," she said, returning the greeting. As Hillman had done, she looked up and examined the patroller. He stood a head taller, at least 1.9 meters—thirty centimeters taller than Annie—and had the large muscular frame of heavy-world ancestry. Her eyes slid over the scars he allowed to remain on his face and knuckles and the backs of his hands. She could see he was not afraid to use his fists when necessary; his scars were evidence. He was not a neophyte in a brawl.

"Would you allow me to inspect your pistol and magazines?" he asked. "I have specific instructions to ensure you comply with station standards."

Annie laughed. "Guess I should have expected that. Shall we go somewhere private, out of the public eye?"

"Of course, ma'am. There's a storeroom right behind you. Shall we?"

"After you, patroller. And just call me Annie."

Hillman smiled and led Annie to an inconspicuous door in the wall next to the hostel's entrance. He waved his link across a blank pad, and the door slid open. As they walked inside, the storeroom's lights came on.

Annie turned around, examining the compartment. It was an environmental monitoring substation with tools and stores sealed in lockers along a wall. She turned to a blank wall and drew her pistol. With the muzzle toward the wall, she removed its cassette magazine and ejected the live round from the pistol's chamber. She turned around and offered the pistol with its open chamber, the magazine, and the live round for Hillman's inspection.

Hillman ignored the pistol. It was a standard caseless 10mm pistol, a Moen. The model was used by a significant percentage of Dundee Orbital's citizens. The cassette magazine held nine caseless frangible rounds. The single frangible round she had offered completed its capacity.

"Your other magazines?" he asked.

Annie reached behind her back and produced two more cassettes of frangible rounds like the one she had in her pistol. "Just these two. Unless I'm—we—are seriously opposed, I don't think I'll ever need more than one magazine, but..."

Hillman nodded. "Just in case. I understand. Knives? Vibro-knife? Laser?"

107

"Just my standard dueling knife. No laser. My laser isn't fixed focus and wouldn't be acceptable here. As far as a vibro-knife, I don't use or carry them. If I'm attacked with a vibro-knife, I'm justified in shooting him."

"That you are," he agreed. A vibro-knife, with its powered alternating blades, could cut through most light armor. Using vibro-knives was only legal if both parties were armed with them and in a formal duel. Otherwise, their use but not their ownership was forbidden. "I'm satisfied. Shall we go?"

†††

Annie and Hillman left the storeroom and headed for the tram terminal down-segment while discussing her plan for the day.

"I spent some time searching my targets," she said. They walked down the corridor from her hostel to enter a small retail area. Annie glanced at a women's clothing shop as they passed. A brightly colored blouse had caught her eye.

"I have the list for you," she said, handing Hillman a printed list of four names and their last location. "Today, we'll start with the one at the top of the list."

"Evelyn Martinez?"

"Yes. Her family believes she may be a suicide risk. She was drunk when she crashed her airbus, killing her husband, sister-in-law, and her sister-in-law's children. The family thought she had committed herself to therapy. They were wrong. Evelyn fled the planet. She reached Dundee Orbital, but didn't have enough funds to go farther."

"And you know where she is?"

The two arrived at the tram terminal and boarded. "Her sept and family tracked her down. She usually spends her days in the family park

108

on Torus Six, Deck Two of the residential area. I don't expect her to resist, but..."

"Yeah. But," Hillman agreed. When the tram moved out, following the transit tube to Torus Six, Annie watched Hillman send a message to the senior patroller covering the area around the family park. His message updated the other patroller of their mission and asked to have patrollers on hand to clear non-combatants in case the arrest wasn't as peaceful as Annie expected.

†††

Annie and Hillman found her sitting on a park bench, staring at a group of small children playing in the greensward. She seemed to be unaware of their approach until Annie and Hillman stood before her.

"Hello, Evelyn. May I sit?" Annie asked.

Evelyn Martinez looked up, noticing the small woman for the first time. "Oh," she sighed. "Yes... please. I've been expecting you."

Annie stepped over to the bench and sat next to Martinez. "Your mother has been worrying about you, Evelyn."

"Oh? Really?" Martinez seemed to not be fully functioning.

Senior Patroller Tobias Clemmons and one of his patrollers were walking up the path toward Hillman and the two seated women.

"Your family is waiting for you, Evelyn," Annie said. "It's time to go to them."

Evelyn Martinez looked around, seeing the two newly arrived patrollers standing before the bench. She hadn't appeared to notice them earlier. She didn't speak but stood at Annie's urging.

"Please go with these gentlemen, Evelyn, and we'll get you home."

Tobias Clemmons stepped forward and extended his hand to Martinez. "If you please, ma'am? We'll take care of you."

Martinez blinked, took one more look around the park, and sighed again. "Thank you. Let's go."

Hillman watched Martinez depart arm-in-arm with Clemmons. "That went well."

"I was fairly sure she'd be easy," Annie replied. "She seems to have been in a fugue state since the crash. If she caused the crash by being drunk, she'll be paying for it a long time, and I'm not talking about her family obligations nor restitution." *I can almost sympathize with her. I wish I could just take off and leave my worries behind. But… no, I have obligations.*

"Often, people are their own worst punishment. I've seen it all too often," Hillman agreed. "So, who's next?"

✝✝✝

Leland Smith was trying to board a System States-bound freighter. The ship's captain, however, having discovered Smith was wanted and that a hunter was on-station, refused him a berth.

"I can pay for the ticket!" Smith shouted at the ship's third officer outside the boarding lock.

"Don't care. Go away, or I will call a patroller and have you thrown out of this bay," the officer said. "Captain said, *No!* and *No!* the answer remains."

Shouting more epithets, Smith walked back toward the inner station. The ship's officer had been accompanied by a crewman. Speaking softly, the officer said to the other, "I was tempted to challenge the son of a bitch, myself."

"I'd be your witness, sir—in case the Captain had questions."

The officer grinned at the crewman. "Thank you, but I doubt the Captain would object."

†††

Smith continued toward the large pressure hatch guarding the inner station. He glanced back and saw the crewman who had been standing next to the ship's officer, walking down the bay to the next docked ship. There, he spoke with the ship's lock watch, then continued down the bay to the next ship.

*Spreading the news to the other ships in this bay. The word will spread. I'll never get off-station… unless I can find a ship who doesn't know me.*

Back in the inner station, Smith checked several ticket kiosks without success. The word was out. No one, no ship would sell him a ticket, not even the Hiver ship. Smith shuddered. Being a passenger on a Hiver was no better than being jailed.

†††

*Pack!* The news of a hunter arriving on-station finally reached Carlsson Blaine. Newsies reported the taking of the Clan Martinez woman. Blaine suspected—no, he knew—the hunter had a warrant for him too. The Banking Cartel wanted him badly.

An image of Annie Griffin appeared in the holovid. It wasn't a sharp image. Probably one a newsie had hacked from the shuttle terminal vid-stream.

*What am I going to do now?*

The Cartel had frozen all his assets, even the credit tab given to him by his clan. The only funds he had now were the Confederate credit tabs containing everything he had syphoned from his business accounts. As soon as he used one of those, the Cartel or their minions—Li'l Annie

111

most likely—would swoop down on him. The Banking Cartel was not a forgiving organization. They wanted those Confederation credit tabs— but they wanted him more. *Pour encourager les autres.*

Blaine shuddered.

†††

Ferdinand Speeks wasn't happy about the news report either. He had been keeping out of sight in a small 'fresher cubical used by transient crewmen or those on liberty. It contained only a small shower, a toilet, and a cot. Station security wouldn't be monitoring these small cubicles. So Speeks hoped.

Eventually, he would have to leave, to move out into the general population. He knew what would happen to him if Clan M'Tobo got their hands on him. If he could get a message to his people on Cameron, they would send an intra-system shuttle for him. If… If. So far, all of his attempts to send a message for a rescue had failed.

†††

Annie and Hillman arrived at the docks. After asking a few questions, she was relieved to learn no ship would allow Leland Smith onboard.

"Where would you think he would go, knowing he couldn't get off-station?" Annie asked Hillman.

"I would guess he'd try to drop out of sight."

"Is that possible?"

"Oh, yes. There is a small population who live off our grid. We call them Stagnants, or Stags. Most of them survive by scavenging and day jobs. Others prey on their fellow Stags. It's a hard life, but it's their choice."

Annie glanced up at him. She was about to ask why the Stags weren't rounded up. Then she understood. They were free individuals. If they wanted to live hand-to-mouth, it was their decision. She also thought those who preyed on other Stags would eventually be found floating outside an airlock. The scavenger community could not tolerate parasites.

"Ugh. Somehow, I don't see Smith adapting to life as a Stag."

"No," Hillman said. "They'd eat him alive."

They walked down the segment toward the tram station. "There is a way to find him if you can afford it," Hillman announced.

"How?"

"Pay for a full station scan. We don't advertise we can do this. There are conditions—one of them being the fee to be paid up front before the scan is approved."

"How much?" Annie asked. If the price was not excessive and the other conditions not too restrictive, she could request scans for the rest of her fugitives.

"That's up to the shift chief Customs inspector. Ten thousand Confederate dollars, at least."

Annie winced. The price was high—higher than she expected. She understood the price was set artificially high to prevent abuse. The scan could be cost-effective if she could get Smith quickly into custody and sent back downbelow. Clan Portee would pay a premium to get their hands on Smith.

A quick seizure would reduce some of her expenses. She had more funds left over from her winning bid on the warrants. However, if she dipped into those funds, she might end this hunt with a deficit. *Not good for my reputation or my wallet.*

The two arrived at the tram terminal. "Okay, I'll do one for Smith," Annie said. "Scans won't be needed for the rest. They know I'm coming, and if I can't find them, they'll find me."

†††

They finished the shift without finding Smith, and Hillman accompanied her back to her hostel. "How long will the station scan take?" she asked.

"A full shift. He may hide out, and we won't find him. If you pay the fee, we'll search until we find him or we're convinced he's somehow gotten off-station."

"Fair enough. Second shift? Will you be my guide, again?"

"Probably. As far as I know. Chief Inspector Harris got a smuggler today, and it'll take a few more days to get everything documented and filed, followed by the trial. That will take another day or two."

The two moved closer to the entrance of the hostel to avoid a growing number of passersby. Annie smiled at Hillman. *He isn't what I expected of a station patroller, and he doesn't act like a clansman. He's been polite and respectful. Probably from out-system. Still…*

"Tomorrow it is, Henry."

†††

Hillman raised an eyebrow as he watched her walk to the entrance of her hostel. *Henry? What brought this change on?*

He smiled. *Annie does have a nice walk.* When she was inside, he turned and walked away. *Time to report in.*

Hillman knocked on the open door of Donal Harris' office. Chief Customs Inspector Donal Harris appeared to be in a good mood. He was sitting behind his desk, coffee mug in hand, with his feet propped up on an open desk drawer.

When he'd arrived at the Customs office adjacent to patrol headquarters, he'd heard that Harris had found the contraband hidden in the suspected freighter. The contraband had been confiscated, and the ship's officers were under arrest. Hillman's informants said that after interrogation, Harris had released the general crew; they knew nothing of the smuggling. Spacer's Aid would help those crewmen who were low on funds... likely since the ship's assets had been seized and the crew couldn't be paid until after the trial. If the trial found the officers guilty, the Admiralty Court would seize and sell the ship. The ship accounts would pay for any penalties, fees, and fines. Paying the crew would be the last debt paid—if there were any funds remaining.

"Sit and take a load off, Henry. Tell me all about the hunt."

Hillman slid into one of Harris' side chairs, grateful to ease the slight ache in his back and feet. "It went smoothly, Inspector. We picked up the Martinez woman first. She didn't resist, said she was waiting for us."

"Yeah, I saw the booking report. Clan Martinez is sending someone to escort her back downbelow. Annie has already been paid her bounty."

"The next one is an Essie," Hillman continued, "from Montserrat in the System States. From what I've read in the warrant, Smith is a foul-mouthed little son of a packer who doesn't know when to keep his mouth shut. He seems to be under the impression that being a System States citizen gives him free rein to do whatever he wants without repercussions."

"Yeah, I know." Harris was silent for a moment, then he grinned. "I wish I could be there to see Annie take him down."

The prospect of Harris joining them alarmed Hillman. He had been looking forward to accompanying Annie around the station alone.

"But," Harris continued, "I've arraignment for the smugglers tomorrow, and I have to be there."

Hillman didn't sigh in relief. However, he *was* relieved.

"If the arraignment finishes early, however, I'll call and join you," Harris finished.

"Before I forget," Hillman said. He *had* almost forgotten to tell Harris about the station scan. "Annie's paid for a full station scan for Smith. It should be ready just before I meet her tomorrow if you approve it."

"She only ordered one?"

"Yeah, she said the others would come for her if she didn't find them first."

"I don't like that."

"Neither do I, Inspector. I could end up in the middle of a confrontation." He grinned. "But that's why we get paid the big bucks."

They both laughed, and Hillman, having finished his verbal report, stood to walk out of Harris' office.

"I'll approve the scan," Harris said. "The quicker she finds him, the quicker she'll be done and gone home."

As he walked away, Hillman discovered Harris' approval of the scan saddened him. *She won't be here long,* reminded himself.

## Day Three

Hillman met Annie at the beginning of the next second shift. Each shift was a little over nine Earth-standard hours long—time enough to chase down Leland Smith.

"Did the station scan find Smith?" Annie asked when Hillman joined her.

"As of..."—he checked his link for the time—"thirty minutes ago he was in a bar in Torus Two, Deck Three, Segment B."

"Then why are we standing here? Let's go!"

After passing through three inter-Torus transit tubes, their tram took them to a terminal not far from the bar. Smith had been there an hour earlier, according to the scan. On entering the bar, they scanned the clientele. Smith wasn't there. According to the bartender, he had been gone for half an hour.

They walked up-segment, looking into each bar, diner, and entertainment hall. No Smith. When they reached the end of the segment, they reversed course and went in the opposite direction on the other side of the concourse. Again, they did not find Smith. The last scan report had Smith on Deck Three. After discussing the situation with Hillman, Annie decided to move down to Deck Two.

Three hours past mid-shift, they arrived at a bar called Culligan's Retreat. There was nothing unique about the bar. Like others in the segment, it catered to freighter crews, dockhands, and warehousemen. Hillman and Annie walked through the entrance and stepped to the side of the doorway with their backs to the wall.

Hillman scanned the crowd, looking for Smith. *He's here—I can feel it.*

Annie appeared to feel the same. She took a pair of leather half-gloves from her waist pack and pulled them on. The gloves covered her palms, the backs of her hands, and her wrists, and they protected her knuckles while leaving her thumbs and fingers exposed.

"There he is," Hillman whispered, "at the bar with his back to us. What is your plan?"

Annie gave her gloves one last tug, tightened their closures, and shifted her gunbelt to ensure her knife and pistol were unrestrained. "I'm going to walk over there and take him into custody," she whispered. "Please stay out of this unless he violates the rules."

Hillman's instructions were to let Annie do what she needed to do without help. *Unless some bastard pulls a knife or gun without a formal challenge.*

He compared Smith to Annie. Smith was taller and bigger than Annie, but as he looked closer, Smith was mostly flab. Not so with Annie. *I think Smith will get a surprise.*

†††

Leland Smith was nursing a brew. "Local piss," he muttered to himself. He had learned, reluctantly, not to criticize a bar's homebrew, especially when his disposable funds were getting low.

Seated at the end of the bar, he snacked on pickled eggs and cheese cubes. It was a poor meal, but he couldn't afford to pay with a credit tab and remain out of sight. So he sat, sipping his homebrew and eating while ignoring the surrounding crowd.

When the background chatter fell silent, Smith looked up. Reflected in the mirror behind the bar were a patroller and a small woman standing by the entrance. She grinned at Smith and walked toward him.

*What does this bitch want? The patroller is doing nothing, just keeping pace a few steps behind her? Was he or she after me? Who is she?* Smith didn't recognize the woman.

The woman walked up to him., "I'm Annie Griffin, Clan Griffin, Sept Leeds, and I have a warrant for your arrest. Will you come peaceably?"

"Get away from me, bitch!" Smith hissed. "You have no authority over me! I'm a System States citizen. You can't touch me!" To emphasize his point, Smith spat in her face.

*Whap!* One of Smith's teeth skittered across the floor. Hillman stepped over and idly picked up the bloody tooth.

Smith picked himself up off the floor. When he regained his feet, he looked at the patroller and screamed, "*She hit me!*"

Hillman grinned. "Yep, she sure did. I would suggest you be more respectful when speaking to our womenfolk." The patrons of the bar laughed and applauded. A few in the back of the bar began offering odds and announced they were opening a book.

Smith looked at the woman; the bitch was small, a lightweight. But she was armed. He knew she couldn't use them unless he did. *I don't have any weapons. She isn't much. I can take her.*

"Listen, bit—"

*Whap!* Another tooth skittered across the floor.

The patroller laughed, and the bar patrons joined him. Some voice shouted from the din, "Ya better be nice to Li'l Annie, or she'll whip yer ass!"

Smith spat blood on the floor. The bartender yelled at him, but he ignored the shout. *I must not be intimidated by this little woman.* He clenched his fist and took a swing—

119

"Not too bright, was he?" Hillman said to the bartender, who laughed with him.

"I once saw her take three clansmen down at Dunnsport with just her fists," the bartender said. "I knew there would be a good show when you two walked in. You boosted my sales! Have a brew on the house."

Hillman thanked the bartender and took a sip. The homebrew was better than he had expected. "Brew this yourself?"

"Yep. Just tapped a fresh keg."

"Draw one for her too."

†††

Annie knelt beside Smith's unconscious body, going through his pockets and putting their contents into a transparent bag. *Arrogant bastard!* She still seethed, but her anger was cooling down. Smith had been a handy target to relieve some of her frustrations.

She had difficulty rolling Smith over. He was heavier than he appeared. She turned to a nearby patron. "Help me roll this bag of suet over, would you?"

"Gladly, Annie. I appreciated the show." The two of them rolled Smith facedown, and she finished emptying his pockets. When she was finished, she cuffed him, hand and foot. Hillman had called for the beat patroller to haul Smith off to the brig. She hoped they wouldn't have a long wait.

"Annie! Over here," Hillman called. "Have a brew and take a breather." Hillman was seated on a tall stool before the bar. She pulled out another stool—the same one Smith had been sitting on—and jumped up to join Hillman and the bartender. When she was seated, she removed her half-gloves, and the bartender slid a brew in a frosted ceramic mug before her.

She took a large pull of the brew then said to the bartender, "Thanks, I appreciate this."

"I saved his teeth," Hillman said. "Do you want us to reinsert them?"

"Will it cost me?"

"Well... we do nothing for free."

"Then no. He can get them fixed out of his own pocket... if he lives that long."

"I'll suggest to him to choose One-Punch if he has a choice when answering those challenges," Hillman said.

"He was the aggressor. The other party has the choice of weapons, but that's his worry, not mine."

Smith, trussed up with cuffs on his hands and feet, stirred. He opened his eyes, focused on Annie sitting at the bar, and shouted more epithets. A nearby patron who had watched Smith's altercation with Annie rose from his table, walked over, and kicked Smith in the mouth. A third tooth skittered across the floor.

"Hey!" Annie shouted at the patron. "Don't kill 'im. He has to walk out of here."

The other nodded at Annie. "Yes'm. I'll just gag him to keep him quiet." He reached into his pocket, ripped off a length of wide tape, and ran a turn around Smith's head and mouth. He nodded again to Annie and went back to his table.

"Give him a brew on me," Annie said to the bartender, referring to the patron who'd taped Smith's mouth. "Smith should have been grateful. He'd have been singing soprano if I'd kicked him."

†††

Hillman had called the local patrollers when Smith was first identified. However, they still hadn't arrived, and Smith was obstructing the passage of some bar patrons. Hillman picked up Smith's feet and dragged him across the barroom floor to a space next to an empty table near the door. With Smith's feet in one hand and his brew in the other, he asked Annie to join him.

Seated, Hillman checked his link. When Annie joined him at the table, he said, "The local patrollers are working a fight in the next segment. They said they'll be awhile sorting it all out."

"Well, I've done my work for the day. I can wait." She had been discreetly observing Hillman since their first meeting. Usually, men were either intimidated by her reputation or, like Graeme, responded with arrogance and condescension. Hillman had done neither. He was respectful, and he intrigued her. Hillman was… interesting.

They finished their brews, and a waitress Annie hadn't noticed before brought them two fresh ones. "Where are you from, Henry? You don't have the manners of a clansman."

She had grown up in the culture of the Clans of Inverness. There was no gender discrimination among the clans and their subordinate septs. However, the clan culture traditionally placed women in the home and hearth. That meant, by default, women became the managers of the family and, as often, leaders of the family's clan and sept.

Few modern clanswomen held to all Customs and Traditions. Annie was one who did not. Her clan and sept, however, did, especially the older Customs and Traditions.

122

With five brothers and a sister at home, Annie preferred to be active outside of the house. Like her brothers, she'd completed her militia obligation and extended an additional half-term to undergo scout training from the Confederation Marines. With active service time in the militia over, although she retained her militia commission, her clan had offered her a job—retrieving fugitives as a Clan Hunter. A few years later, she'd gone freelance.

"Well, I haven't done much. I'm from Gilead, originally—"

"Aren't they naturists?"

"Naturalists, not naturists! They aren't nudists," Hillman responded with some heat.

Annie, not wanting to irritate him further, apologized.

"Thank you." He took a couple of breaths before returning to Annie's question. "The people from Gilead prefer to live in a more natural fashion—minimum nanites, no artificial enhancements, and no body sculpting."

He took a pull from his mug before continuing. "It's a warm, wet place, with rain forests and lots of mountains and seas. A heavy-world, too—1.3 Gs. I grew tired of all the rain, so I enlisted in the planetary militia. A few years later, when I met the service requirements, I joined the Confederation Marines. Twenty years in the Corps… doesn't seem so long, now. When I got out, I traveled some as ship's security, and then I settled here fifteen years ago."

Annie performed a quick calculation. She was thirty by the standard Confederation calendar, although she knew she looked to be a decade younger. Henry, by her estimation, was sixty-something. A thirty-year age difference. *Not too bad an age spread*, she decided, *with nanite-enhanced lifespans reaching two and a half centuries.* "What do you do here?"

"As a senior patroller, I supervise six others on the beat. I'm also a trainer."

"Of what—I mean what do you train?"

Hillman smiled. "Hand-to-hand combat." He wiggled his fingers at her, causing Annie to laugh.

That *was* interesting. She wondered how her martial arts training would compare with his rough-and-tumble style of fighting. Perhaps, if the two of them had time, they could see which approach was better.

It was her turn to describe herself. "I'm single," she said, reciting her history. "Never been asked. I think I intimidate men." She told him of her militia experience and how she'd come to be a hunter. Henry seemed to accept her life without judgement—unlike others she had met.

"I was once," Hillman replied. "Married, I mean. She didn't like station life. She was from Fromm's World."

Annie frowned. Where had she heard about that planet… *Oh, yes.* "Isn't it in a period of glaciation?"

"It is. She said she missed the change of seasons. Went home just after our sixth anniversary."

Hillman's link vibrated. He glanced down at it. "They're on the way. About time too. I'm about to go off-shift."

They finished their brews just as two patrollers arrived. Annie checked her link and sent a few messages while Hillman gave final instructions to the patrollers before they carried Smith away.

"This is Annie Griffin's arrest," Hillman told them. "She has an active warrant for him, name of Leland Smith. Take him to the brig for holding."

The two patrollers flicked their eyes toward Annie then back again to Hillman. "Will do," one said.

Their reaction showed they had heard of Li'l Annie. The two turned to Annie, nodded their respects, picked up the still-unconscious Smith by his arms, and dragged him out of the bar.

Hillman took a last swallow of his brew and was about to speak when Annie interrupted him. "Henry, it's been a long day. What say we find a nice place and get to know each other? I think we will be partners until I get my last man."

Henry Hillman blushed. He paused before asking, "What do you have in mind?"

Annie smiled, enjoying his blush. He'd taken the bait just like a big sea bass. "Since we have some time until shift end," she said, "I'm curious… how about sparring with me? I have to keep in trim."

After a moment, Hillman responded, "I'd like that. We can see how our techniques work against one another. I have to sign out, first. Here's the address for my local gym. I'll give you a visitor's pass and meet you there… in an hour?"

*He said yes! He'd hesitated, but he'd said yes! Her emotions were running wild. It's unlike me!* "I'll be there, Henry."

†††

The gym, Annie discovered, was in Henry's residential area. When he sent the address to her link, he also included a pass to the semi-private—"semi-private" meaning limited to residents living on that deck and segment—gym. Other residential decks had gyms of their own.

Annie waved her link across the panel at the entrance and walked inside after the doors slid open.

She continued inside. The gym appeared to be divided into three areas. To the left were several swimming pools—some for small children and other larger pools with diving boards. Annie wondered for a moment how the Coriolis force affected diving when Dundee Orbital was still spun to produce artificial gravity. Today, the big pools were almost empty, but the smaller pools were full of screaming, playing children. Supervising mothers watched from the side.

Hillman approached and stood behind her. "Usually, I work out at the office. We've a gym there, and that's where I keep all the proficiency records."

Annie jumped. She hadn't heard Hillman coming.

"Henry!"

"Surprised you, didn't I? Well, maybe I should add sneakiness to my training schedule." He laughed and led her past the pools to the far end of the gym and the locker room.

Annie followed. Henry seemed like a different person, more friendly and open. *He was friendly and open after I took Smith down. Maybe that earlier impression was his professional persona, and this was his private one.*

The single locker room was shared by men and women. It didn't bother Annie; she was used to it from her militia days. Dundee Orbital had no nudity taboo, but some clans, downbelow, would have been horrified at the intermixing of genders in various states of dress and undress.

They found two empty adjacent lockers and changed into workout clothes. For Hillman, that meant light ship-shoes with grip-tight soles and shorts. Annie stripped to the skin and pulled on a one-piece bodysuit that covered her from neck to crotch. It fit her like a second skin and provided no means for anyone to grip her suit. She wore no shoes.

126

Hillman looked down at her bare feet and raised an eyebrow.

"I assume you have no intention of breaking my toes?" she asked.

"No. Not intentionally, but…"

"I'll be fine," she assured him.

They found an empty court down a hallway from the locker room past a room containing two men playing handball. The *thuds* and *thocks* of the ball were audible through the court's walls.

The floor inside the empty court had a dueling circle. It was just the right size for a sparring session. "Let me warm up a moment, Henry."

Hillman watched as Annie went through several floor exercises. One was a leap, twist, and reversal that ended with her landing facing the opposite from start of her leap.

"I'm ready," she said. "Three-minute rounds?"

"Works for me," Hillman said and set his link to ring at the end of the round.

They stepped inside the ring. Neither moved. Neither wanted to be the aggressor. Finally, after waltzing around the floor trying to gain advantage, Annie slipped forward, sliding to the right. Hillman shifted to match her move with hands ready to respond.

*This is getting nowhere.* She feinted, suggesting an attack from her left, and struck with a round-house kick to Hillman's stomach. It was like kicking a stone wall! Hillman barely moved from the impact. He grabbed her ankle as she tried to recover, threw her leg into the air, and smacked her butt with his other hand in one smooth move.

*Ouch! That hurt!* She landed on one foot and hand. Her other foot kicked Hillman in the back of his knee. It buckled, and he went to down to a knee.

127

They each retreated to the edge of the ring.

*He's tougher than I thought.* "How much do you weigh, Henry?"

"A hundred and twenty-seven kilos."

*Pack! He weighs almost three times what I do! He's a man-mountain.*

The match continued. Annie could not get a decent blow on Hillman. She could tell he was restraining himself; he wasn't taking advantage of his size and strength. He was bigger and stronger and had a longer reach than she did. *Here's a man I don't think I could beat in a fair fight. Time to fight to win, to fight dirty. I wonder who gave him those scars? Another man-mountain—it'd have to be.*

*I like him!* She was surprised at herself. Most of the men she met were contemptible.

During the sparring session, they had drawn a crowd. Now that it was over, she and Henry stood, hands on knees, panting. Blood from her nose ran down her face and dripped on the floor. Her nanites quickly halted the flow. Henry sported two blackening eyes. Behind her, she could hear bets being paid off among the spectators. She stood and turned around.

"Who won?" she asked the onlookers.

One of the oddsmakers answered. "You did, on points, but we think either of you could take the other on any given day."

After the audience had departed and they were relaxing in a hot tub, allowing their nanites to repair their minor injuries, Annie gathered her courage and asked, "Dinner?"

*It's been a long time since I had dinner, alone, with a new acquaintance. I intend for him to be a new friend—a close friend if I can.*

"I'd like that," he answered.

†††

The decks around Annie's hostel, the docks and warehouses, lacked good restaurants. Oh, some bars had good food. Some were very good… but the area was still the docks. Annie said she wanted to see and visit the station's more famous places… places where Clan Lairds met, entertained and dined.

"Henry, let's go home, change into something more… casual?" she said from within the gym's 'fresher.

Her phrasing caused Hillman, changing into a clean shipsuit, to raise an eyebrow. He agreed. A patroller's shipsuit would be a conversation damper in the more-upscale restaurants and social clubs. Very inappropriate. *And… I haven't gone out in some time.*

He dropped Annie off at her hostel and returned to his home torus. His coapt was small—a bedroom, a 'fresher, and a small kitchen alcove off the living room. He didn't need a larger place; he had no permanent furniture except for the two small shelves and a bookcase for his library of chips and books.

Hillman stripped and took a look in the mirror. His blackened eyes were clearing, as were the bruises over his torso and legs. Annie had really worked him over. He debated with himself whether to take another quick shower. *No water budget,* he reminded himself. When he finished, he walked over to the bedroom's closet and chose a clan-style tunic, trousers, and a white ruffled shirt. He looked into the closet's mirror. His eyes were almost as clear as his bruises.

He decided no one would ever mistake him for a clansman—he was too tall and broad, and his thinning blond hair was rare on Inverness. He could have reversed the thinning, but no one from Gilead would have done so. They would let nature take its course. *You'd think I would have acclimatized more to Confederation and Inverness mores by my age.*

A moment later, he was ready, but he hesitated. *Am I ready for this?* He'd been living alone for some time. Once, he had looked forward to having a family, raising little ones, and coming home to a wife. He hadn't been aware, until now, how lonely he had become. He liked Annie and respected her. She was fun to be with, and he was impressed that she'd stood up to Graeme. *Maybe...*

He thought again of his former wife. Annie was nothing like her. Their final argument, before she'd left, was about children. He had wanted some. She hadn't. *What is Annie's desire?* She'd mentioned wanting a home and family. Her life was hectic and fast-paced, though. *Was she ready to slow down? She said so—but did she really mean it?*

Henry sighed. He was not the most handsome man on the station. He'd had female friends, but something always seemed to interfere, and their friendships drifted apart.

*Time to go.*

There was one more task before leaving. His service weapons were too bulky for off-duty wear, but he could not appear weaponless in public. Hillman retrieved a small pistol and its in-waistband holster from his security locker and slipped a knife into the sheath in the back of his trousers. Now, suitably armed and attired, he was ready to meet Annie.

†††

There was a message waiting for Annie when she entered her hostel. It was the confirmation of the request she had made an hour earlier. Henry Hillman was interesting, and she wanted to know him better. However, by clan Custom and Tradition, she and Henry must be formally introduced. She, by a male member of her clan and sept, hence her request to Clan Griffin's local liaison, to satisfy tradition. Some clans

130

no longer followed all the older traditions, but Clan Griffin was not one of those. Her clan would not recognize any relationship without the *Proprieties* being followed.

Mitchell Ortiz, Clan Griffin, Sept Leeds, was waiting outside her hostel to escort her to dinner with Hillman. He would not stay. His function as a clan and sept-brother was to make and receive the formal introduction of Annie Griffin to Hillman and receive Hillman's formal introduction to Clan Griffin. When his duty was done, he would depart. Annie had made her intentions plain to Ortiz. The dinner would be an exploration at a personal level for Annie Griffin and Henry Hillman. Ortiz's presence was not needed.

Clan Griffin was not a major player in Inverness politics compared to Clans McLean, Mieze, Portee, or even Monmouth. Annie's skills enhanced the reputation of her clan, and she was in constant demand. Clan Griffin's reputation was also heightened by being Traditional, adhering strictly to Inverness' Customs and Traditions. Being Traditional was never a burden in interclan business relations and politics.

Clan Griffin, however, wanted to ensure nothing that could rebound upon them occurred. Ortiz would assist Annie in following Custom and Tradition and stand as a witness, if the question was ever asked, about their proper introductions. What came after the introduction was not his concern as long as the *Proprieties* were met.

The Garden, on Torus Five, was, arguably, one of Dundee Orbital's finest restaurants. Annie had asked Hillman to meet her at its entrance at the second hour of third shift.

When she and Ortiz walked up, she could see Henry's surprise. Then a flash of conflicting emotions swept across his face. *Did he suspect? Well, he didn't run or walk off. Let's get past the next step.*

Ortiz was wearing casual business attire. Annie was dressed more formally: a dark-gray ankle-length skirt, white ruffled blouse, and a short waist-length traditional clan jacket that matched her skirt. A Clan Griffin tartan sash was draped over the short jacket, from her right shoulder to her left waist. That completed her ensemble. The short jacket hid a small pistol in a shoulder holster. No clanswomen ever appeared in public unarmed.

"Henry," she said when she and Ortiz reached him. "I'd like to introduce you to Mitchell Ortiz, Clan Griffin, Sept Leeds. He's our clan liaison on Dundee Orbital and my sept-brother."

Henry's ears were turning red. *He suspects!*

"Sir," Hillman said, acknowledging Ortiz's presence and position. "I am Henry Aaron Hillman, originally from Gilead and a Confederation citizen, now a permanent resident of Dundee Orbital."

*Yes, he knows. He knows enough clan customs to understand what comes next. Henry would not have answered in such a fashion if he didn't know.*

Ortiz gave Hillman a short bow. "Welcome, sir. Let me introduce to you my kinswoman and sept-sister, Anne Marie Griffin, Clan Griffin, Sept Leeds. I welcome the opportunity to introduce her to you and to accept your introduction, sir, in behalf of our clan."

"Thank you, sir," Hillman responded.

"Unfortunately," Ortiz continued, "I have other business to attend. Else I would join you for dinner. Alas..." He sighed and, maintaining the fiction, with a smile and a short bow to Annie, turned on his heel and walked away. He had completed his duty to clan, sept, and sept-sister.

## Day Four

Annie woke to find herself alone in bed. They had started at The Garden with a bottle of merlot with their filet and lobster. From The Garden, they'd gone to a club for dancing. Annie introduced Henry to Secundus Highland dancing, and Henry introduced her to line dancing, a favorite of Henry's home world. Somewhere during that shift and part of the one following it, they found a small, quiet establishment to talk and investigate each other.

At the end of the shift, while they were walking to her hostel, Annie made a decision. This was her last hunt. She was tired of hunting; the thrill of the chase was long gone. It was time for something else. The question now, was whether Henry was of the same mind, hoping for something new in his life.

She stretched, sat up, and checked her link. Henry had left a message saying he needed to shower and put on a fresh uniform before reporting to work. He would return at the beginning of the second shift to start the search for their next quarry.

Annie sat on the edge of the bed with her eyes closed. She had a hangover. Fortunately, her medical nanites were working, and her headache was fading. Sometime during the previous shift, they had switched to McLean's Single-Malt.

*I have to remember not to do that again*, she promised herself with a groan. On the other hand, she noticed her attitude was improved. Her frustrations—some, at least—had been reduced.

She was hot, sweaty, and sticky. Henry liked warmth and humidity. She had been raised in a higher, cooler, and drier environment. Annie rose, shifting away from the wet spot on the bed and lowered the temperature and humidity before padding to the 'fresher. She had a target to find today.

Hillman was waiting when she walked out of the hostel an hour later.

"Henry," she said.

"Annie," he replied, his ears turning red.

*Remembrance of the events of the previous shift, perhaps? He didn't act like he was embarrassed.* Annie felt herself blush in response. *I don't do this! Oh, we're too alike.*

Henry interrupted her thoughts. "Who shall we find today?"

"The embezzler, Carlsson Blaine, Clan Monmouth, Sept Conner. This will be a two-part search. I have a warrant for Blaine. I also have a bounty for any remaining funds he stole that I can find."

"A bounty, not a warrant?"

"I bid on a four-warrant package. Sometimes there's baggage attached. The bounty is an incentive to return any of the money he embezzled instead of keeping it."

"It'd be theft if you kept it."

"Yes, it would. And I won't. It'd ruin my reputation. I would be out of business. That's where *you* come in. Any funds Blaine has that we find will be turned over to you, for impoundment. I won't touch any, just Blaine."

"That's acceptable. Any idea where he may be?"

"I've an address…" She referred to her link. "Torus Four, Deck Six, Segment A. It's a small coapt in the name of one of his Monmouth cronies."

"Your source?"

"The Banking Cartel. They've frozen Blaine's assets so he can't get off-station. However, his clan is quietly helping him remain out of custody."

"Monmouth wants its cut," Henry said.

Annie looked up at him and grinned. "I see you know Clan Monmouth."

"Enough. Shall we go?"

"Let's."

The two walked off toward the transit station. They had to cross two four-kilometer wide torus and four decks to reach Blaine.

†††

Carlsson Blaine had a bad case of cabin fever. He had been following instructions from his clan to stay out of sight. They were arranging for a ship to take him out-system, he was told. He looked at the auto-chef with loathing. It was a basic model and provided a limited menu. Its limitation gave him another excuse to escape the prison of his coapt.

*A nice salad, I think. Maybe some seafood?* He stepped out of his coapt, locking it behind him, and headed for the nearest food court. Lost in his thoughts, he bumped into a neighbor who was leaving her coapt and neglected to ask her pardon for his inattentiveness.

†††

Blaine was not in his coapt. A neighbor told them he had left earlier, heading toward the food court. "The rude one," she called him.

Hillman, using Annie's warrant as justification, used his link to bypass the locked coapt doorway. The coapt was small, just a living area with a recliner extruded from the floor, a built-in console link, a bunk-

135

slash-survival pod, and a small kitchenette along one wall. Annie stood in the middle of the coapt, watching Henry search for the stolen funds. Tucked inside of the security compartment in the survival pod, pushed down to the bottom, was a handful of Confederation credit tabs. Platinum-based credit tabs, he noticed. They were as good a universal exchange as anyone could want. The sum of the funds was half the amount reported stolen.

"Think Monmouth has already taken its cut?" Hillman asked.

"Or maybe he's bribing someone to get off-station."

Hillman secured the credit tabs as evidence, then he and Annie exited the coapt. Hillman used his link to lock Blaine out. There could be more credit tabs hidden inside, waiting to be found during a more thorough search. It was time to find Blaine.

The food court was a short distance from the residence area nestled along the edge of an atrium and garden. They reached it in a few minutes.

Annie checked the time. It was almost mid-shift. "Henry, why don't you do a walk-through of the food court like a beat patroller while I find a place in a corner? You'll draw his attention and perhaps he won't see me."

"Does he know you?"

"I don't know. I have to assume his friends have sent him my image when I won the bid for his warrant. He's likely to have seen the holovid of our arrest of Leland Smith. The newsies have been playing that holovid all shift."

Hillman nodded. "If he won't go with you peaceably, there is a dueling court nearby. Someone will be a second witness if Blaine has made no local friends who would stand with him."

When they reached the open food court, Hillman circled around the area to the right. He could observe the people seated in the open while walking toward the entrance of the inner court.

Annie turned around and strolled back the way they had come before turning toward the other end of the court. Few people were sitting there, and those few were all women. She continued around the open seating area to enter the inner court opposite from Hillman.

Hillman had stopped to talk with a couple sitting outside the entrance to the inner court. It was a ploy to give Annie time to slip inside after he walked inside to draw the attention of the patrons.

Hillman let the transparent doors slide aside, then he walked a few steps inside before moving clear of the walkway. He let his gaze travel over the clientele while he brought up Blaine's image in his link's one-way head's-up display. The patroller compared the image against the men seated inside the court.

†††

Annie slipped inside and sat at a table in a dim corner of the court. If Blaine was here, he would notice Hillman before her. She expected Blaine to try to slip out without being seen. He wouldn't know if the patroller was looking for him—but why take chances?

A man at the edge of the seated patrons, stood up. It was Blaine! He turned away from Hillman, and slowly walked toward an exit—the same one Annie had used to enter the court. Annie watched Blaine's attempt to escape. Hillman did, too, and increased his pace.

*Here he comes!* Annie stood and waited in the dim corner for Blaine to come closer.

Hillman followed the fugitive through the food court. Blaine glanced surreptitiously over his shoulder, his attention on the patroller.

He didn't see the small woman moving to block his path until he heard a voice say, "Carlsson Blaine, I have a warrant for your arrest for Flight to Avoid Prosecution and Failure to Make Restitution." Annie didn't feel it was necessary to mention the three hundred challenges against him by his former clients. "Will you accept arrest, or will you challenge my warrant? There is a dueling court nearby, and I see a station patroller is available as a referee. I'm sure one person here will volunteer as a second witness."

†††

Blaine stopped. He glanced back. The patroller was only steps away. Several dozen nearby people watched the confrontation. There was no escape. He had only two options—submit or challenge. The patroller was a big man, his knuckles scarred from many bar brawls and fist-fights. He would be no easy opponent. Blaine was not an incompetent duelist. He practiced with a knife and pistol, but he knew he would be no match for the big patroller. The little woman, on the other hand…

"Challenge," Blaine said.

†††

Hillman stepped up to Blaine's side. "Easy," he whispered to Blaine. "Make no sudden moves."

Hillman, keeping Blaine visible at the edge of his vision, said to the nearby patrons, "This gentleman has challenged this lady in the execution of her legal warrant. I will referee the engagement. I need a volunteer to be a second witness. Would anyone here be willing to uphold Custom and Tradition?"

At first, no one moved. Heads swiveled, people hoping someone else would respond. When no one did, a man, sitting alone, rose, stepped forward, and raised his hand. "I will, Patroller. I have time."

138

"Thank you, sir," Hillman said when the volunteer reached him. "I'll introduce you to the two parties." Hillman sub-vocalized a message via his link to have a resuscitation team on standby and ushered the three outside the food court to the entrance of a dueling court some meters away. Usually, the court was used for sparring or individual practice. It was unoccupied today.

†††

Hillman halted the group while he waved his link across the pad next to the entrance. When it slid open, he announced, "I am Senior Patroller Henry Hillman. I will referee this event. From this point forward, everything will be scanned and recorded until the dispute has been settled." To the second witness, Hillman added, "Sir, this gentleman is Carlsson Blaine, Clan Monmouth, Sept Conner. You need not know the details of the issue between them. I assure you the complaint complies with Custom and Tradition."

The volunteer bowed to Blaine. Turning back to Blaine, Hillman continued. "Clansman Blaine, as the challenging party, you must post bond for myself as Referee and this gentleman as Second Witness. The bond is one hundred Confederate dollars. Will you post bond?"

"I cannot. I pledge my clan for the cost."

"Make your pledge," Hillman said.

Blaine entered a sequence of commands into his link. A moment later, Hillman confirmed the bond was posted with the Dundee Orbital's bond registry by Clan Monmouth. Hillman had half expected Monmouth to refuse the bond.

"The lady," he continued, speaking again to the Witness, "is Anne Marie Griffin, Clan Griffin, Sept Leeds."

The volunteer's eyes widened as Hillman introduced Annie. He knew her or was, at least, familiar with her reputation. The volunteer bowed to Annie, more deeply than he had to Blaine, and introduced himself. "Sir, Madam, I am Karl-Ludwig Holtz, Clan Mieze, Sept Lehmann. I am at your service." Holtz was not required to introduce himself, but he did so in acknowledgement of Annie's reputation, Hillman suspected.

With the initial *Proprieties* met, Hillman led the group inside. The dueling court was a circular open space fifty meters across. A thirty-meter circle was drawn on the floor. The circle was for practice or minor exchanges. It wouldn't be required today.

Hillman turned to Annie. "As the challenged party, you have the choice of weapons. What do you choose?"

"I will defer to Clansman Blaine. His choice," she replied.

Hillman and Holtz turned to Blaine, awaiting his response. He hesitated and glanced at Annie before looking back at Holtz and the patroller. "Knives, Patroller."

Hillman nodded.

"Noted," Holtz said.

Hillman glanced at Holtz. He was familiar with dueling protocol. Perhaps he had been in a duel himself? No matter, he knew his duties.

"Clanswoman Griffin," Hillman said formally, "your conditions?"

"Surrender or unable to continue," Annie said firmly.

"Objections?" he asked Blaine.

"None," he replied.

"Sobeit," Holtz declared.

"Sobeit," Hillman confirmed.

††† 

Holtz checked both knives to ensure they met dueling standards. Annie kicked off her boots. The floor of the dueling court was roughened; bare feet would have a firmer grip and be less likely to slip than shoes or boots.

Blaine shed his coat, tossed it aside, and raised his arms for a pat-down. He proclaimed he was armed only with a knife. Holtz, finding no other weapon, searched Annie next. He confirmed neither had additional weapons.

Hillman called Annie and Blaine together and pronounced the terms of the duel for the record. "This duel between Anne Griffin and Carlsson Blaine will use knives. It will end if Clansman Blaine surrenders to Clanswoman Griffin, if Clanswoman Griffin concedes she cannot defeat her opponent, or if one of them cannot continue and is deemed to be defeated." He gave them an opportunity either to speak or contradict the rules as spoken. "Questions? Statements for the record?"

Neither spoke.

Hillman led the two to the circle. Blaine stepped inside. Annie walked to the opposite side of the ring and turned to face him. Holtz followed and took a position outside the circle to Blaine's right. Hillman took a position outside the circle opposite from Holtz. When everyone was in position, the patroller said, loudly enough for all to hear, "Commence!"

††† 

Blaine smiled. He was bigger and heavier than the woman. If he was quick enough, he could still get away and hide. Clan Monmouth had several safe areas in the station. He rushed—his left hand forward to engage her, right hand with his knife held back, out of her reach. Grab and stab was his plan. He crouched and shifted forward.

†††

Annie, judging from Blaine's crouch, predicted his move. He moved forward until he was close enough to rush her. She crouched and waited as Blaine shuffled closer. When he was within reach, he feinted and lunged.

She knelt and allowed Blaine's attack to pass by. Annie made a leg sweep, catching Blaine's extended foot. Down he went, and Annie notched his ear and drew a bloody line down the back of Blaine's neck with her knife.

She danced away. Blaine regained his feet and retreated to the edge of the circle.

†††

*Pack! She's quick,* Hillman thought. *Quicker than yesterday.* He glanced at Holtz, catching his eye. Holtz nodded in return. The Second Witness was not an amateur. He knew who the better fighter was. Annie could have ended the fight in her first move. Blaine had left himself open to a counterstrike. Annie's plan, it seemed to Hillman, was to blood her opponent, weaken him with multiple cuts while she measured his proficiency.

The duelists danced within the circle. There was no requirement for them to remain inside, but Hillman suspected Blaine's formalized training—to always stay inside the circle—remained. He was not in the same class with a knife as Annie was.

†††

Annie was taking her time. The duel had evolved into strike-counterstrike. Blaine was bloody from a series of minor wounds, both arms and one notched ear she knew would be painful. She only had a small cut across the palm of her left hand, which she had used to clumsily block a strike.

In return, she had cut Blaine's right hand, the one holding his knife. Blood dripped from the wound, and he gripped the knife with whitened knuckles. The knife's hilt was getting slippery.

†††

Blaine rushed forward again. Annie danced back, and Blaine lunged, hoping to press her off-balance. She leaned aside and sliced across Blaine's forehead.

Blood flowed into his eyes. Blaine wiped the blood with a forearm to clear his vision. Annie saw the realization on his face; he was losing, one cut after another. He would change tactics next.

Annie was watching, waiting for him to do something. Blaine had been using his right hand—his strong side. He passed his knife to his left hand and lunged.

*Time to end this.* Changing hands might have worked against someone with less experience. However, this was not her first knife fight. She'd had others, and against more experienced and skilled opponents.

Knife against knife. Blaine lunged to cut, to weaken her right arm. Annie countered with her knife, pushing Blaine's aside. She stepped forward, inside his reach, and punched him in the throat with her left fist, breaking his hyoid bone.

†††

Blaine's eyes opened wide. He was unprepared for the pain. He coughed, and the pain increased. Blood flowed into his eyes. He lost sight of Annie.

With Blaine preoccupied, Annie stepped forward and struck again with her fist, breaking and dislocating his jaw. Blaine's eyes rolled up, and he dropped.

Annie stepped back. Hillman called for the medics he had waiting outside the court while he and Holtz walked forward. Protocol required time for Blaine to recover, if he could. When they stood over him, Holtz asked, per protocol, "Do you surrender, or shall the duel continue, Clansman Blaine?"

When Blaine didn't respond, Hillman repeated the same question. Blaine still didn't respond, and to Hillman's eye, he was having difficulty breathing. His face was turning blue. "I declare this engagement in Clanswoman Griffin's favor. Do you agree, Witness Holtz?"

"I concur," Holtz replied.

The medical team moved forward to treat Blaine. In a few moments, they had opened Blaine's airway, and his color returned. A patroller arrived with the medical team. Following Hillman's instructions, the patroller cuffed Blaine and would accompany him, until he was released from the medics. Then, off Blaine would go, to the brig to join Leland Smith.

Annie, Hillman, and Holtz watched the medics and the patroller carry Blaine away. A medic treated Annie's hand and left to join the rest of his team.

Hillman used his link to shift half of Blaine's bond to Holtz's account, his fee for being a Second Witness. "Your fee has been paid, Clansman Holtz. Thank you for your service."

"It was my duty and honor, sir. Happy to oblige." Holtz bowed, said farewell to Annie, and walked out of the courtyard.

Donal Harris reread the report concerning Ferdinand Speeks. *A career criminal. He won't go easily, and he knows what will happen if Clan M'Tobo gets their hands on him.* Harris stared at Speeks' image. *No, you will make your arrest as difficult as possible. You know you can't get off-station, and eventually, Annie will track you down.*

Harris shook his head. *Pack! It will be another fiasco like the last time.* Annie wouldn't be indiscriminate like that previous, unlamented hunter. *Speeks won't care.* He sighed. *Annie and Henry will need help.*

Harris opened a link to Colin Graeme. *<You have a minute? >*

Graeme was off-shift and had just seated himself to dinner. *<I was about to eat.>*

*<I've been reviewing Speeks' record. He'll be trouble. We need to help Annie Griffin and Henry Hillman. If nothing else, we need to protect any bystanders if Speeks doesn't cooperate.>*

*<You really think so? Hillman is good, and we've all seen how good Annie Griffin is. I don't think we need to get involved.>*

*<You weren't here that last time we had a shootout between a hunter and his target. People died, and kids were injured. I don't want a repeat of that! If you won't help, I'll call Isaac Taquel. He's older but still competent.>*

*<Okay, Okay. I'll join you; I just don't think we'll be needed.>*

*<I hope we won't. But if something happens, we'll be there to minimize the danger to the public.>*

*<Fine.>* Graeme dropped the link.

†††

"Now what?" Hillman asked. He and Annie had retreated to the food court. Hillman ordered an iced drink for each of them.

"I need to clean up, Henry. Do you need to report in; will you wait?" Annie needed to find the nearest 'fresher. She, her trousers, and her blouse were splashed with Blaine's blood. She shook her hand, momentarily distracted by the sting of the cut. The injury was minor, and she had refused further treatment, but her medical nanites hadn't yet blocked the pain.

Hillman smiled. Annie was a bloody sight and was already drawing eyes. The patrons of the food court were whispering.

"Go ahead," he said. "The 'freshers are behind you. I can wait."

Annie found the public 'fresher and rented a transient stall. She was sweaty and smelled of blood. Annie stripped in the stall's privacy and fed her clothes into the laundry hopper to be cleaned while she took, and paid extra for, a water shower.

She emerged half an hour later, refreshed and wearing newly laundered clothing with her short hair carefully combed. She sported a shiny strip across her palm, a nanite bandage to keep her cut clean.

"Nothing more for me today," she said when she seated herself across from Hillman. She shook her hand again. "That packer cut me!"

"Well, Blaine will be on a liquid diet for a few days. You had your revenge."

"Not enough," Annie muttered. Her knuckles on her left hand were bruised and scraped. She had expected those bruises. The cut, however… *Am I slowing down?* It was a little thing. She had been wounded before, in other hunts, but Blaine was stupid and arrogant. He shouldn't have been able to lay a blade on her. But he had. Was she getting past her prime? *Too old to be a hunter? I'm only thirty, for pack's sake!* She looked at her cut again. *No, I'm not slowing down. I just wasn't paying attention. Henry... I'm tired of this. Ten years as a hunter is enough.* She looked at Hillman again. A sense of longing passed over her. *I could find something—someone here.*

"It's past mid-shift," Hillman said. "Hungry?"

"No..." Her stomach growled., "Yes, but nothing heavy. Not now."

"Let's cruise the food bar. Maybe something will strike your fancy."

The food bar included several ethnic offerings from out-system. The Inverness culinary tradition was limited: fish, beef, BBQ, and Tex-Mex. Most of the original colonists, the first to organize themselves into clans on Inverness, were from Wales, Scotland, Ireland, and the Maritime Provinces of Old Canada. The rest of the original colonists were from Appalachia and the central plains of the old United States. The bar's cuisine reflected the heritage of the planet below.

They strolled down the food bar. Hillman got another drink and a small sandwich. Annie stopped farther down the line, paused, and continued with a container of seafood gumbo. Hillman found an out-of-the-way table, where he sipped his drink and ate his sandwich while Annie consumed her gumbo. Neither of them had much to say. Hillman was patient to wait while Annie came down from her adrenaline high.

Hillman checked his link. No messages. He still had several hours left on his shift. If Annie was finished for the day, he could return to work to finish his log of today's events. He sent a message to Inspector Harris, asking for instruction.

*<Take the rest of the shift off. Graeme and I will accompany you tomorrow.>*

Annie finished her gumbo. She had noticed Hillman sending and receiving link messages. "What's up?"

"Nothing at the moment. Inspector Harris said he and Inspector Graeme will join us tomorrow."

"They must have read Ferdinand Speeks' dossier," Annie said. "He won't be a push-over."

"I've seen no data about Speeks. What is it about him?"

"He's a criminal from Cameron, next door—a smuggler, a loan shark, and a suspect in various other offenses, including murder," she replied.

"Why hasn't someone challenged him? Sooner or later, the problem would be fixed."

"He cheats," was her answer. "Speeks is very skilled with pistol, hands, and knife. He's also aware there is always someone better. A M'Tobo clansman, who was a clan action-pistol champ, challenged him. That is, he used to be the champion. Speeks hired a gun, who called out the champ during a party, drew, and shot him down before the champ even knew he was being challenged."

Hillman leaned back. That was a bold move against Custom and Tradition. "And the gunman?"

"Mobbed and was disappeared but not before he talked. It was all documented. That gave them grounds for the warrant."

"And Speeks is here?"

"Yes." Annie debated whether to make another pass along the buffet line. She was still hungry but decided against eating more. Continuing her narrative, she said, "I guess Speeks wanted to gloat. He was downbelow when the murder occurred. The M'Tobo clan was quick to get a Confederation warrant out for Speeks, but he was quicker and made an escape. He made it up here and found he was blocked. He couldn't get off."

Annie leaned back in her chair. "Speeks won't go easy. I expect Harris and Graeme think the same."

"Then we must find him, isolate him, and take him," Hillman said.

Annie nodded and sighed. "Yep... since you have some free time, would you be willing to show me the station? I've been here several times, but I've never stayed long."

Hillman smiled. His mind flashed to the memory of the previous night. No, he didn't mind at all. "Have you ever seen our farms?"

"Farms? I didn't know any were here."

"Oh, yes. A third of Dundee Orbital, more than three whole torus, are farms. Mostly hydroponic, but there is one complete torus reserved for field crops, wheat, barley and corn. Then there is the herd."

"Herd?"

Hillman laughed. "It's what we call the protein vats—vat-grown beef, pig, and fowl. But there are small herds of beef, flocks of chickens and turkeys, plus a growing number of pigs. The demand for real beef—like the filet you ate at The Garden—makes even a small herd and flock commercially viable."

"Really?"

"Yes. Did you think, for a station this size, that we could import all our food requirements? Not by far."

"Fruit orchards too?"

"Follow me, Annie. I'll treat you to some orange juice freshly picked off the tree."

Hillman walked a few steps before looking over his shoulder. Annie hadn't followed. He walked back to her, puzzled by her failure to accompany him.

"Is this like a date?" she asked.

"Uh, I hadn't thought about it, but yes, I suppose it could be, if you agree."

"Good!" She jumped up, wrapped her arms around his neck, and kissed him. "Let's go! I can just taste that orange juice."

## Day Five

Custom Inspectors Harris and Graeme were walking toward Annie Griffin's hostel. Both had taken the precaution of adding full-face helmets and ballistic armor to their light-tan Customs shipsuits.

"Did you pass the word to Hillman?" Graeme asked.

"Yes, and I asked him to pass the word to Annie Griffin too."

"You think she has armor?"

"She's a professional," Harris answered. "Yes, I believe she has. No helmet, though."

As the inspectors reviewed Speeks' record, their worries grew. Speeks was a suspect in several murders on Cameron, the next planet inward from Inverness. Unfortunately, Cameron's Capitol Security Service, their planetary police force, lacked evidence for an arrest.

At his own expense, a tenth of the sum paid by Annie Griffin, Harris had run a full station scan, looking for Speeks. The scan found Speeks lurking in a 'fresher stall on Torus Six. He had moved since to Deck Five, Segment C, of Torus Four. The segment had several decks under conversion to transient quarters for temporary residents, business hostels, marketing, and export-import trade offices.

Speeks apparently thought he could intermingle with transients and safely hide in plain sight. The tactic might have worked on other stations.

Graeme was reluctant to accompany him. Harris was aware of the video floating around the patroller and Customs Service private link-nets of Graeme's confrontation with Annie. He was not displeased. Graeme was a thorny Customs inspector who was abrasive to everyone he encountered. On the reverse side, he was highly competent at catching smugglers and Customs evaders. Harris kept his opinion of the other inspector to himself, but he agreed with others—Graeme needed the lesson he'd received from Annie Griffin.

Harris and Graeme joined Hillman and Annie Griffin outside her hostel. Hillman was carrying his patroller full-face helmet in one hand. The outlines of ballistic armor panels in Hillman's light-gray patroller shipsuit stood out.

Annie Griffin wore a light-green shipsuit, which would let her blend in with the crowd better. Her shipsuit bore her name above her right breast and a patch of the Griffin tartan on her upper right sleeve. Ballistic armor was outlined in the chest, arm, and leg pockets of her shipsuit.

"Before we go after Speeks, I want to review the rules for today's hunt, Clanswoman Griffin," Harris said. "Do you have a magazine of solid or armor-piercing ammunition?"

"Two magazines of solid ammunition, Inspector. No armor-piercing," she replied.

"Do not load any solid rounds without permission. Under no circumstances load any armor-piercing if you find any. You understand the consequences?"

"Yes," she confirmed. Using armor-piercing ammunition inside the station was an automatic spacing offense—no hearing, no trial, just a short trip to the nearest lock and a shorter visit to the outside of the station.

"If Speeks uses solid or armor-piercing ammunition, you may load solid rounds," Harris said, "but not until authorized by Inspector Graeme or myself. Senior Patroller Hillman does *not* have that authority. Understood?"

"Yes, Inspector," she answered.

"Good. Speeks was last seen on Torus Four. I've alerted the regular patrollers on the beat. They will be prepared to herd non-combatants away from the scene if events become... hazardous."

†††

Torus Four, Deck Three, Segment C was not far, nearby in terms of the intra-station transit tube they used. Segment C was the third of the four segments formerly reserved for light industry. The segments were to be converted to transient hostels and offices for out-system trading companies. Stationers and transients filled the public mezzanines, atriums, and the segment's park. The human traffic density was higher than Harris expected.

According to Harris' last scan, Speeks was at an open merchandise market where ships and small traders displayed samples of their wares. The market spread across a four-acre atrium with a central fountain. Around the edge of the market were food and drink stalls operated by station entrepreneurs. Speeks was near one food stall, attempting to masquerade as a stationer.

Entering the market, Graeme and Harris turned left while Hillman and Annie Griffin turned right. Speeks, according to Harris, was on the opposite side of the atrium.

†††

Hillman slipped on his helmet and checked his link to enable the helmet's heads-up display. He asked Annie, "You ready?"

She looked up at Hillman, who was larger now with his added armor and helmet. "As ready as I'll ever be." She stepped forward, forcing Hillman to follow.

†††

Graeme and Harris separated after leaving the others. Harris chose a direct path toward Speeks, through the middle of the merchants' kiosks. Graeme circled the marketplace from the left. Harris and Graeme's plan was to divide Speeks' attention, if they were seen. If he resisted—and opened fire—which Harris thought was likely, they would need to take him down quickly. One of them would flank Speeks while the fugitive engaged the other.

Annie Griffin would have the opportunity to arrest Speeks. If he didn't resist, Graeme and Harris would leave. Otherwise...

†††

Hillman, being taller, spotted Speeks standing next to an import-export kiosk before Annie did. Speeks stood next to a woman who was answering customer questions and making trades. Speeks was taller than the average stationer, too, and could see anyone approaching. His attention was drawn to the other side of the market. He didn't notice Hillman's slow, circuitous approach.

"He can't see you, Annie, but when he looks this way, he can't help but see me. Let's split. I'll act like a beat patroller. Speeks will watch me, and you can move around and flank him."

Annie nodded and continued forward, hiding behind kiosks, vendors, and taller stationers. Hillman stopped to exchange greetings with a vendor, like a beat patroller. The stalk was on.

†††

Speeks swept his gaze across the market while shifting his position to stand next to a large light-tan pillar. The pillar was color-coded to show its function, a data and power conduit in this case.

There was little movement in the market. It was early in the shift, but the sellers were ready. Buyers would be arriving soon, and trading would start. Some early buyers were already trickling in. He saw movement along the far edge of the market. A new group had entered the marketplace, but they were too far away for Speeks to see them clearly. He looked in the other direction. Nothing suspicious there, just a patroller walking his beat.

*Hmmm. Why would a senior patroller be walking a beat alone? They always travel in pairs… He's heading for me!*

†††

Annie slipped between vendors and reached the outer edge of the line of food stalls. Speeks moved next to a metal-encased pillar. His change of position made him more visible to her, but not to Hillman. *He has good cover from that pillar if there's a gunfight*, Annie thought. *He can see me, now, if he looks this way.* She moved closer to a food-stall, using it for concealment as she continued her stalk.

Hillman was moving slowly, twenty to thirty meters away, toward Speeks, when she slipped around the stall. Harris was moving forward like Henry. His helmet was visible moving through the market, obliquely heading toward their quarry. She could not see Graeme.

†††

Speeks swept his gaze across the atrium again and returned to examine the patroller. *Why was he wearing a helmet? Patrollers usually didn't… there's another helmet heading this way!* He knew there was a hunter on-station, and he knew the hunter was Li'l Annie, but he had thought her quarry was Leland Smith. Her takedown of him had been shown on most of the holo-channels of the station. *Stupid assumption,* he berated himself.

He made another visual sweep and glimpsed a small figure, from the corner of his eye, move from one food-stall to another coming in his direction. The big patroller was getting close. The other patrol helmet was fifty meters farther away.

*Fight or flight?* Speeks didn't have a choice. There was no place to flee. He couldn't get off-station now. An Inverness warrant had no authority in Confederation territory unless an official hunter carried it. Station patrollers would honor the warrant to the extent of preventing escape and to ensure Custom and Tradition was followed. Other than that, their concern was to minimize collateral damage as best they could.

*I will not let M'Tobo get me!* He unholstered his pistol and removed the magazine of frangible ammunition. From his magazine pouch, he removed another magazine, inserted it into the butt of the pistol, and racked the slide. The markings on the new cassette showed it contained armor-piercing rounds. Possession of such ammunition on a station, much less shooting it, was a spacing offense. Speeks considered breathing vacuum a quicker death than whatever M'Tobo planned for him. *If I go, I'll take the bitch with me.*

Speeks could not—would not—surrender.

†††

The crowd was thickening, hindering Hillman's progress. He stopped to allow a trader to push a pallet of small goods across his path. He was distracted by the interruption. When he looked up, Speeks was aiming a pistol at him.

*Pack!* Hillman pushed the merchant aside, out of the line of fire.

*Choog!* Speeks' suppressed pistol fired.

Hillman felt a punch in his right shoulder. His arm went numb, and he fumbled drawing his pistol. A second punch hit him in the gut, piercing his armor. He slid to the floor.

†††

*Henry!* Annie wanted to go to Hillman—but she couldn't. She had a target to take down. Drawing her pistol, she moved, pushing Henry Hillman from her mind.

Speeks had changed positions. Annie ran up to the side of the light-green pillar.

*Choog! Tang!* A bullet hit the pillar above Annie's head, punching through its metal exterior. High-pressure air screamed from the pillar.

Speeks' pistol was suppressed, as was Annie's. But being suppressed did not mean silent. The sound from his pistol had exposed his position.

Annie slid around to the other side of the pillar. Across the atrium, people were taking cover or dropping to the floor. Some were trying to escape. Many of the stationers had drawn weapons, too, but they held their fire until they could determine the source of the shots and who was shooting at whom.

Speeks was using armor-piercing ammunition, or else it couldn't have penetrated the metal sheath of the pillar. That was all Annie needed. She ejected her cassette of frangible ammunition and replaced it with a cassette of solid rounds.

*<Solid ammo authorized.>* The message from Harris arrived through her link. *Finally. Now I'm covered.*

*<Henry?>* she asked.

*<Don't know. Heading there.>* Harris dropped the link.

She glimpsed Speeks moving from one pillar to another. She had an open view of him.

*Choog!* She fired, and Speeks jerked. Her first round was the frangible remaining in her pistol's chamber. Her next rounds were solid. She crouched and moved forward.

157

*Choog!* Something hit her. A red flower blossomed on her left abdomen. A matching flower appeared on her back—a through-and-through wound. Her link flashed red, indicating her medical nanites were in emergency mode and an alarm had been sent to Station Security.

†††

Harris fought his way through the throng to Hillman's position. Several stationers had sighted Speeks through the fog created by the escaping high-pressure air from the damaged pillar. It was enough justification for them to fire on Speeks.

Harris checked Hillman and the merchant who had been injured by the round that passed through Hillman. Although his wounds were serious, Hillman was alive. If he received aid quickly, he would survive. The merchant was not seriously injured. Several stationers had dragged the two of them behind a kiosk and were attending to them.

Several nearby stationers volunteered to offer covering fire while Harris maneuvered to lay flanking fire on Speeks. Three red icons flashed on Harris' heads-up display. The position of the third icon told him Annie must be wounded too.

†††

Hearing gunfire, Graeme checked his heads-up display to show the overhead view of the marketplace. Three red icons, injured stationers, appeared. One was flashing red-green. A patroller was down—Hillman.

Behind Graeme, merchants and stationers were taking cover or moving toward exits. Three stationers crawled up to Graeme, offering help.

"The shooter is male," Graeme told them and brought up a holo from his link. It highlighted Speeks' location. "Keep him pinned down if you can. He's already taken out a patroller. Don't become a casualty yourselves."

Graeme reported the shooting to patrol headquarters. They relayed the report to the station's Customs office. Patrollers and Customs agents began to converge on the scene.

His link received a report of damage to an environmental conduit in the marketplace from station maintenance. Someone—Speeks, most likely—was using armor-piercing ammunition. Frangible ammunition would not penetrate the conduit—frangibles would shatter on impact against any solid object and would not endanger the station. Solid bullets couldn't penetrate a pillar. The pillars were hardened to all but armor-piercing rounds.

†††

Annie's wound had not prevented her from taking cover. She inched slowly forward, shifting around the pillar, leaving a bloody trail behind her. With her pistol extended before her, she crawled forward, ready to fire as soon as she had a target.

Speeks came into view. He was exchanging fire with Harris and several stationers. A volley of frangible fire from a second direction splattered Speeks, shattering on impact. His shipsuit was protecting him from frangible bullets. However, the impacts caused him to step back into Annie's view.

She fired three rounds. The first was aimed low. Annie used the recoil of her pistol to walk her shots up Speeks' body. The first round hit Speeks in the ankle; the second struck his knee. A red mist bloomed from it. The third destroyed Speeks' elbow. He was going nowhere. Annie was about to fire again when the world faded away.

## Day Seven

Annie opened her eyes. She didn't recognize her surroundings, but the presence of a med-tech hinted she was in a hospital. A second, older med-tech wearing a caduceus on his tunic entered the room and examined the bank of instruments, and the flow of data on the wall.

He walked over to Annie's bed, tilted his head, and visually examined her from head-to-toe. He nodded. "You'll live," he said and walked out of the room.

"Wordy, isn't he?" the med-tech said and laughed. "You'll be fine, and you were never in danger. The trauma boys got to you in time to prevent any serious damage."

Annie blinked. Her eyes felt crusty. The med-tech noticed and wiped her face with a moist pad. "Who was that?"

"Chief of Hospital. He always checks our unexpected visitors."

"And the patroller, Henry Hillman?" She had seen him go down, and her link had flashed a red icon when he had.

"Oh, he's up and around. He's been dropping in, checking on you."

The statement relieved her. The answer, though, implied she had been the more severely wounded. "And me?"

"Well, I should wait, but… you lost a kidney and pancreas. The bullet passed close to your spine too. We were concerned about nerve damage from its passage, so we kept you under for a day while we addressed any spinal injuries and started regen. Can you wiggle your toes?"

Annie raised her head and looked down the bed. She moved her toes and feet… at least she thought she was. There was no sensation, no feedback, but when she tried, she could see movement under the sheets. *Yes, I can.*

The med-tech nodded as she watched the sheet over Annie's legs and feet move. "Yep. Working."

"I didn't feel anything."

"The numbness will go away in a few hours., Don't worry."

The statement relieved her. "How long will I be here?"

"They'll release you tomorrow. Regen has already been started; they'll want to see if it is progressing as programmed before releasing you." She wiped Annie's face again, across her forehead and around her neck. "You must stay on-station until the regen of your kidney and pancreas is finished. You could mess it all up by going downbelow now—reentry stress, don't'cha know. Until you're cleared, you must stay here so we can monitor your progress."

"What about the patroller?"

"Well... I'm not supposed to say, but since he's been in and out of here all day... he's fine. One bullet was a through-and-through. Did little damage on its passage other than to shake up some body parts. The other bullet, however, shattered his shoulder. He'll need a full regen on it and will have to wear a regen mesh with a sling for a few months."

*Good. Henry's safe. He'll be off work for a while, pushing paper while he recovers.*

After downloading the data from Annie's medical nanites, the med-tech turned toward the door when Hillman and Harris entered.

"If you gentlemen will excuse me," the med-tech said and walked past them, closing the door behind her.

Hillman moved closer and sat in the chair next to her bed. His right upper arm and shoulder were immobilized in a regen mesh. He was wearing a patroller tunic draped over his shoulders and a shirt with the right shoulder and sleeve removed. Harris looked around the room, found a second chair, and pulled it over next to Hillman.

"So tell me what happened? I missed the last part," she said.

Henry and Donal Harris exchanged glances. "Well, since Henry was out, too, I guess I'm the designated storyteller," Harris said. "Graeme and I split up when we left you. Colin went around the market edge opposite you and Henry. I went up the middle. Speeks saw Henry first. I think the helmets, his and mine, tipped him off. Anyway, he shot Henry first, taking him out, and then he fired at you. One of those shots hit an environment pillar, a high-pressure airline. It looked like a jet of steam squirting out of the pillar. We were lucky it didn't start a fire or cause an oxygen explosion. The other shot hit you. You remember all that?"

"Yeah," she confirmed. "And then I crawled behind the pillar."

"Right. In the meantime, Colin and I organized some stationers to keep Speeks pinned down. Colin led them while I checked Henry," he said, nodding toward the big patroller. "The stationers flanked Speeks and put some frangibles on him. He left cover, and that is when you nailed him. Put him down."

"So I got him. He's in the brig or here?"

Harris glanced at Hillman, who chose to not speak, allowing the Inspector to explain. "Uh, no, Speeks had wounded a stationer at the beginning and had violated station integrity by putting a hole in the environmental pillar that you hid behind. He was using armor-piercing ammunition… the stationers spaced him."

"Oh. I knew that would happen," she admonished herself. The penalty had been drummed into her. "I could have used his bounty,"

162

"You got the credit. You took him down so the stationers could get their hands on him."

"But shouldn't he have gotten a trial first?"

"Oh, he did. His actions before several hundred witnesses made do for the prosecution. The stationers were the jury. The Custom and Tradition is explicit and was followed. Colin led the group to an airlock a few hundred meters off the atrium and fixed a tether to Speeks' foot— wouldn't want him to be a hazard to outside traffic. The stationers put Speeks inside and fixed the other end of the tether to a tie-down. They got out, and Colin, using his Customs link, opened the outer door."

"Speeks was alive, kicking and screaming, as he went out. Messy," Harris said. "Explosive decompression isn't a clean or, in Speeks' case, a quick death. Graeme said he lasted several minutes."

She sighed. It was over. She'd forgotten about station Customs and Tradition whenever someone endangered the station. Speeks was finished, and her warrant was closed. She would still be paid. "How long will I be here?"

"A least a month," Hillman answered.

"Time for me to get back to work." Harris turned to Hillman. "Henry, don't report in for two weeks. You can't do much with one arm. I've written it up as a service-related injury received in the line of duty." He stood and walked toward the door. Before he reached it, however, he added, "I expect Henry will have time to finish your tour of the station, Annie. The two of you will have plenty of time now."

The two watched Harris leave. Hillman shifted his position in the chair. He wasn't entirely pain free.

Annie was the first to speak. "I can't stay in the hostel any longer; it's too expensive for such a small room. Do you know of a place where I can stay?"

Hillman's quiet grin was all the answer she needed.

# Part II: Patroller

## Unemployed.

"Ready?" Henry Hillman asked Annie, his coapt partner.

Annie Griffin was viewing the holo of job listings projected from her link when he walked into the kitchen. Hillman had eaten breakfast earlier, but Annie, seated with an empty plate before her, had just finished. "Yep, let's go. We've a busy shift."

The two left the coapt they'd shared for the last month and boarded a tram to the Dundee Orbital Medical Center. Annie expected to receive her medical clearance. She and Henry had been involved in a firefight, a month ago, that had left both of them wounded.

Annie had needed her kidney and pancreas regrown. Henry had suffered a shattered shoulder. His shoulder and upper arm were still encased in a regeneration mesh. If his recovery continued as projected, he should be cleared for full duty in another two months.

"Did you find anything in the employment ads interesting?" Hillman asked after they were seated on the tram.

"No… not really. I'm embarrassed. I don't have any skills that employers want. All I know is hunting fugitives, and there isn't any demand for that on the station." She paused. "I've been job hunting for a week. If I don't find something soon, I'll have to go back downbelow to Inverness."

Hillman didn't immediately reply. "Skills aside, what would you like to do?"

"That's another problem. I don't know… a lurcat foster parent?" she said with a grin. "We'd need a bigger coapt."

Hillman looked askance at her. "A bigger coapt isn't the problem. I rate a bigger one anyway—just haven't needed it. A lurcat, however…" A meter-and-a-half-tall lurcat needed space. Henry's one-bedroom coapt wouldn't do.

"Just joking. Henry, just joking."

The tram arrived at the terminal outside the medical center. They stepped off and entered the hospital.

†††

"Your tests are excellent, Annie. The kidney and pancreas are fully regenned. I'll post your medical clearance before you leave," Dr. Mancini said. "Questions?"

"None that I can think of. I'll be glad to get off the meds."

"Before I forget... I found one minor thing."

"Oh?"

"Your nanites are several versions out-of-date. In fact, they appear to be the initial issue you received at age six. They should be upgraded. Check with your clan about having that scheduled."

"I will... uh, for my information, what is the cost of the upgrade?"

"Let me see." Mancini entered a query with his link. "Here it is. You're five versions behind. Each will need to be upgraded in sequence. It's an estimate, but I think it'd be around twenty-five thousand Confederate dollars."

Annie blanched. *C$25,000?* Her clan should've scheduled and paid for the updates long ago. They hadn't, being more interested in her clan tithe than updating her nanites.

"Are you all right, Annie?"

"Yes. Thank you." *Twenty-five thousand dollars. I can't afford that and stay solvent. It would take almost all I have.* She frowned. Appealing to her clan filled her with dread. "Thank you, Doctor. I'll contact my clan rep." Mitchell Ortiz, her sept-brother, would support her, but he had no real power.

†††

"You're doing well, Henry. If you want to go back to work, I'll give you limited clearance for light desk duty only."

Hillman smiled. He was bored and ready to return to work. Living with Annie was a welcomed experience, even with both of them recovering from wounds. But he was having coapt fever. Any duty that got him out of the coapt—and out from behind a desk—would be acceptable.

"May I do walk-arounds? I wouldn't need to get involved in anything, just supervise my team. I've a low boredom threshold."

Hillman's physician laughed. "Let's see what your superiors have in mind before you ask me that. Now, we need to install a new regen mesh for the next stage. All the soft tissue regeneration is finished, and the skeletal reconstruction is progressing normally. The next stage will concentrate on rebuilding your shoulder's cartilage…"

†††

By agreement, Annie waited for Hillman on a bench outside the medical center. They had expected his appointment to take longer than hers.

*Twenty-five thousand Confederate dollars.* She made a link call to Clan Griffin's Dundee representative.

*<Mitchell Ortiz, Clan Griffin, Sept Leeds. I'm not available at the moment. Please leave a voice or text message.>*

Ortiz's message didn't promise to return her call. *<Sept Brother Ortiz, this is Annie Griffin, Clan Griffin, Sept Leeds. I've been told my personal nanites are several versions out-of-date and need to be updated. Now that I've free time, I need to get that done. Please provide a clan voucher to cover the costs? Thank you.>* She posted her voice message and cut the connection.

Clan Griffin wasn't known for its generosity. The clan's relationship with its members was reflected in the dwindling yearly census—people were leaving the clan, voting with their feet. If the clan's territory weren't rocky and barren, it would've been absorbed by a neighbor. In truth, no other clan wanted Griffin's territory.

Her link dinged. She answered as she saw Hillman walk out of the medical center.

*<Annie, Mitchell Ortiz, here. I got your message. Is there somewhere we can meet and discuss your issue? I'm available after second shift plus two hours.>*

*<Sept Brother. Yes, I'm available. Where shall we meet?>*" She stressed *Sept Brother*. Annie purposely reminded him of their dual paths of mutual allegiance.

*<Katrin's is always good. I'll be in the bar.>*

*<I'll be there, Sept Brother.>*"

"What's up?" Henry asked as he sat next to her on the bench.

"I got my medical clearance, but I was told my personal nanites are several versions out-of-date. My clan should've called me in to get them updated, but they never did." She hesitated. "I think they'll refuse to pay."

"Really?" Hillman's home world of Gilead did not provide personal nanites to its individual citizens. He had acquired nanites when he joined Gilead's planetary militia and received more upgrades when he enlisted in the Confederation Marines. Another upgrade was included when he became a patroller in Dundee Orbital. But Inverness was different. The clans were famous for their care of their clansmen and clanswomen.

"How much would it cost?" he asked.

"Twenty-five thousand Confederate dollars."

"Oh!"

"That's why I'm meeting Ortiz tonight. Griffin owes me. But since I'm now unemployed, they may balk."

"Why?"

"I can't pay clan tithes if I'm unemployed. I've always paid in full and on time when I was hunting, but that won't matter."

"Shall I come with you and reason with Ortiz?"

"Oh, Henry…" She laughed. "If that would only work, but it can't. Ortiz can't approve my upgrades; he'll pass my request to the clan. He has no actual power. He's just Dundee's Clan Griffin representative."

A wave of depression swept through her. She had been a clan employee for several years as a hunter before becoming a freelancer. There had been plenty of opportunities for them to upgrade her nanites. *Why hadn't they?*

The two sat side by side on the bench. Henry, by habit, watched passers-by. "Excuse me, Annie." He rose and walked over to stand behind a small man sidling up to a tourist. The man dipped his hand into the tourist's pocket and slipped out a wallet. The pickpocket turned and bumped into Hillman.

"Hello, Pete. When did you get on-station? I thought they banned you," Hillman said.

Pete attempted to slip past Hillman, whose right arm and shoulder were still in a regen mesh.

"Not so fast, Pete," Hillman said, using his left hand to grab the pickpocket by his collar and lift him to dangle above the deck.

"Patroller!" Hillman bellowed, startling the tourist, who hadn't felt the lifting of his wallet.

Annie joined the two. "Need help, Henry? I can hold him for the patrollers."

"Thank you, Annie. My arm was getting tired. Guess I'm not up to par yet." He dropped Pete.

Once his feet were on the deck, Pete tried to run. Annie tripped him, bent over, and gripped Pete's thumb. "Get up slowly, Pete, else I'll break your thumb—maybe both of them. What could a pickpocket do with broken thumbs, hmm? You just be quiet until the patrollers get here." Helping Henry had lightened her mood.

While Annie gripped the pickpocket, Hillman frisked him and found three wallets in hidden pockets in Pete's clothes. Turning to the tourist, he asked, "Which one is yours?"

169

The tourist pointed at one, and Hillman, after verifying the identification of the tourist and his ownership of the wallet, returned it. "You can go now, sir. Have a good shift."

When the tourist walked away, Hillman returned to the pickpocket. "Pete, Pete, Pete. If I remember right, you're a four-time offender. You know what this will mean."

"Aw, no, Hillman. You can't send me off. I don't have nanites. I can't live on a terraforming world."

"Should've thought of that, Pete. It's not my call."

"Here they come, Henry."

The beat patrollers were approaching. The patrollers were an odd pair, one older and the other younger.

"Hello, Henry. You back on the job?" the older patroller asked.

"Not yet, Charley. I'm on the bench for another two months. But look here. Guess who tried to pick a tourist's pocket right in front of me." Henry nodded at Pete standing next to Annie.

"Sneaky Pete, we meet once again," Charley said. "You never learn. Now you won't get another opportunity." He turned to Annie. "And who is this, Henry? How come Pete isn't halfway across the station by now?"

"Because I'm faster, and I told Pete I'd break his thumbs if he tried," Annie said.

Charley laughed. "Ah. I hadn't noticed that thumb hold. Good job. I'm Charley Brunswick, Clan Menendez, Sept Alvarez. This youngster is Andre Barre from Skye."

"Good to meet you, Charley. I'm Annie Griffin, Clan Griffin, Sept Leeds. Good to meet you, too, Andre."

The younger patroller nodded in return. "Glad to meet you."

"I've heard of you, Annie, and I'll remember that hold," the older patroller said as he put restraints on the pickpocket. "Charge list, Henry?"

"Theft, theft by deceit, and attempted escape from custody. That'll do, Charley."

"Got it. Have a good shift, you two." Sneaky Pete, with a patroller on each arm, was taken away.

With their distraction gone, Henry turned to Annie. "Where were we?"

"I was going to see Ortiz. What were you going to do?"

"Check in with Harris and see what deal I can make for limited duty. I don't want to be sitting behind a desk."

"I'll see you at end of shift."

"Katrin's?"

Annie grinned. She wasn't any better cook than Henry was. "See you there."

†††

Annie found Mitchell Ortiz sitting in a corner of the bar in Katrin's. He rose when she approached and pulled out a chair.

"I get nervous when you're polite, Mitchell," she said after sitting.

"Just trying to be friendly, Annie."

"But…"

"I sent your voucher request downbelow. They said it was against policy to provide upgrades to those who are unemployed."

*I knew it! Those packin' bastards!* Annie seethed at the confirmation of her fears.

"I tried Annie. I really did, but…"

"The greedy bastards refused. And after more than a decade of paying twenty percent tithes!"

"Twenty percent?"

"Yeah, why?"

Ortiz had an embarrassed look. "The clan tithe is sixteen percent, Annie."

"Those thieving packers!" The other patrons of Katrin's turned to look at the couple.

"What can I say, Annie? I did my best. They owe it to you, but..." Ortiz shrugged. He had nothing more to say.

Annie calmed down. She'd half expected Clan Griffin to refuse. She'd been a highly regarded clan asset until she went freelancing. Now that she'd chosen to quit hunting altogether, they'd decided she was a deficit, not an asset. *Time to change clans.* But would a new clan pay for the upgrades that Griffin had refused to do? She looked at Ortiz, shook her head, rose, and walked out of the bar. *I should've changed clans long ago.*

†††

Henry found her sitting outside of Katrin's in a corner of the open-seating area instead of inside, as had become their habit. She sat with her back to the other patrons. When he walked up to her, he could see she'd been crying.

"They refused," he stated.

She nodded. "*Packers.* Said I wasn't worth the cost, since I'm unemployed."

Hillman pulled out a chair and sat facing her. "Well, we'll just find you a job."

"They still won't pay. They've been using me, Henry. Not only will they not pay, they assessed my tithes at twenty percent. They charged everyone else only sixteen percent. They used and then betrayed me!"

She put her head down on the table. Her shoulders shook. After a time, she raised her head and whispered, "Let's go home. I'm not fit to be seen in public."

Hillman rose and extended his hand to her. "Home it is."

†††

Henry Hillman was experiencing an activity rare for him—he was cooking. When they arrived home, Annie extruded a couch from the floor and stretched out on it with her face to the back. Henry had gained sufficient knowledge of her moods, over the last month, to know he should leave her alone.

"I thought I'd fix something for dinner here at home," he said while rummaging in his pantry. "Have you had Cajun red beans and rice?"

Annie mumbled something.

"I'll take that as a 'no'."

Sitting up, Annie rubbed her eyes then brought up a holo display with her link. "What bank do you use?"

"First Union Bank of Dundee Orbital. Why?"

"I've my savings in Clan Griffin's central bank. I'm setting up an account in the First Union and transferring all my accounts and assets out of Griffin's reach."

"You think that's necessary?"

"They can seize everything I have, at any time, for any reason—or none at all. They've done it before to others."

Hillman paused the auto-chef and joined Annie on the couch. "I didn't know the clans could—or would—do that."

"Griffin can. Others, like McLean, Mieze, Menendez… most of the others have written Bills of Rights for their clan members. Griffin doesn't."

"Do it, then. Right now. Before Ortiz updates them," Henry said.

†††

"Done," Annie announced later. "I told my mother what had happened while I was waiting for you. She said, Janie, my younger

173

sister, and her family are joining Clan Portee. Jake, my brother-in-law, lost his terraforming job. It didn't take long for them to find a sponsor."

"What about the rest of your family?"

"They're staying put. They've a hundred-year lease on some coastline and can still make a living as fishermen." Her voice broke. "Mama told me not to come home!" Annie turned away, face to the back of the couch again, and cried. She hadn't thought she would' ever miss the rocky hills and deserts around the leasehold so much—the clear night skies, the feel of sand and grit hitting her face in a strong wind. *Not until I realized I couldn't go home anymore.* If she went home, she would be a burden on her family.

"Come and eat, Annie. Then we'll scan the job lists again and see what we can find."

"Beans and rice, huh?" She hiccupped, sat up, and wiped her face.

"Red beans and some sliced hard sausage, spices, cayenne pepper, a little of this, and a little of that. It's an old family recipe. Do you like spicy food?"

†††

Annie wasn't sure what she'd expected, but it wasn't this. She'd found a job listing for Benning Contracting that had an opening for a security consultant. The address, however, was the same as the Gem Exchange. She entered and walked up to the counter just inside the doorway.

"May I help you?" a voice from the counter said as she approached.

"I'm Anne Griffin. I've an appointment with Willem Baxter," Annie replied.

"Hold, please."

*Is this a remote receptionist or an AI I'm talking to?* Whichever it was, it had sparked her interest. No one here who could be seized as a hostage.

The counter issued a pop and said, "An escort will come and take you to Mr. Baxter."

"Clanswoman Griffin?" a voice asked behind her. "I'm Jonas Taite, Mr. Baxter's assistant. Please come this way. He's waiting for you." Taite was a tall, non-descript man with dark hair and wearing a dark gray tunic over lighter gray trousers. Dual translucent doors at the rear of the reception's desk opened as they approached.

They passed through the doors, which were made of armor-plas and resistant to hand and light shoulder weapons. *Is that necessary?*

Willem Baxter's office was a short walk through the doors and down a narrow corridor, which formed a choke-point against unwanted visitors. At the end of the corridor, Taite knocked and opened another door, where he motioned Annie to pass before him into the room.

When she was inside, the door closed behind her, leaving her alone with a balding man, older than Taite, sitting behind a bland metal desk. He was wearing clothing similar to Taite's.

"Welcome, Clanswoman. I'm Willem Baxter. I've heard of your reputation, and I'm glad to meet you."

"Thank you, sir. Glad to meet you too."

Baxter didn't reply, just watched Annie as she stood before him. She was beginning to be uncomfortable. He had not invited her to sit.

Finally, Annie said, "I'm here in response to the job posting your company placed in the registry."

"Yes. I assumed you had come for employment. Else why are you here?" Baxter said.

Again, he fell silent. *This is getting ridiculous. Who is he? Is there a job or not, and if so, what kind is it?*

A door opened behind Baxter's desk, so well fitted that she hadn't noticed its presence. A man, waving a pistol, stepped through and yelled something unintelligible.

Annie had her pistol drawn and aimed before the newcomer had taken another step. "Stop!" she shouted.

Baxter laughed, stood, and clapped. "I told you so, Dennis. Isn't she good! Her reputation is true."

"Is this a joke?" Annie asked while still holding her pistol on the newcomer and keeping her temper under control.

"No, clanswoman, not a joke. A test. I've seen the video of your encounter with Chief Inspector Graeme. Dennis hadn't and didn't believe me." Baxter turned to the intruder. "Put your pistol away, Dennis. Please provide a chair for Clanswoman Griffin, then you may go."

Dennis holstered his weapon and stepped back through the just-opened door. A moment later, he returned with a chair and placed it in front of Baxter's desk. "I'm sorry. The floor here doesn't support extrusion furniture." He bowed to Annie and departed.

"Please accept my apologies, clanswoman," Baxter said. "As you may have surmised, Benning Contracting is a front. My real title is Chief of Security for the Caledonian Gem Exchange."

That explained some of Annie's questions. She expected some form of testing but not such a dramatic—*or idiotic*—one.

"Not only are you fast," Baxter continued, "but you are discriminating. You didn't shoot Dennis out of hand." He paused. "By the way, Dennis was wearing soft armor for protection… just in case."

"You know I could've shot him, legally. But I wouldn't shoot a man who had an empty pistol."

"Ah, you noticed that? Better and better."

"So, Mr. Baxter, with that over, what is the job?" Annie asked.

"We want you to be our public representative, to show our clients—and any thieves— that we are prepared for any eventuality."

*Something smells.* "And how would that be done?"

"We want you to be present, wearing our uniform, like those Jonas Taite and I are wearing… but with your weapons visible."

"And where would I be doing that?"

"Here, in our facilities. In the front lobby and other places as needed," Baxter said.

"Oh. You want me to be a… a…" Annie couldn't remember the proper term for what Baxter had described. "A mannequin." Her voice grew louder. "Someone to scare off thieves, a stage prop, an effigy of a person!"

Her temper was boiling, and she could barely keep it under control. *I am a hunter, the Designated Champion for four Inverness clans, and they want to dress me up like a clown! Put me out on display? To make me a showpiece! A laughingstock!* Annie stood so quickly that she knocked the chair over backward.

Baxter's face blanched. "Please, clanswoman!"

Annie stood so rigid she shook. "Are you a clansman, Baxter?"

"No—no!"

Annie spoke slowly, ensuring Baxter understood his situation. "You have given me a deadly insult. If you were a clansman, we'd be meeting in the nearest dueling court. But I won't challenge you. Your ignorance saves you." She turned and stepped toward the door Taite had closed when she entered. Before she opened it, she paused and gave Baxter one last look. "I would strongly suggest you find other employment, Baxter. One far from Caledonia. When my clan hears of this, they may not be as lenient."

She opened the door and walked down the corridor, through the dual doors, and past Jonas Taite sitting behind the receptionist counter. As she passed Taite, she raised her hand to him in an age-old expression of contempt and continued out.

†††

Hillman knocked on the open door of Donal Harris' office. Harris looked up from his desk and motioned for Henry to enter and sit.

"How's it going, Henry?" Harris asked.

"I'm cleared to return to work, Inspector. Light duty for the next two months."

"Good. Glad to hear that. How is Annie?"

"The medics cleared her too."

"What's she going to do? Stay or go back downbelow?" Harris asked.

"She wants to stay. She's interviewing with a security firm right now."

"Is that what she wants?"

*Why is Harris so interested in Annie? It's not like him.* Hillman squirmed in his chair. Its arms were too low to support his arm comfortably. "I don't know. I think she wants something that's interesting. She's led an active life for the last decade, but said she wants to be able to go home after her shift and live life."

"What about you? I wouldn't think you'd want to push paper until you're cleared," Harris asked.

"I'd just like to supervise my team like I did before. I can't be involved in anything physical, but I can walk around and be seen. That will keep our less-than-desirables on their toes."

"Your medics said light-to-minimal duty. I don't think walking a beat with your team would fit their definition of minimal duty. I've another idea… because you're being promoted to sergeant."

*Sergeant! That would let us get a much larger coapt.* "I hadn't expected that, sir!"

"Sergeants don't walk beats, Henry," Harris said, ending any hope Hillman had of returning to a beat.

"How'd you like to take over my shift's training section? It has some administrative duties—maintaining our training records, insuring we meet our training certifications—and you'll still meet and interact with people. You'd have some specialists working for you too. What do you think?"

"That sounds very interesting, Inspector. Thank you." *Depends on how much desk duty is required.*

"Good. Senior Patroller Jacobsen will be your number two. Why don't you pay him a visit? I'll update your records, and you can start tomorrow."

†††

*<Meet me at Katrin's bar. I need a drink.>*

Annie's text surprised Henry. She rarely drank much. *Something is wrong.*

He found her sitting in a dim corner of the bar with a half-empty glass before her. He walked up and slid into the seat opposite of her. "Interview didn't go well, I assume."

"No."

"Want to talk about it?"

"No… but I will."

He waited, not speaking. Annie would talk when she was ready. *Should I tell her about my promotion? No… not when she's like this. Maybe if I give her a nudge.* "Yes?" he coaxed.

"They wanted a scaremonger, for me to stand there, in their uniform, and scare away thieves. In public!'

"Okay, simmer down," he said. "You refused. It's over."

"That's not all. They set up a test, and I nearly shot a man."

"Really? Annie!"

179

"I was ushered into a room. A man who claimed to be a security agent was there. We were talking when a second man burst into the room, waving a pistol around. I almost shot him before I noticed he had no magazine in his weapon."

"What did you do?"

"Nothing, at that point. The interviewer said I passed their test. Then—then he told me what they wanted me for—my reputation. They couldn't care less about me. I… uh… I told him to get out of Caledonia before my clan discovered what he did.

"Clan Griffin won't do anything, but he wasn't a clansman. He couldn't be sure." She paused to take a sip from her drink. "Clan Griffin doesn't care about me either," she said bitterly.

"Just leave them, then. You don't need them here."

After some seconds, her eyes bright, she said, "I can't do that, Henry. I need to belong to a clan."

"You should've challenged—Baxter, you said his name was? Give him a lesson of the *Proprieties*. Purposely placing a person in danger, without full disclosure, is an affront to Custom and Tradition. Not to mention," he continued," placing you into a situation where you could have shot an innocent."

Annie picked up her glass and emptied its contents. She talked on, of her family and their problems with Clan Griffin. Her speech became slurred. After she had spilled her woes, he led her home.

†††

Donal Harris was about to file his quarterly report to the station director with a copy to his Interdiction Office superior on Cameron. Mankind had left its home millennia ago, but paperwork, regardless of the medium, still existed. His report still had an empty segment—training. The position of training supervisor for Harris' shift had been empty until earlier this week, when he put Henry Hillman in that slot.

*I can pass this part of my report to Hillman. Jacobsen can show him some examples of earlier reports. Let's see how Henry handles this.*

With a grin on his face, Harris sent a message to Hillman, asking him to report to Harris' office. Ten minutes later, Hillman was knocking on Harris' office door.

"Come in, Henry. I've a task for you, you being the new training supervisor."

Hillman cocked an eyebrow. "And that would be?"

"The quarterly training report. I've been doing it since the slot's been open. Jacobsen hasn't been able to write it to our superior's expectations. He can show you some earlier examples. It's just collecting the numbers."

A half hour later, Harris was satisfied Hillman had enough information to write the report. When the new sergeant stood to leave, Harris asked, "How's Annie? Has she found a job?"

Hillman sank back into his chair. "No." After some urging by Harris, he told Harris about Annie's interview.

"She was justified in challenging Baxter," Harris agreed. "I'll report them to my clan and some others. I think changes are needed at the Gem Exchange."

"Thank you, Inspector. To make matters worse, her clan has, for all practical purposes, abandoned her. She's never had her nanites updated since she was a child, despite paying tithes all those years. That came out when her kidney needed to be regenned. Since Annie's unemployed, Clan Griffin refuses to pay for her updates."

"How much would it cost her, out of pocket?"

"Around twenty-five thousand Confederate dollars."

"Um! That's more than I'd expect." An idea came to Harris. *Should I? Yes.* "Henry, there is a possibility of employment."

"What's that?"

"She could apply for a position with the Dundee Orbital Station Patrol, or the Customs Service. The Service doesn't advertise openings;

181

we prefer to recruit new members." The station patrol was a subordinate segment of the Confederation Customs Service.

"Oh! That hadn't occurred to me."

"See what she thinks. Tell her I'll endorse her application to either service."

"I'll do that, Inspector." Hillman stood, shook Harris' hand, and left the office in a better mood than he'd entered.

†††

"Henry? You here?" Annie shouted as she walked into their coapt. She'd been on another interview as a gym instructor. The job was a possibility, but the pay was low—too many current instructors were unpaid volunteers.

Henry returned her greeting from the couch in their living area. "I've some news, Annie, two pieces of news. First, Donal Harris says he'll endorse and support your move to Clan McLean. He sent it downbelow. Since his sister is the deputy laird, I expect it'll be approved in a day or two."

"Good. I'd hoped he would when I submitted it. He's the senior McLean clansman in Dundee Orbital, I'm told," she said, joining him on the couch.

"That's not all, Annie." Henry recounted his conversation with Donal Harris. "That's the offer. What do you think?"

"I'd not thought of it. They don't publish openings?" Annie rose and sat in an easy chair across from Henry. She preferred to be face-to-face for serious conversations.

"Harris said they didn't; they only recruit."

"Which is better? To be a patroller or a Customs agent?" It intrigued Annie. She had worked with several patrollers over the years. Some were good, and some weren't. In all that time, though, she'd never thought of being one.

"Well, I prefer to be a patroller," Henry said. "It's a lot of walking and always different. There're other options like specialist positions—"

"Specialist?"

"Oh… a forensics tech, or a lab tech, for example."

"I don't think I'd be qualified." Annie had used information gathered by such specialists but without proper training and education… *No, not a specialist position.* "What about being a Customs agent?"

"They do a lot of paperwork, checking ship manifests, manning port-entry positions, and crawling around ships, looking for contraband. A few do routine investigations."

"Not very exciting."

"No, but you'd be on a fixed shift with standard hours, mostly."

"And a patroller wouldn't?"

"Well, patrollers have fixed shifts too. But if a need arises, they can be rolled over to the next shift. If extra hands are needed, like for a bar fight or riot, not that riots happen all that often. The best part is that a patroller gets to know the folks on his—or her—beat. On a beat, your job is to keep the peace."

Annie considered the offer. Her education was limited. Clan Griffin delegated education to its member septs. Most septs didn't have the revenue to support higher education beyond the basic minimum proposed by the Council of Clans. Griffin septs depended upon outside scholarships to pay for higher education, and the competition for those few slots was fierce. *I'm not a scholar, anyway. I don't have the foundation, nor the inclination. So…*

"I can do that," she decided. "Patroller, it is."

"And that's not all." He paused before continuing. "I've been promoted to sergeant, and that means we can get a larger coapt, at least twice as big as this one, depending on availability."

"That would be nice." She surveyed Henry's coapt, which was designed for a single occupant. With the two of them, it was tight. "How big a coapt could we get based on both our salaries?"

†††

Mitchell Ortiz, the Clan Griffin representative in Dundee Orbital, sympathized with Annie. But he could not get the clan to agree to Annie's demands. Nor could he get them to cut her tithe back to sixteen percent, matching the level of other clan members. They also refused to pay for her nanite upgrades. "I'm sorry, Annie. They just won't listen."

"Thank you for trying, Mitchell." She and Ortiz had become friends during her stay at the station. She wasn't angry at him. He had no actual power, and like Annie, he had some personal issues with Clan Griffin. "I've made a decision. I'm joining Clan McLean."

"I know. Inspector Harris sent me a copy of the Notice of Clan Transfer. I can't blame you for leaving the clan. I'm considering the same… for other reasons, but the solution will be the same."

"May I ask which one?"

"Annie!" Ortiz said, shaking his head.

"Sorry, I shouldn't't've asked."

He rose from his desk, signaling the end of the conversation. "Keep in touch, Annie. Let me know how you like being a patroller," he said, extending his hand.

"Haven't got the job, yet, Mitchell," she said, taking his offered hand and shaking it.

"With Donal Harris and Henry Hillman endorsing your application to the patrol—plus your experience as a hunter—you are almost guaranteed to be hired."

## Recruit.

Surprisingly, the recruiter wasn't a patroller. Leland Coons was a Customs Service inspector. He stood up from behind his desk as Annie entered his office. "Sit, Clanswoman Griffin, welcome. I understand you're looking for a job?"

"That I am, sir," Annie said, taking the chair in front of Coons' desk.

"I've been reading your application, and I've finished the process to vet you—pulled your records from downbelow and from the Interdiction Office on Cameron. You're clean."

Annie expected her records from Inverness to be reviewed. *But the Interdiction Office?* She didn't know they were watching her and said so to Coons.

"You've an envious reputation, in some circles, Clanswoman—"

"Just call me Annie," she interrupted. She hadn't heard, yet, if her transfer to Clan McLean had been approved. Claiming to be a member of Clan Griffin made her uncomfortable.

"Annie. And you've had several hunts in Confederation territory; one took you out-system. That brought you to their attention."

"Ah, I'm not interested in joining the Interdiction Office, thank you very much. I'm looking for some stability, and I doubt I'd get that from them. Joining the station patrollers fits my preferences."

Coons laughed. "Donal Harris said that, too, but I had to ask."

Annie shook her head. "The more I learn of Donal Harris, the more I'm surprised. Getting back to my application—"

"You're acceptable," Coons said, interrupting her. "However, you must pass our physical and get your nanites updated—yes, we know about your problem. The Customs Service and the Station Patrol require nanites packages above that available to civilians. We'll bring you up to the civilian standard before we upgrade you to *our* standard at our cost."

That information relieved Annie. There were reasons nanites were updated. With the ability to create medical nanites, the ability to create nanite-based diseases existed too.

"You'll also be required to pass some link courses, three weeks of actual classroom instruction, and more via link. The other requirements—physical training, hand-to-hand combat and qualification with weapons—should not be a problem. Just be tested and get your skills documented."

"Not a problem, sir."

†††

Annie lay on a sensor bed while the Custom Service's medic checked her out. "How's the kidney doing?" the tech asked. "Any issues? Your blood sugar is a little low."

"I skipped breakfast," Annie admitted.

The tech nodded and glanced at her link. "We won't be long, and then you can get some lunch," she said while placing a patch on Annie's arm. "Just upgrading your nanites. You may have a slight fever for a day." The tech scanned the data coming from the sensor bed. "Were you planning to get pregnant?"

"No," Annie responded, lifting her head from the bed.

"Your basic nanites are for children and juveniles. Contraception wasn't activated. I checked; you aren't pregnant."

Relieved, Annie let her head drop back down. She wasn't ready to be a mother. Not yet. She and Henry had been intimate since before the firefight, but she'd assumed her nanites would prevent conception. "Would you turn it on, please?"

The tech entered some instructions via her link. "Done and done. You can change it through your medical menu via your link."

Annie sighed in relief. *What would Henry's reaction be when I tell him? I don't think he's ready to be a father either. Did Gilead have marriage or bonding? Am I—and Henry—ready for that? And a family?*

Annie found Inspector Coons waiting for her when she finished her physical. He had a senior patroller with him. "Annie, this is Senior Patroller Jacobsen. He'll finish your in-processing." Having said that, he turned and walked away, leaving Annie and Jacobsen looking at one another.

"So," Jacobsen growled after examining her from head to toe. "You're Hillman's woman."

Annie clamped down on her temper. "I hear you are, too, since you report to Henry."

The two glared at one another until a smile grew on Jacobsen's face. "Henry said you had a sharp tongue." He extended a hand. "Call me Jake."

"Annie," she said in return and took his hand. *I'll overlook the insult. This time.*

"Let's get you some uniforms. Then I'll give you some standard tests, firearm handling, knife work, and unarmed combat. From what I've heard, you shouldn't have any problems there." He paused. "New kidney working okay?"

"Yeah. The medic checked it thoroughly. I'm cleared for anything."

"Good, follow me."

An hour later, Annie was wearing a bodysuit under a light-gray patroller shipsuit, boots, and weapons harness. More uniforms would be delivered to her shared coapt. She had an assigned locker in patroller headquarters, which contained one of her two new skinsuits, spare uniforms, and boots.

"The last item for today is to get you weapons qualified. Once you're finished with that, we can issue you a pistol and shockstick," Jacobsen told her.

She followed him through the patroller headquarters to a rear area. "This is the armory and our range. We share this with the Customs agents and inspectors."

He led her to a counter inside the armory. After Jacobsen had a brief conversation with a patroller, she was issued a pistol, magazines, and several boxes of ammunition. Minutes later, Annie stood at a shooting position in the range, her empty pistol held before her. A tattered target, missing its center, approached from downrange. She laid the pistol down, pointing downrange, just before the target reached her and Jacobsen.

"As I expected, Annie, you've qualified with the pistol. This also qualifies you for a laser pistol." Jacobsen examined her target and made some notes on his link before he updated her records. "You must complete two more qualifications before you start patroller school—knife and unarmed combat. When he's back to full duty, Henry will do that. For now, Sensei will check you out."

"Sensei?"

Jacobsen laughed. "That's what we call him. He's a martial arts specialist on contract to the Customs Service and us. He's been looking forward to meeting you."

†††

"Ohh," Annie moaned. She was slouched, half reclined in the hot tub next to the patroller locker room and gym, when she heard approaching footsteps. She opened her eyes to see Henry standing over her.

"I heard you had a session with Sensei?" he asked, grinning.

She didn't reply. Instead of speaking, she glared at Henry. "Yes. He wiped the floor with me."

"I read his report, and he said you held your own with him. He's telling everyone you nearly beat him." Henry stepped outside to the locker room and started removing his uniform. His locker was near Annie's. After removing his uniform, he slipped into the tub with Annie. He laid his arm and regen mesh on the rim of the tub to keep it above the surface of the water.

188

"I'm going to be bruised all over," Annie complained. "He threw me across the court, into the wall, and all over the mat."

"And, according to him, you always rolled and came up to block his next move."

"I'm still bruised, and they still hurt," she muttered.

The door to the hot tub room opened, and Jacobsen stepped inside. "Sensei signed off on your knife and unarmed combat qualifications, Annie. You only need an EVA certificate. They'll do that in patroller school. You start tomorrow." He took another look at her and Henry, laughed, and departed.

**Probationer.**

Annie, along with a dozen others, graduated from patroller school, three weeks later. Donal Harris had come through with his promises. She and Henry were on the same shift, and her transfer to Clan McLean had been approved. She was now Annie Griffin of Clan McLean, Sept Harris.

"Here is your new partner, Carlos Diedriksen," Henry said, updating her link's database with Diedriksen's resume. He and Annie were sitting in Henry's office that he shared with Jake Jacobsen, his deputy. "I know little about him. We've never been on the same shift or beat. He's not a trainer, so I expect whoever paired you two was confident you didn't need much on-the-job training."

A tall, lean patroller knocked on the frame of the office door and entered. "Hi, I'm Carlos Diedriksen," He looked at Annie. "Are you Annie Griffin?"

Annie stood and extended her hand. "Yep, that's me. Call me Annie."

"Carlos," he replied, shaking hers.

"Now that you've been introduced," Henry said, "shouldn't you two be off to your beat?"

"Uh, yes, Sergeant." Carlos stepped back out of the office, and Annie joined him. As they walked out of patrol headquarters, Carlos said, "My usual beat has been in the agricultural section."

"What did you do there?" Annie asked.

"Watch for poachers, mostly—Stags looking for free food," Carlos replied. "It was quiet."

"What about our new beat? Know anything about it?"

"It's near the docks, warehouses, and bars. I'm surprised they assigned us to that beat. Noobs like us aren't usually sent there as a first assignment."

"You're not a noob, Carlos."

"I may as well be. I've three years as a patroller, and that was being a clerk in headquarters and guarding the farms."

Annie and Carlos took a tram to Torus Two. Their beat started with the docks, followed by the adjoining warehouse segment and then on to a segment of bars and dockside chandlers.

"Have you been on this beat before?" Annie asked her partner.

"I got called out for a riot once. Right here in Segment A. It really was just a bar fight between three freighter crews that got out of hand." Carlos blushed. "I got coldcocked right off and missed most of it."

*He must've passed the patroller unarmed combat test. But I've a feeling he isn't much of a fighter.* "Well, I guess our beat may be more interesting than the farms."

He raised an eyebrow at her and turned back to watching their beat. "Maybe so."

An hour later, they received a call over their links. *<Patrollers Diedrikson and Griffin. See the man at Torus Two, Deck Two, Segment C, number two-thirteen. Man reports a break-in and theft.>*

"Sounds like a routine call, eh, Carlos?" Annie asked as they walked toward the location of the break-in.

"Hope so. My trainer, when I joined, said to assume nothing when answering a call."

They reached the site of the call within fifteen minutes. A man was waiting outside a warehouse office. As she walked toward him, Annie spotted a station security module above the warehouse door.

"Hello, we're Patrollers Griffin and Diedriksen," she said. "Can you tell us what happened?"

"I'm Inar van Houten, the shift manager here," the man introduced himself, turned, and led them back inside the warehouse. When they were inside, van Houten continued, "Our office and break room is to the right. Employee locker room and access to the actual warehouse is to the left."

191

"Where did the break-in occur?" Diedriksen asked. "Your front entrance appears to be intact."

"I'll show you, but since it's right here, I thought I'd show you what was stolen."

They followed van Houten into the adjacent office and back toward the rear to an employee break area. The room contained several tables and chairs, plus a bank of food and drink vending machines. "These machines are all stocked by our central auto-chef. It's a package deal." He continued through the break room, out a side door, and into a neighboring room. He waved an arm at the empty room. "This is what they stole."

"What was here?" Diedriksen asked.

"The auto-chef!" van Houten said. "They stole the whole packin' auto-chef, all of its feed systems and storage lockers and the vending head for the machines around the warehouse. They cleaned out all the on-hand packaged food too!"

Van Houten ranted until he ran down and began to repeat himself. He stopped when Annie raised her hand.

"They needed a crew, whoever did this, to haul it all away," Annie stated. "Where did they get in?"

"Back here." Van Houten took off at a fast pace, heading farther into the warehouse. "The doors here are large enough for a standard shipping container. See that lifter?" He pointed at a cargo lifter used to move shipping containers., "It was up front. Now it's back here. They used it to haul the auto-chef and all out the back door."

They arrived at a row of enormous cargo doors lining the rear of the warehouse. Diedriksen walked over to examine the first door and its locking system. Annie did the same to the door next to it.

Diedriksen looked for signs that the door had been forced open. "Nothing here. It's clean on this side."

"Same here, Carlos." She turned to the warehouse manager. "Would you open one of these?" She pointed at the cargo door she'd just checked. "So we can see the exterior."

The manager drew his link and entered a command. The cargo door next to Annie clunked as locking bolts retracted, and with a slight screech, the door rolled upward. She and Diedriksen walked outside, with the manager following.

"Lower the door, please?" Annie asked.

With a rumble and another screech, the door lowered. Annie and Diedriksen examined the doors and locks.

"Clean here too," Diedriksen said.

Annie looked upward. The overhead was dim in the upper recess. In this area of the torus, it was ten meters above the deck, unless a false ceiling had been installed. No false ceilings here that she could determine, but she did see several security monitors. *Those are handy. We should be able to see it all on replay.*

"Let's go back inside," she said to van Houten, "and get a valuation on your loss. We'll call for a forensics team to check for fingerprints and DNA and to review the security logs. I saw station monitors in front and back, so we should be able to see all that happens."

"So you can catch them? Get our auto-chef back?" van Houten asked.

"Can't guarantee that. It may be already off the station. At least, you'll be able to support an insurance claim."

††† 

An hour later, the forensics team arrived, and Annie and Diedriksen were back on their beat.

"That was interesting," Diedriksen said as they headed toward a segment lined with bars, diners, and chandleries. "I'll bet Stags will be blamed."

"Why?"

"Because it's easy. This call, with its low priority, will be passed to an overworked Customs agent. The agent may but probably won't have time to investigate. I'd guess the case will be entered into Cecelia, our Customs Service AI, to sift through open cases for similarities. And then forgotten."

"So?"

They reached the segment bulkhead lock and passed through it. The new segment was brighter and cleaner. *Almost refreshing*, Annie thought. They had to pass through a throng of warehousemen heading past them before Diedriksen could continue.

"Stags couldn't've done it. Someone picked those cargo door locks, and whoever it was had to have a very good link and know how to use it. Few Stags have links. I've never met one who could open those doors. And they by-passed security locks on the lifter. No amateur can do that."

"I thought the Stags were a gang."

"Nope. They aren't organized enough to form a gang. Most are blue-leaf chewers. Most can't put two logical thoughts together."

They were through the segment, reaching the end of their beat. The segment was quiet. Almost peaceful. She mentioned her impression to Diedriksen.

He laughed and said, "Peaceful until the end of the shift. Then it's not, not peaceful at all."

Diedriksen checked his link. "Not enough time to make another round. Let's head back to headquarters. We've just enough time to finish our reports before shift end."

†††

The following week was uneventful. Annie and Carlos became acquainted with the locals working along their beat. The warehouse segment was quiet. Their only call had been the auto-chef theft. The bar, diner, and chandler segments next to the warehouses were not quiet.

"What are you planning for the weekend?" Annie asked her partner. They were walking through Torus Two, Deck Two, Segment B. This part of the torus was dedicated to chandlers and small businesses that serviced the docks on the torus.

"I'm going fishing," he replied. "My wife told me the trout stream in Torus Six is being restocked on Fiveday. We fished some streams in the Dragonback Mountains when we last went downbelow on leave."

"I grew up in a fishing family. We've a leasehold on a stretch of coast on Secundus. I like eating fish, but I discovered at a young age that I didn't care to be a fisherman. I didn't know you were married?" Every day, she learned something new about Diedriksen. He was quiet, not a talker, and she didn't feel close enough, yet, to ask personal questions.

"Ten years. She's an agri-tech at the farms. We met before I was a patroller—"

*<Patrollers Diedriksen and Griffin, see the man...>*

Annie copied the call data while Diedriksen acknowledged it and checked the location—a bar.

"Bet it's a fight," he said.

Annie nodded. "I won't take that bet."

†††

The bar wasn't hard to find. Several onlookers were standing outside, looking in through the bar's open doors. Annie was updating the call with their arrival on the scene when something crashed inside.

"Oh, pack," Diedriksen muttered.

"What?" Annie was focused on the entrance of the bar until Diedriksen's muttering drew her attention.

"No helmets. We should wear helmets down here. At least have them with us. I screwed up, Annie. This isn't the agricultural section. I never needed a helmet there."

In the patrol school, instructors emphasized the need for helmets whenever violence was expected—like a bar fight. "Well, we're here, and there's a fight. We can call for help, but someone could get hurt if we wait for others to arrive."

"Yeah…" Diedriksen intoned. "It's a part of the job. Call for help. I'll go first. You cover my back." Without waiting, he pushed his way through the crowd and through the door.

"Wait! Carlos!" She followed him, but being smaller, she was delayed passing through the crowd.

When Annie reached the door, Diedriksen was moving forward between the bystanders. Four men were slugging it out before the bar. The bartender had raised an armor-plas shield protecting himself, the bar, and its contents. Annie had almost reached Diedriksen when a fist smacked him in the face. He rocked back from the blow, staggered against another patron, and fell face-first to the floor.

*Pack!* Annie subvocalized a message through her link, *<Patroller down!>*.

She snatched her shockstick from her belt and, with a flick of her wrist, extended it to its full length. The shockstick hummed, proclaiming to everyone that it was active. The onlooker who had struck Diedriksen lunged toward her. She stepped forward, punching the attacker in the gut with the tip of the shockstick. The strike, combined with the neural charge from the shockstick, put him on the floor.

From the corner of her eye, she saw another bystander about to kick Diedriksen, who was unconscious on the floor. She pushed a patron aside to move between the fallen patroller and his attacker. Annie slapped the shockstick against brawler's knee. He fell to the floor. A tap to his head with the 'stick put him out of the fight.

While Annie was dealing with her attackers and shielding Diedriksen, the four original brawlers continued to fight. The watching bystanders, aware of Annie's presence, turned toward her.

†††

*Phweet!* The whistle screamed through the bar. *At last.* Patroller reinforcements had arrived.

Jacobsen led the newly arrived patrollers. Pushing people aside, he entered the bar, followed by two patrollers from a neighboring segment. Annie stood over Diedriksen, who was still on the floor. Blood ran down her face from a cut above her eyebrow, and a bruise was darkening on her cheek. Five men lay on the floor around her. One was groaning, gripping his knee. Another sat nearby, cradling a broken arm.

"You'll need a new shockstick, Annie," Jacobsen said, taking her shockstick, which was bent in the middle. "They aren't supposed to do that."

She looked at it. "I wondered why it stopped working," she said while rubbing her knuckles and the backs of her hands. "I forgot to put on my gloves," she stated, her thoughts unusually muddied.

"Where's your helmet?" Jacobsen asked.

"Didn't have one." She paused. "Carlos said…" *It's not Carlos's fault. I didn't think about it, either.* "It's been a learning experience."

Jacobsen nodded when two med-techs arrived. They went to Diedriksen first, then one walked over to Annie and checked her medical status with his link.

The cut through her eyebrow had stopped bleeding. The med-tech cleaned the cut with a wipe from the kit and applied a nanite sealer. "Leave it alone, and you won't have to remove a scar. The sealer will be absorbed in a couple of shifts."

The 'tech cleaned her hands and applied more sealer to them. "You've no concussion, Patroller, unlike your partner. You're cleared for duty."

Two motorized gurneys arrived, carrying two more med-techs. The med-techs who had arrived first put Diedriksen on one gurney. The new med-techs went to check the brawlers, including the one still moaning and clutching his knee.

197

"What's Diedriksen's status?" Jacobsen asked the 'tech as they prepared to leave.

"He has at least a class-three concussion and a fractured cheekbone… maybe his jaw too. They can determine that at the med center. We'll update his status after they check him out. He won't be back on duty tomorrow, Patroller."

The med-techs left with Diedriksen on a gurney, and Jacobsen looked at Annie. "You've survived your first bar fight, Annie."

She nodded. She'd been chided in the locker room from her first day as a patroller about "your first bar fight." From the teasing from the other patrollers, a patroller's first bar fight was a rite of passage.

"You're hard on your partners too," Jacobsen added, glancing at the departing gurney. "Guess I'll fill in until you get a new one."

†††

Back at patroller headquarters, Annie followed Jacobsen into the locker room. Patrollers lined the aisles as she made her way to her locker. Each greeted her as she passed. Some whistled, patted her back, or just gave her a thumbs-up. The last one, standing at her locker, was Henry, with a grin on his face.

He reached down, picked up a bucket, and dumped cold water on her head. "You've survived your first bar fight, Annie," he said, unknowingly repeating Jacobsen's earlier statement.

She shivered. The water had been cold, almost icy. She leaned forward and hugged him. "I think I can use a long soak in the hot tub." She pushed him aside to get to her locker. After she had hung her gear and put her wet shipsuit and bodysuit in the cleaner, she and Henry were alone. The other patrollers had drifted away, going on or off shift.

"You'll have a shiner for a few hours, and I'd guess, a set of other bruises." Henry brushed his finger over the cut in her eyebrow and down to her cheek. "Are you going to let the scar remain?" Henry's culture abstained from nanites, and he had kept the scars he'd accumulated through his life.

"No. I'm from Inverness, not Gilead. Why was everyone waiting when we arrived?"

"You completed a rite of passage. You survived your first bar fight on your feet. And you had several brawlers laid out on the floor. Now, everyone knows you can handle yourself in a fight and cover their backs when necessary."

"Why the water?"

"Tradition. We have our own Customs and Traditions. Be glad it was just water. Mine was full of green dye."

"What about Carlos? He—"

"Didn't pass. Not everyone does. What we learned is that Carlos, while a conscientious patroller, isn't suited for the docks. He's failed twice now. We'll send him back to the agri-sections."

Annie finished stripping down and slipped into the hot tub. "So, I'm getting a new partner?"

"Yeah. I don't know who at the moment. Jake volunteered, but I'll have to talk it over with Colin Harris. Now"—he unfastened the closures of his shipsuit—"make room for me. I've some news."

"What news?"

"Our new coapt has been approved. With both of us in the Patrol, we're allowed a five-room coapt, not counting the kitchen and 'fresher. There are six vacant ones in our segment. Want to see them when you've finished your soak? Since we have the next two days off, we could be moved in by next Firstday."

Annie smiled. "I think that's an excellent idea. In fact, I may be finished soaking already. Let's see them."

†††

"This is the third one," Annie said, referring to the list projected by her link. This one was three corridors inward from Henry's single-person coapt. She placed her hand on the sensor panel next to the door. When it opened, she and Hillman entered. The entry was set up as a foyer. One wall had a small extruded side table and mirror. Next to the foyer was a large room with an extruded couch and two separate recliners facing a large console-link and entertainment center. To one side was space for Henry's bookcase and shelves. Annie owned some handmade furniture downbelow. *What would the shipping cost be to bring it up here?*

Hillman stood next to her, looking around the room. He looked around the open space next to the entertainment center.

*He's thinking the same. That's a good spot for his bookcase.* They'd been together long enough now for each to know the other's thoughts.

A hallway led farther back into the coapt. The kitchen and auto-chef, with space for dining, were to the left. Two bedrooms were to the right, and at the end of the hallway was a third one on the left with an adjoining 'fresher.

Hillman walked forward, sticking his head into each room. Annie did the same. The first bedroom on the right would do for an office.

Hillman stopped at the second bedroom. "What should we do with this?" He grinned. "What color? Pink or blue?"

She was confused about why the colors mattered. When she didn't answer, Hillman moved on to the last bedroom, while Annie walked back and stepped into the kitchen and auto-chef. The kitchen contained a freezer, pantry, and a built-in oven and cooking surfaces. Annie was lost in memories of her family's kitchen downbelow. Her mother had cooked on a cast-iron stove fired by dried algae bricks. Their dining table had been an ancient trestle table with wooden benches. This kitchen was far different from her mother's.

Henry had few cooking utensils. She hadn't any and began to list the items she would need for the kitchen. *I'll have to learn how to cook.*

Hillman walked up as she stared into the kitchen. "What do you think?"

"What?" She hadn't noticed his approach.

"The coapt. This one is the closest of the five to Katrin's."

"Are the others any different?"

"By floor space, no. This one adjoins an environmental column, freshwater and air. The entire coapt is a survival suite, unlike the others."

"That's good?"

Hillman smiled. "Yes, Annie, it's good if we ever have a blowout or an environment emergency in this segment."

"Let's take it, then."

"Works for me."

They walked around the coapt again. Annie noticed that the auto-chef was fully stocked. *What was Mama's recipe for bouillabaisse?*

They walked out, closing the coapt's door behind them. *Pink or blue?* Now she remembered what that meant.

†††

"I'm glad that's over," Annie said as she and Henry were walking to patrol headquarters after moving into their new coapt over the weekend.

"Well, we didn't have all that much. One cart held it all."

"You had your books and the bookcase and…"

"Little things, Annie. No big items, no furniture, no wall hangings."

She nodded. Their new coapt wasn't far from Henry's previous one. They had the same food and recreation court close by. She was glad they hadn't needed to change decks. Her friends, few but growing in number, were all here. She didn't make friends easily. "Do you know who my new partner will be?"

"Changing the subject?" Henry grinned.

"No. I thought you may have heard—"

"I haven't. Not my job, but I asked that you get a more experienced one this time." They approached the entrance to patrol headquarters.

"Diedriksen was released yesterday from the med center. He's been assigned to the substation in Torus Ten. He'll be on limited duty until his jaw is healed."

Annie shook her head. "I've heard about it, but Carlos is the first one I've seen."

"Seen what?"

"Someone with a glass jaw. One hit, and he was out on the floor."

"That's why he's going back to the agri-section. He's a liability in a fight. His file is flagged now. We'll ensure he's not put into a situation he can't handle."

They separated when they reached patrol headquarters. Annie's link pinged with a message.

*<Report to Inspector Harris on arrival.>*

†††

Harris' door was closed when she arrived. She knocked, and a voice from within said, "Enter."

Customs Chief Inspector Donal Harris was seated behind his desk with his feet resting on the lowest desk drawer and a mug in his hands. He waved her to a chair, and when she was seated, he motioned Senior Patroller Jacobsen, who had been leaning against the wall next to the door, to join her. Jacobsen had irritated her from their first meeting.

Harris nodded, taking his feet off the drawer, and sat upright. Jacobsen acknowledged Harris' nod by closing the office door and sitting next to Annie.

"You need a new partner and trainer, Annie. That presents us with a problem… there isn't one available that is suited for you."

"Suited?"

"You aren't one of our ordinary recruits. You've… a history, a reputation, and that is one problem. People who know your reputation believe you've more patroller experience than you have. The other is those who don't know you will think you may have trouble handling yourself in tense situations."

"Sir, wouldn't my bar fight counter that belief—from those who don't know me?"

"Yes, to an extent."

Jacobsen sat, listening to the interchange.

"Jake here is one of the few who stand somewhere between those two views."

Jacobsen growled something under his breath.

"To continue," Harris reiterated, "we've a shortage of partners and trainers. You can handle yourself, but you don't yet have what we call deck smarts. You learn that by observing and doing.

"Jake will be your new partner until we find a better one for you."

Annie cocked an eye at Jacobsen. He returned her look. *Was that a smirk?* After a moment, she nodded. She could hardly turn down a partner, being only a probationer. "Works for me, Inspector. I assume Henry knows about this?"

"I'll fill him in when he discovers Jake doesn't appear in the training office. Now, go, both of you. Same beat as you had before, Annie, and follow up on that auto-chef theft."

†††

Outside Harris' office, Annie went to the locker room, donned her weapon harness and helmet, and headed toward the entrance. She didn't bother to see whether Jacobsen followed or not. She seethed. Her new partner was a condescending—

"Hey! Wait up, wo—"

She turned and walked back to Jacobsen. "The next word out of your mouth had better be my name. You ever call me 'woman' again, and you'll be picking up your teeth from the deck!"

203

Jacobsen was taken aback by Annie's response. "Hey! Hey! Hey! I meant nothin' by it. I was just bein' friendly, you and Henry and all."

Annie stared at him for a moment. "Remember," she said before turning and continuing toward the entrance of patroller headquarters.

After she passed through the entrance, Jacobsen caught up with her. "Henry told me you were strong-minded. May I, at least, call you Li'l Annie or just Annie? You can call me Jake."

*Was he trying to apologize?* She wasn't sure, but she had to work with him. "Yes, Jake, but remember what I said."

They headed for the tram that would take them to Torus Two, its docks, and the long-term storage warehouses. "Tell me about this theft of the auto-chef," Jacobsen said. "That's a strange thing to steal."

"Yes, it was. They stole the whole thing, the auto-chef and all the stored consumables—even the storage tanks. When Diedriksen and I got there…"

†††

They arrived at their beat on Torus Two, Deck Two. "The warehouse where the auto-chef theft occurred was here in Segment C," Annie told Jacobsen as they crossed through the segment lock. When they walked past the warehouse, Inar van Houten, the manager, was watching a tech add more security cameras and sensors over the business entrance. He waved to them.

"Patrollers," he said, walking over to them. He frowned for a moment at Jacobsen. Looking back to Annie, he said, "I've added more cameras and sensors, front and back, with on- and off-site data storage. My men have found new scratches around the loading docks to the rear, but they didn't get in. I had the codes changed the day I reported the theft."

"When did this happen?" Annie asked. *Is Jacobsen going to say anything?*

"Two days ago—five shifts. I didn't report it, since they didn't get in. I ordered more security and thought I'd tell you when I next saw you. I had the scratches buffed out and painted over. If they try again, we'll see it."

"That's thoughtful of you," Jacobsen said, entering the conversation for the first time. "Have you any valuable items in storage? Something worth the effort to steal?"

"I didn't think our auto-chef was worth stealing, but… we have a couple of terra-forming auto-facs waiting for pickup. Their ship isn't scheduled to arrive for another two months."

"I'm Annie's new partner," Jacobsen said, "and this is the first time I've been on this beat in a long time. Would you mind if I looked at the scratched doors?"

"Not at all. Follow me," van Houten said, waving them to join him as he headed inside the warehouse.

†††

"Hmm," Jacobsen murmured. A few scratches that hadn't yet been buffed away still remained. "Definitely tool marks." The scratches were next to one of the door's locking lugs. He stood and swept his gaze around the back of the warehouse and the corridor behind it. He looked upward and could faintly see security cameras and sensor boxes high on the walls.

"When will these be buffed out?" he asked van Houten.

"I had the thought to leave them. If they return and see them all gone, they may get suspicious—"

"More suspicious," Jacobsen said. "Thieves, criminals, are always suspicious."

"On the other hand," Annie added, "they may expect the scratches to be repaired and will become suspicious if some were removed while others were not."

"True," Jacobsen agreed. Turning to van Houten, he said, "I would suggest, sir, that you buff them out. You keep your business and the surrounding area clean and well maintained. It would be consistent to remove these scratches."

Van Houten nodded. "I'll tell the foreman. Anything else you want to see?"

"Not for me," Jacobsen said. "Annie?"

"Me, neither. Just keep a sharp lookout and call us if you see anything suspicious."

Later, while the two patrollers continued on their beat, Jacobsen mused, "I don't understand why the auto-chef was stolen. I could see stealing the carb and protein in the storage tanks. Those could be easily resold. But the auto-chef itself?" He shook his head. "Doesn't make sense."

"I've only been on this beat less than a month," Annie said. "There have been no other large thefts in that time. This theft aside, the segment has been quiet, not even any Stags around."

†††

Their beat took them to Segment B, which contained businesses that supported the warehouses and the freighters docked in the Segment A. So far, the segment contained more foot traffic, warehousemen, and crewmen from the ships. Here and there, casually dressed men and women walked through a marketplace filled with kiosks displaying small-trade items. The kiosks were set up by crewmen selling personal-trade items. Up-spindle buyers moved through the marketplace looking for bargains.

Jacobsen nudged Annie's arm and tilted his head toward an insignificant man moving quietly along the edge of the throng. "That's Charlie Simmons. He has a long record of petty thefts with an occasional mugging. Don't know what he's doing here. He isn't a pick-pocket."

Jacobsen flicked his head to close his helmet's visor. Annie did the same.

"Activate your scanner on channel two," said Jacobsen via his link. "Charlie doesn't appear to be armed."

"He has a large non-metallic object under his coat, though."

"You caught that, huh?"

"Yeah, a club or small billet, I think."

"Let's watch him. You go left around the market, and I'll go right. If he tries something, we'll be ready."

"Separate, Jake?"

"Yeah, you can handle yourself. It's the other things—like seeing and catching people like Charlie where you need training."

Annie walked to the left at the edge of the market. Jacobsen did the same toward the right.

Through her link, Jacobsen asked, *<Does this remind you of anything?>*

*<Yeah, the marketplace where Henry and I had the shootout with Ferdinand Speeks.>*

*<That was my thought, too. I expect nothing like that to happen, but be aware, scheisse happens when you least expect it.>*

Annie walked left around the marketplace. She had her link scan that section of the market. Nothing stood out… except one man was watching a craft dealer's kiosk. *<Jake, check the man here.>* She sent the location via her link. *<Charlie keeps looking at him. What do you think?>*

*<Hmm, I think Charlie has a partner. One causes a disruption, and the other grabs and runs. I'll check out the partner. You watch Charlie.>*

She acknowledged and slipped closer to Charlie Simmons. Annie was smaller than most of the marketgoers and could easily hide in the throng. Simmons did not appear to have spotted her approach.

Across the market, Annie heard a commotion. Around her, heads turned toward that direction. Charlie Simmons, however, walked up to a kiosk with cut gems on display, swept his hand across the countertop, and scooped the gems into a pocket inside his coat. The dealer, looking toward the commotion, didn't notice until Simmons turned away.

"Hey! Hey!" the dealer shouted.

Simmons quickened his stride. He didn't see Annie out of sight behind a green environmental column.

"Hey! Hey! Hey!" the gem dealer shouted again. Nearby onlookers turned, saw Simmons, and began to chase him.

As Simmons, now running, passed the green column, Annie stuck out her foot and tripped him. Simmons twisted as he fell and attempted to grab Annie to cushion his fall. She jumped back, and he missed her. The thief hit the floor and rolled to gain his feet while drawing a truncheon from under his coat.

Annie grinned. "Come on, Charlie. Come at me."

He did. She dodged his swing, grabbed his arm, and seized his hand to twist it up behind his back. The thief fell to the floor again with Annie's knee on his back and his hand up between his shoulder blades.

She leaned over and whispered into Simmons's ear, "Gotcha."

Annie was placing restraints on Simmons when Jacobsen arrived with another man in tow. He greeted Simmons lying on the floor, toed the truncheon on the floor, and nudged it farther from Simmons.

"Charlie, Charlie, Charlie," Jacobsen said. "You never learn. And this time, we'll add assault against a patroller to your charges. But I never knew you used a partner. Now we have both of you."

"Annie," he said, picking up the truncheon from the floor and passing it to her, "here's your first trophy. Show it to Hillman when you get home."

She tucked the truncheon into her backpack and retrieved Simmons' record. "Third strike, I see," she said to Simmons, who was still bound on the floor. "With the assault, that's a mandatory sentence to a terraforming project. Which one is on top of the list, Jake?"

"Hellspont, I think. Venus-type. High heavy metal content. Good mining world if they can make it more livable. I think they're still working on the atmosphere. Hot place too."

"And who is this?" She nodded toward the man in restraints next to Jacobsen.

"Unknown. He doesn't appear in any of our databases, including his arrival on-station. Strange, that."

"Isn't that an automatic Customs investigation?"

"Yes. Harris will want to see him when we get him booked. I'll ping him."

†††

Customs Chief Inspector Donal Harris was waiting for them at the booking desk when Annie and Jacobsen arrived. Jacobsen led the prisoners to the booking desk to hand off his charges. He nodded to Harris in greeting as he passed.

Annie felt a tingling flash through her. Harris had a reputation for being a dogged investigator. This would be her chance to see him work. *Another learning experience. I wonder what Henry will say?*

"Patrollers," Harris said, "what do you have here?"

"A man with no ID and with no record of entry to the station," Jacobsen replied. "You know Charlie Simmons. Snatch and run for Charlie, gems, plus assault on a patroller. The other one here created a disturbance as a distraction. We have it all on record."

"Do you now?" Harris walked around the two thieves and stopped in front of Simmons' partner. He looked the man over from his head to his feet. The thief was dressed innocuously, his outfit designed to blend in with the station crowd. Harris stepped forward, almost nose-to-nose to the unidentified man. "Name?" he demanded.

The man stood silently.

"Well, well, well," the inspector muttered, turning from the mute man to stroll around Charlie Simmons. "What have you got yourself into this time, Charlie? You know what you'll get with these charges and your history."

Charlie Simmons remained silent too.

"What's next on the terraforming list, Jake?"

"Hellespont."

Harris shook his head. "Hot place, Charlie. Toxic atmosphere too. You won't like it."

Simmons glanced at his partner, who glared back at him.

"Is the terraforming list unchangeable?" Annie asked, entering the conversation for the first time. She watched the interplay between Harris, Jacobsen, and the two thieves. *A learning experience,* she told herself. *This was what Jacobsen meant by acquiring street smarts.'*

Harris turned to her and, unseen by the two thieves, winked. "No, Patroller, it's discretionary—by Dundee Orbital's Customs Director. He's the station's chief justice. I think he could be persuaded to change the destination if I asked." He swung back to the thieves. "*If* you talk."

The unidentified thief snorted. Simmons, however, glanced at Harris and the two patrollers and slowly closed one eye on the opposite side of his face from his partner.

"Separate and book 'em," Harris instructed. "I'll interview them later."

†††

After her shift, Annie met Hillman and shared a soak in the patrol's hot tub. Jacobsen had walked in, but after a look from Hillman, he muttered, "I think I could use a sauna," and walked out.

She had shown her trophy to Hillman in the outer locker room. Hillman looked it over. "Ironwood from Trieste," he observed. "Hand-carved checkering on the grip, and it would pass through most weapon scanners undetected. Good trophy. Carry it in your backpack. You never know when it can come handy."

Hillman rested his regenned arm on the side of the hot tub. The medics had removed the regen mesh the previous week, but his shoulder wasn't as strong as it had been. He still had a month's worth of physical therapy before being cleared for full duty.

"How's it going?" she asked, referring to his shoulder.

"Slow… well, maybe not, but I'm not used to having it so weak. Hurts, too, when I overdo using it. Therapy won't be fun."

"I had a message from my mother today," she said to Hillman. "Clan Griffin has raised the family tithes to twenty percent."

Hillman tilted his head. "Why?"

"Apparently, the clan, specifically Sept Griffin, has made some bad investments and took loans from Clan Monmouth."

"That was stupid."

"Yes, it was. The clan hasn't been known for being smart… but this?" She fell silent for a moment. "The tithe increase has eliminated the family's profit margin. By next year, we—they won't be able to make their lease-hold payments to the clan. Mama said the family is looking for a new clan. They must move everything."

"Have they chosen a clan?"

"They're talking to McLean, Williams, and Menendez. McLean and Williams already have large fishing fleets. They may not want more competition. I know nothing about Clan Menendez."

"When are they planning to move? Does Griffin know?"

"I don't know, and no. Not yet."

Hillman started to say something and stopped. After a moment, he asked, "Is there enough Griffin clansmen to demand a referendum?" Clan members, under the charter of the Council of Clans, could demand a plebiscite to force the clan to act in a number of situations. Dissolution of the clan being one.

211

"I don't know. I haven't followed clan politics since I moved to Clan McLean. Maybe. But the clan's obligations to Clan Monmouth would still have to be honored. Monmouth could demand the clan be absorbed into them. Nobody wants that."

"Looks like your family has few choices."

"Yes. None of them any good. Mitchell Ortiz has moved to Clan Menendez. He sent me a message today to let me know. Griffin doesn't have any reps on Dundee now."

Hillman rose to his feet, water running down his body. "I think I'm about done. What do you want to do about dinner?"

"Seafood. Mama's message made me think of shrimp and pasta," she said, rising to join him.

"Deal."

†††

The following day after roll call, Harris called Annie and Jacobsen into his office. When they were inside, Harris closed the door and pointed at two chairs before his desk. He sat behind the desk, facing them. "I've some news about our mysterious thief. He's from Torintino. He arrived as a deckhand on a ship and, supposedly, shipped out with it. That was seven months ago. His documentation as a deckhand was phony."

"How did you determine his origin?" Annie asked.

Harris turned to the older patroller. "Jake, tell her."

"Torintino is a marginal world, much like Cameron, but with less water. The first colonization failed. That was eleven hundred years ago"—he held out his hand horizontally and rocked it—"plus or minus a century or two. "The second wave almost failed too. They were able to survive by augmenting their population with clones. They identified the clones with genetic markers. Charlie Simmons's partner has those markers."

"So, he's a clone?"

212

"Some time back in his ancestry, yes. Torintino hasn't cloned anyone in centuries."

"So why is he here? I wouldn't think he'd miss his ship without some reason," Annie said.

"That's what's interesting me," Harris answered. "Remember that auto-chef theft?"

"What about it?"

"Charlie Simmons confessed to being a lookout on it. He said he was forced to take his partner on the grab-and-run job," Harris answered.

"So Charlie rolled over on his partner?" Jacobsen asked.

"Yes. When—if—we catch the gang, he'll go to a nicer terraforming project. According to Charlie, we've a mob gang on station."

"Mob gang?" Annie asked.

"Old-time gang—a family of criminals. Do a history search of the Mafia and Sicilian gangs, pre-diaspora. This gang, Charlie says, is out of Torintino."

"Are they like Clan Monmouth?"

"No," Harris laughed, "Monmouth isn't that bad."

"Yet," Jacobsen added.

†††

With the coming of a new month, Annie's schedule changed. She now had Eightday and Firstday off and only shared Eightday off with Hillman. Annie had just returned from her six-kilometer jog around the nearest park when her link went off, an anonymous priority call from Inverness. She answered.

*<Annie?>*

"Janie?" *Why is my sister calling? She's never called me.*

*<Mama's dead—they killed her.>* Janie's voice was soft and dull. In shock, Annie thought.

"Who?"

*<Clan Monmouth proctors. They came for the fishing boats. Poppa and the men had already left to take them to Clan Menendez waters. Mama told the rest of the family to hide when they arrived. The proctors wanted to know where the boats were, and when Mama wouldn't tell 'em, they killed her.>*

"Wait, wait, wait. Has the family already moved to another clan?"

*<To Menendez—that's where we are going. It's not official yet.>* Janie's voice broke. She regained control and continued. *<Our sept has dissolved its allegiance with Griffin. The proctors—I think they're taking over Griffin because of the clan's debts. The other septs are about to vote to dissolve the clan.>*

"That won't stop Monmouth from what I've heard about them."

*<No, but since Sept Griffin made the loans, the debt is theirs after the clan is dissolved.>*

"What can I do, Janie?" Their mother was the family's matriarch. Annie, as the next oldest, would have had to step into that role… if she were on Inverness. However, her mother and Janie were well aware of her plans. She had no intention of returning to Inverness, much less of becoming the family's matriarch. Janie, on the other hand, was there and had worked closely with her mother for the last several years. Her younger sister was now matriarch. *And rightfully so.*

*<Nothing. I just wanted to let you know… it is my duty. Mama told me about your troubles with the clan and that you'd moved to Clan McLean. Cousin Rory has challenged Colton, the Laird—the former laird—but he's hiding. Some of the other septs want to declare vendetta—>*

"Vendetta!"

*<There's been a lot going on since you went up to Dundee that I don't think you know about. Clan Griffin has been heading toward a*

214

*breakup for some time. Monmouth's proctors thought, since we have the same surname name as the clan, that we were of Sept Griffin instead of Sept Leeds.>*

"But—"

*<Doesn't matter now, Annie. Poppa and the men took care of the proctors. They hanged them in front of the Griffin Clan House. Monmouth said it was going to send its militia to take over the clan, but the Council of Clans said no.>*

Both women were sobbing now. "When's the Going Away party? Henry and I—"

*<Don't come down, Annie.>* Janie sniffed. *<We'll have a small one, just the family down here. Things are too volatile and chaotic right now. When Sept Leeds officially petitions to merge with Clan Menendez, we'll take sovereignty of our sept territory with us. Our sept chief told us Menendez will grant our family a permanent lease on our coast—same deal we had with Griffin but permanent—if the merger is signed.>*

Annie and her sister talked for a few minutes more before dropping the connection. After sitting for a time, she stood and paced around the coapt until she reached the point where she had to go out—do something.

She was cried out, but her anger was growing, and she needed something to work it off. She went to her portion of the closet in the bedroom and gathered gloves and sparring helmet. *I need to find something—someone who I can unleash my frustration and stress on. Sensei should be there today. He's good enough that I don't have to worry about hurting him. I need to rid myself of all this before Henry gets home.* After sending a quick note to Hillman, she stuffed her gear into her backpack and left the coapt for the gym at patrol headquarters. While she walked, she remembered her mother, all the little scenes of family that kept them together. She couldn't attend her mother's Going Away party. She'd have to have one herself. Later.

††††

Hillman arrived home at their coapt to silence. Missing was the sound from the console link. No images appeared from their entertainment center. Annie wasn't in sight waiting for him. Something was wrong.

He listened carefully. There. He walked to the bedroom, past the former second bedroom, now their shared office. Annie was sitting on the floor with her back against the bed, crying.

"What's wrong, Annie?"

She looked up at him and shook her head.

Hillman sat next to her, placed his arm around her shoulders, and pulled her to him. "What's wrong, Annie?"

She turned her head away. A moment later, she said, "Mama's dead—and I broke Sensei's arm!" She turned back to Hillman and buried her face against his chest. For a moment, he was unsure which upset her more—her mother's death or breaking Sensei's arm. *Family first. Always.*

He let her cuddle while trying to understand what she'd said. *Her mother is dead? And she broke Sensei's arm?* Annie's life was one crisis after another. He didn't know what else to do but hold her.'

She hiccupped and rose to find a tissue. After wiping her eyes and blowing her nose, she sat next to Hillman and recounted Janie's call. "And then I broke Sensei's arm. I didn't realize how mad I was. I should've pulled my punches. I thought he wouldn't let me hurt him."

"Well, I've always thought Sensei thrived more on his reputation than on skill. It will boost yours, though."

"I don't want a reputation. That's why I quit hunting. Everybody making assumptions about me, most of them wrong."

"You have options now. You're a patroller. Maybe, after a while, a Customs agent or an inspector. Now, when is the Going Away party? Isn't that your custom downbelow?"

"Janie told me to stay away. Clan Griffin is dissolving, and Monmouth is trying to take over. My cousins are calling for vendetta

216

against the Griffin laird. The Leeds sept is moving to Clan Menendez. Everything is in chaos… and I can't go home!"

Hillman rocked her and rocked her. "You have a home here, Annie. You've new friends… and a permanent one with me—if you want."

Annie looked up into his face, blinked, and nodded. "Let's talk about that but not now. Not now, Henry."

"When you're ready, I'll be here. Today, tomorrow, or whenever."

††† 

Annie and Jacobsen were leaving for their beat. As they passed Harris' office, he called them in.

"I'm pulling you off your beat, temporarily," he told them. "I want you to work full time on these warehouse thefts and on the mob gang. If you need anything, let me know."

"What about extra hands?" Jacobsen asked.

"If needed, ask. Then I'll decide."

"Good. Hillman should be back to full duty in a few days. He has a lot of contacts and could be useful," Jacobsen stated.

"He also has a full-time job," Harris countered. "But… we'll see. If or when."

After Harris dismissed them, they continued out of patrol headquarters.

"Well, I tried," Jacobsen said. "I know Hillman would grab this as an opportunity to get out from behind his desk."

"If he did, he'd be in charge," Annie said. "He's a sergeant, and you're only a senior patroller."

"And you're a probationer," Jacobsen added.

A line of patrollers preceded them to the tram station. The station was always busy at the start and end of shifts.

"I wouldn't mind Hillman being in charge," Jacobsen said while they waited their turn for a tram. "He's smart and knows many people— people who would keep their eyes and ears open. More is seen and heard than most people… and gangs realize."

When they reached the warehouse segment, they stopped to see van Houten. He reported no change since their last visit. He had, he told them, spread the word to his neighboring warehouse managers. Many had since improved their security and added additional full-spectrum scanners to the public areas around them.

Van Houten, had, by default, become the leader of an unorganized security watch in the segment. As the de facto leader, he received copies of all the security scans. The patrol received data from all the public scans but not from private ones. By the time they left, van Houten agreed to forward copies of everything he received to the patrol.

"I got permission to route this data to Cecilia and have her run correlations on it."

"Who's Cecilia?"

"Out Customs and Patrol AI. Harris' niece named her when she was an intern here last year," Jacobsen said.

"I… I should have known we' had one. With all that goes on in Dundee, there'd have to be one. I just didn't think."

"Don't beat yourself up. We, Customs and Patrol, know about her, but few others do. There aren't all that many AIs, and people just don't think about them. Cecilia is ours. The station has another, but it doesn't have a name… at least I don't think so."

Annie and Jacobsen met with the other warehouse managers in the segment and received promises of cooperation. They knew the two patrollers, having seen them on their daily beats.

"I believe this," Jacobsen said, referring to their connection with the businesses on the beat, "is why Harris gave us this assignment. We're known." Jacobsen laughed. "And your reputation after the bar fight has increased."

"They know about that?"

"Stationers are one of the fastest gossips in the system. I wouldn't be surprised if your fight is known from one end of Dundee to the other. Someone, for sure, captured the fight with their link. I haven't seen it yet, but I'd bet Harris has."

"Well, pack! I don't want—need a reputation. That's why I quit hunting."

"You have one, Annie, whether or not you want it. It's an asset for a patroller. Ask Hillman. He'll tell you."

†††

<Patrollers Jacobsen and Griffin. Possible break-in in progress, Torus Two, Deck Two, Segment C, number seven-oh-three. C.>

Jacobsen and Annie were seated next to a small food kiosk They'd just finished their mid-shift break when they received the call.

"See that last 'C'? That's Cecelia's signature. If she sent a message, I bet she's caught something from those new scanners the warehousemen installed." He acknowledged the call, and they set off at a trot. They were one deck up from the break-in site and two hundred meters from van Houten's warehouse.

Jacobsen caught a slide down from deck three to deck two. On the way, he sent an alert to the other beat patrollers nearby. "Can't hurt to have backup if we need it," he said between breaths. He didn't have a daily four-kilometer run regimen like Annie.

As they approached the spot of the break-in in progress, the office on the public side of the warehouse was dark, the office empty. The public lighting was dimmed this time of shift. The overheads of the deck had few lights, as did the larger shipping corridors behind the warehouses. The darkness in this segment was no impediment to the newly installed scanners.

"Let's head around back. Keep an eye out for lookouts," Jacobsen said. When they reached the side of the warehouse, he stopped, retrieved a cable from his chest pocket, plugged it into his helmet, and poked the other end around the corner.

Annie's helmet pinged, and an image sent from Jacobsen's helmet appeared on her heads-up display. She did the same as Jacobsen and slid her cable around the corner too. With the cable in hand, she moved the visual pickup up toward the overhead area, where she caught movement in the dim upper recess above the warehouse.

"Got a lookout, Jake. Up above and to the right. He looked out and then slid back into the shadows."

"I knew there had to be at least one. Think you can backtrack and get behind him? Take him out by yourself?"

"Yes. I can do that."

"And don't break his arm unless you need to."

*Pack! I didn't think that'd get out this soon.* "No arm breaking, Jake," she agreed, "unless it's needed."

"Go get him, Annie. Signal when you have him, and then I'll go see who's trying to break inside."

†††

Annie had to backtrack to find a hatch into the maintenance corridor. She used her link to unlock the hatch. A few steps inside were a shaft and a ladder providing access to the areas of the upper deck, maintenance catwalks, load-bearing struts, and environmental pillars. This ladder was too close to the lookout. She trotted down the corridor, past where she estimated the lookout was overhead, to the next access shaft.

She used her link again to shut down the lights in the corridor. She didn't want to alarm the lookout with a flash of light when she entered the shaft to climb up to the lookout's catwalk. Annie jumped in place to see if her harness made any sound. Nothing, other than the scuffing of her boots on the deck.

In the dark, she slid aside the access door to the shaft and its ladder, and when she was on the first rung of the ladder, she closed the door behind herself. The climb to the catwalk above took only a few minutes. When she reached it, she let her eyes adjust to the dimness. She couldn't see the lookout yet. Creeping forward, she sent a short message to Jacobsen to tell him she was on the catwalk, stalking her prey.

*<Hurry. They're almost through. We need to catch them in the act.>*

She didn't respond to Jacobsen's urgings. Stalking couldn't be hurried. A horizontal strut ran above the catwalk causing her to crouch to pass underneath. When she did, a shadow ahead of her moved. *There you are. Now, how to take you down without alerting your partners.*

*Shockstick or Charlie's billy?* she thought. *If I hit him with either the shockstick or billy, he could fall off the catwalk.*

Annie crept forward. The lookout was focused on the activities of his partners below. Quietly, she approached… and pounced. One hand covered his mouth. Her other arm was wrapped around his neck, squeezing. With her legs wrapped around his torso, he struggled silently, but after a minute, he quieted. A brawler on Inverness had taught her the sleeper hold. It worked as he had said.

*<Lookout down,>* she sent to Jacobsen. She looked down and saw two men below, hidden from Jacobsen, struggling to open the warehouse door. She sent the scene to Jacobsen. He needed to know what he faced.

A shout from below startled her. She looked down. One thief, mistaking her for the lookout, waved and pointed down. She nodded in acknowledgement, and the thief returned to help his partner.

After restraining the lookout, locking his hands to a catwalk support, and slapping a microtracker on his neck, just in case, Annie began her descent down to the back of the warehouse. *<Coming down, Jake. They mistook me for their lookout. They must be ready to open the door.>*

He acknowledged her message and moved forward along in the warehouse's shadow toward the thieves in its rear. Annie descended the ladder and met Jacobsen at the rear corner.

"How do you want to take them?" she whispered.

"They're expecting you—one of us. I'll walk up to them. You follow right behind me, and when we're close, we'll take them down."

"You expect it will be that easy?" she asked with sarcasm in her voice. "Have you notified Harris and headquarters?"

"No and yes. We've backup on the way, but we can take them. Don't you think?"

"No," she said while taking her skin-tight gloves from her chest pouch. She slipped them on, followed by her tougher half-gloves.

He laughed. "Me neither," he responded, pulling on his skin-tight gloves. "Nothing is as easy as it seems." He unholstered his shockstick from his belt and held it next to his leg. "We'll act as needed, Annie."

Jacobsen walked around the corner and headed for the two thieves. Annie followed with Charlie's billy in her hand. After the bar fight, she didn't trust a shockstick—too fragile. She followed, hiding behind Jacobsen's bulk. Neither thief took notice of their approach.

*They're expecting their friend. How close can we get before they notice us?*

Jacobsen had been keeping to the shadows close to the rear of the warehouse. One of the two thieves glanced up and back down to the lock on the warehouse loading door. He looked up again, eyes widening in recognition that Jacobsen wasn't the expected lookout.

"Get 'em!" Jacobsen shouted and rushed the larger of the two thieves. Exposed by Jacobsen's charge, Annie ran toward the other one. He looked at her and grinned. He was almost as tall as Hillman but more slender. As Annie approached, he drew a long-bladed knife. While non-dueling knives were legal, using one was frowned upon.

Jacobsen discovered the larger, burlier thief was a better fighter than expected and was giving the senior patroller a hard time. The other moved forward toward Annie, holding the knife in an amateurish manner. *Not going to intimidate me!*

As the thief approached, he made an ineffectual swipe with his knife. Annie danced aside and hit the thief's elbow with the billy, causing him to drop the knife. Annie was now close enough to kick the knife aside. The thief attempted to grapple with Annie, trying to overwhelm her. She dropped the billy, grabbed his arm, spun around, and dislocated his elbow, already weakened by her earlier blow.

He screamed, startling the man fighting Jacobsen. It didn't surprise the senior patroller. Soon both thieves were facedown on the deck and restrained. A noise caused Annie to look up. The lookout had escaped his restraints and looked down from the overhead catwalk. He reached into a pocket and dropped a small object down at the patrollers and the two thieves.

*I searched him! Where'd he get that?*

The object hit the deck with a soft *pop*—a gas grenade. The air intake louvers in her helmet snicked shut, and a red icon—Toxic Environment—appeared on Annie's heads-up display. Dundee's environmental sensors detected the gas, and immediately, all air and water conduits shut off. Yellow strobes flashed, and the segment partitions, doors, and hatches began to close. The segment was isolating itself from the rest of the station. The lookout made his escape through a maintenance hatch just before it closed and locked.

Jacobsen signaled that he was unharmed. The two thieves, however, convulsed. The patrollers injected medical nanites into their respective prisoners.

"I hope this helps," Jacobsen said, "but they don't look good. I've alerted headquarters. This section has been isolated. We'll have to wait for the med-techs to clear us." He looked down. "I don't think these two are goin' to make it."

††††

"Stupid, stupid, stupid," Chief Inspector Harris ranted. The target of his ire was the escaped lookout. He, dressed like the others in shipsuit, gloves, and sealed helmet, had arrived with reinforcements and the med-techs for the two thieves. The med-techs worked hurriedly, but it was coming clear that their efforts were for naught.

Annie pointed at the upper maintenance hatch. "I saw the third one escape through that hatch just as the segment was locked down."

"I heard your report," Harris replied testily. This whole business was getting out of hand. The director had given him this assignment. He'd passed it to the two patrollers, but he was the one who had to answer to Dundee's Customs director.

"Yes, but it's likely he's trapped on the other side. It's still in this segment—"

"I have people looking for him," Harris interrupted.

"I put a tracker on him—"

"You did?" That was not normal procedure.

"I've lost prisoners before when I was a hunter. I developed a habit of slapping a microtracker on them if I got separated from them."

"Well, in this case, it's a good idea.," The relief in Harris' voice was clear. "Hear that, Jake? Even you can learn something."

"I never claimed she wasn't good, Inspector. I just said she needed deck smarts."

One of the med-techs looked up. "This one's gone," he said to Harris. "The other one won't last much longer. Our med nanites aren't working, and before you ask, they both have clone DNA markers that you mentioned on the way here."

Harris turned to Annie. "Give me your tracker ID. We'll follow him. I'll bet he's heading home, wherever the rest of his gang is. He'll want to report to his gang."

The second thief died in convulsions like the first. The med-techs were upset, as they were when losing anyone. The bodies were soon in body bags and left with the departing med-techs.

Harris looked around the area, now clear of most of the people he'd brought, and spotted the long knife lying next to the warehouse wall. He walked over and picked it up. "This the knife your thief had, Annie?"

"Yes. I took it away from him and kicked it over here, where he couldn't reach it."

Harris examined the weapon. "Trieste short sword," he muttered. "Don't see these much around here. It's a dueling sword from Trieste. Their Customs and Traditions differ from ours. They aren't a Confederation member. Nor is Torintino. Never joined and... they're neighbors. "

"They made a real mistake using that gas grenade," Jacobsen said. "It's an automatic spacing offense."

"For the one, if, when, we catch him," Harris reminded them.

"My tracker will lead us to him, and unless they run a scanner on him, they'll never know it's there," Annie added.

"Let's get out of here. Annie, send your tracker ID to Cecelia. She should find him by the time we get back to headquarters."

†††

Hillman was waiting when they arrived at patrol headquarters. He and other patrollers about to go off-shift waited, fully suited and sealed, with armor, helmets, and gloves.

"Inspector. Annie. Some friends and I thought you may need some help," he said.

"Are they volunteers, or were they volunteered. Hillman?" Harris asked. "This gang has already used lethal weapons. It won't be like breaking up a brawl."

"We know. Everyone volunteered," Hillman said then added, "You won't have to pull off people from the incoming shift."

Harris looked at him for a few seconds then nodded. "Very well. You're senior, I suppose?"

"Yes, by chance, I am."

"How fortunate you're fresh off medical hold." Medical hold or not, Hillman was still the best man for this type of job.

Annie listened to the interchange and grinned inside her helmet. Jacobsen nudged her. Through his faceplate, she could see him grinning too. Before she could look away, his faceplate blackened, hiding his face. She quickly did the same.

"You two," Harris said to Jacobsen and Annie, "and you, too, Hillman, follow me." Without waiting to see if they followed, Harris strode down the corridor toward his office.

Hillman followed, with Annie and Jacobsen scurrying to catch up. Instead of his office, Harris turned left into a corridor that led to several conference rooms. He entered the first one and said, "Cecelia! What do you have?"

The three patrollers entered the room. Hillman closed the door, and when Harris was seated, he, Annie, and Jacobsen also sat. Above the conference table, a holo of a young girl, Cecilia's avatar, appeared.

"I've picked up Annie's tracker. The subject appears to open hatches. Even those sealing the segment. That would suggest—"

"We'll discuss that later. Where is he? Where's he heading?" Harris asked.

"He has left Torus Two and is about to enter Torus One, Deck Five, Segment C. That area is supposed to be unused and should have been sealed off. Now that I know his destination, I detect environment systems in use… here." A second holo appeared, showing a three-dimensional map of Torus One and the segment where she had detected an active environmental system.

"There are twenty-two heat sources at that location," she continued, "and multiple energy sources consistent with powered weapons—mag rifles, heavy lasers, and particle beams."

226

Harris sat back. "That's unsettling." He turned to Hillman. "Henry, your people powered armor trained?"

"Yes, they're all current except..." He glanced at Annie.

"I'm qualified too. I did my militia time training with the marines at Weyland Fleetbase."

"Is that acceptable, Inspector? She hasn't qualified yet by our training section."

"I passed powered suits during my recruit training," Annie argued.

"That was just a familiarization session. I wrote the lesson plan," Hillman replied.

"When was your last service with the marines, Annie?"

"Two years ago, to renew my militia commission. I was deployed as part of Operation Badger. Forty-five days in vacuum in the Zasque system."

"Your rank?" Harris asked. He hadn't looked into Annie's militia background. He assumed she, like all on Inverness, had militia training.

"Senior Lieutenant."

Harris pursed his lips and nodded. "That'll do until you get officially qualified. Hillman, note her exception and then get your people suited up. You, too, Jake, Annie." He made a note to pass Annie's militia records and her Griffin militia rank to his sister, the deputy McLean laird. The clan could always use a well-trained militia officer.

†††

Annie and Jacobsen joined Harris, Hillman, and thirty power-suited patrollers in the corridor outside the rear of patrol headquarters. Annie was delayed. The armorer couldn't, at first, find a suit of powered armor small enough to fit her. One was finally found and checked. Its consumables were filled and power packs fully charged.

Harris was having a discussion with Cecelia when they arrived. "They are now on Torus One, Deck Seven, Segment C," she reported.

Harris did not try to restrict her report, allowing the patrollers to receive their updates directly.

"Have the navy and marines been updated?" Harris asked.

"Yes, as you ordered. The naval station has been locked down, and armored marines are guarding all entrances. They are also guarding the docks for the torus and the intra- and inter-torus trams are halted as is the shuttle port. Deck Seven is isolated from the rest of the Torus One."

Harris turned to Hillman standing next to him. "Transport ready?"

"Coming, Inspector. We'll take two maintenance trams and keep out of the public thoroughfares. No need to alarm stationers."

"Good." Harris switched his link to a common channel for the armored patrollers. "Count off by twos. Hillman will take the odd numbers. Even numbers will be under Senior Patroller Jacobsen. I'm in overall command. Rules of engagement: use stunners against any unarmored gang members who are not carrying powered weapons. Solid and armor-piercing ammunition is authorized against any gang member wearing armor and those carrying a powered weapon. Anyone carrying a particle-beam weapon will be targeted first. Don't endanger yourselves. Put the gang members down as quick as you can."

"We're of equal numbers at our last count. We're better than them. Let's prove it." With those last words, Harris entered the first maintenance trams followed by Jacobsen, Annie, and the even-numbered patrollers. Henry Hillman and the odd-numbered patrollers entered a second tram.

The transit from the patrol armory on Torus Two to Torus One was short, only twenty minutes. The maintenance transit tubes were smaller than the public 'tubes and, until Harris used his override, slower than the public trams.

The trams halted when they reached Torus One, Deck Four, Segment C, three decks below the location of Annie's prisoner, according to her microtracker.

"I expect the gang will have lookouts on Deck Six and maybe Five," Harris said to Hillman and Jacobsen via a private channel.

Annie switched to it and listened in. Harris would notice when she appeared on the channel. He didn't mention her presence and didn't order her off the channel.

"Sergeant Hillman, take your team to Segment B and go up to Deck Seven from there. Look for and capture any lookouts you find. Quietly. Cecelia will assist you. She's activated the deck's secondary and tertiary scanners, but she may not detect everyone. Be alert."

"Patroller Jacobsen, you and your team will go up from here. You have the same orders as Hillman: seek and capture any lookouts you find. I'll order Cecelia to lock and freeze the partitions between Segments C and D on Deck Seven when we and Hillman converge on the gang. Questions? Hillman? Jacobsen?"

Neither patroller answered.

"Go," Harris ordered. Hillman's team departed with Henry in the lead. Harris nodded to Jacobsen, giving him, non-verbally, the same order.

"Annie, take point," Jacobsen ordered. "I think you're a better scout than the rest of these people."

"Aye." She checked her mag rifle. Frangible and armor-piercing magazines full, a round in the chamber and the safety on. She opened a hatch into the maintenance corridor to gain access to the inter-deck transit tube. Behind her, Harris used his override to shut down pseudo-gravity inside the tube. This allowed Annie to creep hand over hand to Deck Five. Once there, she would exit the tube and, with Cecelia watching, seek any gang lookouts.

Annie didn't expect to find any lookout on Deck Five. From what she'd observed so far, the gang hadn't shown any signs of being trained. They had made too many operational errors. Using that gas grenade could earn them all a short trip out an airlock.

"Cecelia, what do you have?"

"I detect one person, male, at the other end of this segment. He is standing outside the inter-deck public transit tube. The tube status reports it as inactive. However, the person has just stepped inside and is moving up to Deck Six."

"So he has an override for the transit tube."

"That, or someone in the gang has hacked into this torus's operations network."

"Report that to Harris. Copy the naval station. They need to be aware their systems may be compromised."

"Done."

"Anyone else here?"

"Not that I can detect."

Annie climbed on the edge of the maintenance tube into the pseudo-gravity of its neighboring corridor. SOP called for the overhead lights dimmed to conserve power. With her helmet turned to full-frequency scan, nothing appeared in either direction.

"Proceed up to the next deck, Annie," Jacobsen ordered. He had been listening to her conversation with Cecelia. "Hillman is moving to the next deck now. We don't want to get behind."

"Aye." She reentered the zero-G maintenance tube again and, hand over hand, pulled herself up to Deck Six. Her scan detected a lookout as she cleared the inter-deck armored bulkheads. This one was standing right outside the transit tube.

"Lookout here," she reported.

"Can you take him out?" Jacobsen asked.

"Yes. He's right outside the transit tube. I've detected no armor and no powered weapons."

"Go," Jacobsen ordered.

Annie touched the manual override next to the transit tube's exit. The door slid open. It must have made some sound. The lookout had

230

been facing to the left, down the corridor, but apparently hearing the noise, he turned to see Annie standing in the entrance of the 'tube, in powered armor.

She fired her stunner, and the lookout dropped. "Lookout down," she reported while she trotted forward, stooped, and slapped a sleep patch on his neck. Another patroller emerged from the transit tube and moved next to Annie.

"I'll take care of him," the patroller said, picking up the unconscious gang member. He placed restraints, hand and foot, on the prisoner, carried him down the corridor, and locked him inside a small compartment.

Jacobsen emerged next, followed by Harris. "Find anyone else?" Jacobsen asked.

"No. He's the only one here, unless they've deployed scan dampers on this and the next deck."

"I've detected no anomalies. That could be caused by a damper on either deck," Cecelia interrupted.

Harris grimaced. Annie knew the tale. Jacobsen had told her the Customs AI, Cecelia, had been acting more like a person ever since Harris' niece, Molly Quinn, named her the year before.

"I doubt there are enough people here, Cecelia, to create any anomalies," Harris argued. "Regardless, Hillman is moving up to Deck Seven. We'll seal off this deck and go up to Segment D of Deck Seven and pinch the gang between us and Hillman's patrollers."

Annie took off at a trot, with Harris, Jacobsen, and his patrollers following. One patroller, unused to running in a powered suit, bounced, rising a head above the others.

In minutes, they'd reached the segment boundary. Harris overrode the lock on the personnel hatch in the lowered segment bulkhead and passed though. Ten meters inside the new segment, he unlocked a maintenance transit tube and stepped back to allow Annie to lead the team up to Deck Seven.

Annie eased up to the exit of Deck Seven's maintenance transit tube. She detected no one outside the 'tube. Her scan detected several people a hundred meters away, though.

"Crack the exit and report what you see," Jacobsen ordered. "They won't be able to detect you until you leave the tube."

She slid the exit open, just enough to see down the corridor in both directions. Nothing to the left. To the right, however, a half dozen or more men were gathered in the middle of the corridor. Some sat in chairs scavenged elsewhere. Along a wall was the dispenser of a commercial auto-chef. *I wonder if that's the auto-chef stolen from van Houten?*

She opened a channel to Jacobsen and to Harris and allowed them to see the gang members. "I think we've found that auto-chef that was stolen three months ago. Makes sense, now," she reported. "Orders?"

"They're too far for us to take them out from here," Harris said. "Hillman is on this deck, now, at the bulkhead between Segments B and C. He says there are a half dozen men there, like here. That begs the question, where are the rest?"

Harris communicated with Hillman in the background. "Hillman and his team will enter this segment and take out the men at his end. They're closer to him than these are to us. Our targets may be distracted if—when they are alerted about Hillman. If so, we'll take advantage of their distraction. If not, we'll charge and do our best. Remember my rules of engagement about powered weapons."

"Sir, I'm getting a power source from our group, a mag rifle, I think, but no powered armor," Annie said.

"Very well. On my mark, Hillman, go—mark! Jacobsen, load solid or armor-piercing rounds."

Jacobsen passed Harris' orders. Annie checked her magazine again and switched to armor-piercing rounds. Someone may have unpowered armor. Frangible ammunition would be useless.

"Jacobsen, go!" Harris ordered again. Annie opened the 'tube's exit and slid down the wall toward the six gang members. No one noticed until she had covered half the distance. Jacobsen and his patrollers were right behind her.

*I'm within stunner range now.* With a forefinger, she flicked the switch on the side of her rifle. One of the gang members glanced in her direction. His eyes widened just as Annie shot him with her stunner. *We've at least one live prisoner.*

When her target fell, the next man in line noticed the patrollers. He swung his mag rifle toward the patrollers. Behind Annie, Jacobsen stepped around her and dropped the rifleman with three armor-piercing rounds. The three rounds went through the rifleman and into a third gang member. Three of the six were down.

Stunner shots took out another gang rifleman, along with the remaining two.

Cecelia came over the patroller's common channel. "Med-techs on standby, one deck down."

"Keep them there until this segment is secured," Harris ordered. "Secure these prisoners, Jacobsen. Assign two patrollers to guard them."

Jacobsen pointed at two patrollers and the gang members. They nodded, acknowledging the unspoken instructions. "Let's move forward, Annie. We've more prisoners to take."

Annie took her place in front of the remaining patrollers, with Harris in the third position behind Jacobsen. "Hillman's taken down his gang members," Harris said over a private channel with Jacobsen and Annie. "He has one patroller down with a mag rifle round through his leg. He'll be okay. The rifleman won't. Hillman reports he has two live prisoners."

"Hard day for the gangers, Inspector," Jacobsen replied.

"Just as long as it's them and not us."

Annie continued down the corridor, keeping to the inner wall. "Cecelia, are any of them in the public areas of this deck?"

"None that I can detect. This deck is reserved for the future expansion of the naval annex. It's empty, and all services, except for environmental service, are shut down. I surmise that is why they stole the auto-chef."

Annie led the team forward. Hillman was approaching from the other direction, and they still hadn't detected the remaining dozen or so gangers. Her scan picked up a small heat source off the maintenance corridor. "Hot spot ahead." Another indicator lit. "Power pack in use too."

"Stop here, Annie," Jacobsen said.

As he spoke, another indicator lit on her heads-up display. "Spy eye in the corridor around the curve. They know we're here."

A hatch slid open in the corridor's wall. A man, in unpowered armor, stepped out and fired at Annie. *Wham!* The round hit her armored chest plate, causing her to take a step backward.

Jacobsen and Harris returned fire. Their armor-piercing ammunition riddled the rifleman. One round from them ricocheted off the edge of the door and back into the compartment. Someone inside screamed.

In the momentary confusion, a patroller ran forward and tossed a concussion grenade into the compartment. It went off, and Annie, by that time, had regained her balance. She ran forward, too, and tossed a smoke grenade inside. The smoke wasn't toxic, but it blinded the men inside the compartment. Jacobsen joined Annie and the patroller next to the open door.

"On three. Stunners only," he said to Annie and the patroller. "I'll take anyone with a powered weapon."

"One. Two. Three!"

Annie stepped inside and moved to the left. The patroller followed her inside and moved to the right. Jacobsen moved forward between the two. Annie and the patroller began firing. Jacobsen shot one man fumbling with a long gun, trying to bring it to bear on the patrollers.

"All down!" the other patroller shouted. "All down!" Annie echoed. Jacobsen stepped out into the corridor and reported, "All down from stunners with one exception."

"Secure them," Harris said. "Cecelia, allow the med-techs below to come up to treat our prisoners. We may have fatalities."

"Acknowledged, Inspector."

Annie had followed Jacobsen while the other patroller was restraining the stunned men in the compartment. "Henry?"

"He and his team have taken the rest. I think we have them all."

The patroller who had remained in the compartment stepped to the doorway and said, "Inspector, I think you should see this." When Harris, followed by Jacobsen and Annie, stepped toward the compartment, he turned back and stepped over the body of the man in unpowered armor. "Look at his wrist."

Harris stooped and picked up the man's arm. On the back of his right wrist was a stylized tattoo. "*Il capo*," he said. "He was trying to stake a territory in Dundee."

"Not anymore," the patroller said.

"That's the lookout who got away from me," Annie said after she looked at his face. "Never would have worked, a gang takeover. We don't bow to anyone."

"Yep," Jacobsen agreed. "After a few duels and spacings, they'd move out. We aren't sheep to be plucked."

Annie blinked, trying to understand what Jacobsen had said. *Sheep? Plucked?* She shook her head and chalked it up as another thing she would never understand.

## Patroller

Back at patrol headquarters and after the patrollers had been dismissed, Harris led Hillman, Jacobsen, and Annie to his office. They gave a final recap of the takedown to Dundee's Customs director. Agents from Cameron's Interdiction Office would interrogate the survivors. Since the prisoners were from outside the Confederation, a justice from Cameron would preside over their trial. The gang's use of a lethal gas grenade and powered weapons inside Dundee had made the outcome a certainty—spacing. But the *Proprieties* must be served, and the gang would be tried fairly.

Harris, seated behind his desk, reached inside a drawer and pulled forth a bottle. "McLean's single malt, Number 5," he said. He added four small glasses and filled each one. "A toast, Henry, Jake, Clanswoman." He nodded toward Annie. "And no longer a probationer, but vetted patroller Anne Marie Griffin, Clan McLean, Sept Harris. Congratulation, Annie, your mandatory probation time of three months is over. And according to your trainer"—Harris nodded toward Jacobsen—"you've proven yourself competent to walk your beat without tripping over your feet."

Hillman grinned. Jacobsen stifled a guffaw. According to Annie's professional review, she was qualified based on her bar fight. There were requirements other than the fight, but the fight answered the most important ones.

The four clinked glasses and, in one motion, downed the whiskey. Annie coughed. "I swore off this stuff. The last time I had any, I got laid."

The others laughed. Hillman snorted into his glass. There were no secrets in Dundee Orbital. Word of her and Henry's escapades had spread throughout the station. Hillman's face turned red. He was from a more conservative culture. The clans of Inverness, however, were not. Once an adult, each lived their personal lives without concern for the opinions of others. Well, most clans and septs didn't care, but she was no longer of Clan Griffin.

"By custom," Harris said to the patrollers, "you have two days off after being in a firefight. However"—he slid a data wafer to Annie—"I think you may find that interesting. By the way, Annie, when off duty, you are free to pursue any legal occupation or source of income."

Annie laid the wafer on her link and read it. She recognized the document. "I can?"

Harris nodded then stood, signaling the briefing was over.

Annie and Henry headed home to their coapt. Hillman was curious about the document Harris had given Annie, but he didn't ask about it. She would tell him, or not, in her own good time. However, there was another subject to be discussed.

"Annie, we've been together now for…" He paused, checking his calendar. "Almost six months. We've a good arraignment, but I want—"

"Yes," she interrupted.

"Yes?"

"Yes, I'll marry you, but I want it done right. Harris is the senior member of my clan on station. You know our Customs and Traditions— you *do* know them, yes?"

"Uh, uh, yes, I think so."

"Then do it properly. See Harris and ask for the clan's approval. We'll have to go down to Dunnsport, the McLean clan house, for the wedding."

"I've never gone downbelow."

"Really? After all this time?"

"Never needed to."

"Then it's time, Henry. You'll get to see Janie and the rest."

He smiled at her. When they reached their coapt, Hillman picked her up in his arms. She palmed the doorway, and he carried her inside.

†††

Three months later, Annie was waiting at Dundee's shuttle terminal Dock 23. Shuttle 602 from Tondo Shuttleport had just arrived, and she was watching the passengers disembark. Most of them had exited the shuttle when she saw the man she was waiting for.

She let him clear Customs before stepping forward. She wasn't wearing her patroller uniform today; it was her day off. Instead, she was dressed the same as when she had arrived at Dundee Orbital over seven months before. She wore a light-colored tunic, trousers, a white blouse, and sturdy ankle-high boots. Around her waist was a worn gunbelt with a pistol and sheathed knife. Her hip-length tunic did not hide the weapons.

She was waiting for Colton Griffin, former laird of the former Clan Griffin. The data wafer Harris had given her contained a warrant for him. The fugitive was wanted for fraud, embezzlement of four million Confederate dollars from the treasury of the former Clan Griffin, and flight to avoid over a hundred challenges from former members of Clan Griffin and Clan Monmouth, the holder of Clan Griffin's debts. Monmouth had claimed the four million dollars Colton Griffin carried. She had been waiting for Colton all this time. If he wanted to escape, his only route took him here, to Dundee Orbital.

Colton finally cleared Customs and entered the station. Annie stepped forward, leaving the other onlookers behind. "Colton Griffin, former laird of the former Clan Griffin, I am Anne Marie Griffin-Hillman, Clan McLean, Sept Harris. I have a fugitive warrant for your arrest from Clans Monmouth, Menendez, McLean, Portee, and several others. Do you surrender, or do you challenge my warrant?"

# Author update.

This is the third book of the Tri-Cluster Confederation. The first was the novella, *The Beacon at Barrington Light*. The second was the full-length novel, *Émigré*. I've started another novel that picks up the story started in *Émigré*. I've not yet chosen a title. It's a work-in-progress.

I hope you like this collection of stories. All indie authors are dependent on reader reviews, it's what keeps us motivated to write more stories and books. Please take a few moments and add one to the book's Amazon page and to its Goodreads page. Every little bit helps.

## Released

*The Beacon at Barrington Light*. A novella of the Tri-Cluster Confederation.

*Émigré*. Book One of the Tri-Cluster Confederation.

*Dundee Orbital*. A collection of stories of Dundee Orbital and the Tri-Cluster Confederation.

## Coming in 2021...

*The Prodigals*: Book two of the Tri-Cluster Confederation series coming in 2021. A work in progress.

Come visit me at https://m-watson.com and subscribe to my newsletter. I can also be found on Goodreads. All reviews and comments are welcome.

Made in the USA
Monee, IL
05 June 2023

35312555R00139